James Barnett was born in 1920 in Glasgow and was educated at Glasgow's Calder Street School. He joined the Territorial Army in 1939 and served in France and later in the Middle East, Italy and Austria. He joined the Metropolitan Police in 1946 and retired in 1976 with the rank of Commander in the CID. During this time he was awarded the Queen's Police Medal for Distinguished Service. *Diminished Responsibility* is his sixth novel.

James Barnett is married with two sons.

Also by James Barnett

THE FIRING SQUAD
MARKED FOR DESTRUCTION

JAMES BARNETT

# Diminished
# Responsibility

Futura

A Futura Book

Copyright © James Barnett 1984

First published in Great Britain in 1984
by Martin Secker and Warburg Limited

This edition published in 1986
by Futura Publications, a Division of
Macdonald & Co (Publishers) Ltd
London & Sydney

ISBN 0 7088 2852 3

Printed and bound in Great Britain by
Collins, Glasgow


Futura Publications
A Division of
Macdonald & Co (Publishers) Ltd
Greater London House
Hampstead Road
London NW1 7QX

A BPCC plc Company

Section 2, Homicide Act, 1957, provides a defence to a charge of murder if it can be established that the accused was suffering from such abnormality of mind as to substantially impair his mental responsibility.

The onus of proof lies upon the defence to demonstrate the existence of what is referred to in the Courts as:

DIMINISHED RESPONSIBILITY

# One
‧‧‧‧‧

The small coastal town of Marovic lies on the Yugoslavian side of the Istrian Peninsula, some twenty miles south of the Italian port of Trieste. Henry Teasdale rather enjoyed his occasional trips to Marovic. He always went by sea, much preferring to travel aboard the steamship that sailed once a week, and needed two hours to get there. The alternative was the daily hydrofoil that sped across the Adriatic, covering the same distance in less than forty minutes. But in that vessel one was confined to a small seat in a cramped cabin and subjected to Muzak of the most dreadful banality. It was rather like being in an airliner; and Teasdale did not care much for airliners either.

There was an additional advantage to travelling by steamship. It left Trieste early on Friday mornings, dropping passengers at Marovic, then continuing its journey down the Slovenian and Dalmatian coastline to Dubrovnik; the ship returned to Marovic on Sunday night, thereby permitting Teasdale a pleasant weekend at the Grand Hotel. For all its present imperfections, Teasdale adored the Grand Hotel. It had been constructed at the turn of the century, the heavily arched and columnar façade oddly blending into the more subtle architecture of the town, built by the Venetians over four hundred years before.

Inside the hotel, dark polished woods rose to a rococo ceiling and massive chandeliers. A curved staircase made its dignified ascent to the mezzanine, where loungers could survey the comings and goings at the reception desk through richly bevelled windows. Once Bosnian princes, Serbian dukes and Macedonian counts had paced the corridors. Now, in the socialist penury of Yugoslavia, it was the temporary abode of the char-à-bancers, as Teasdale called them, the package holidaymakers of Thomson, Horizon and Yugotours from Britain, and those of Neckar Reisen, Linde Reisen and others from Germany, most of whom, to Teasdale's absolute disgust, did not even wear a tie to dinner, let alone a jacket.

Nevertheless they provided useful cover; for Teasdale was in a profession where cover was an essential part of its practice. Not that he would stoop so low as to dress or behave like the other holidaymakers. By day, he wore a light linen jacket, a cravat and a straw hat, and spent his time examining the murals and carvings in the sixteenth-century church, sometimes visiting the Maritime Museum or simply sitting at a café in the square reading a newspaper. If one watched him carefully on his perambulations, one would observe that he fastidiously dropped the paper bag containing the remnants of his packed lunch in a litter bin by the bus station, and occasionally he would carelessly leave his folded newspaper tucked under an empty chair at his table outside the café. In the dining salon at night, he wore, if not a dinner jacket, at least a dark mohair suit and a bow tie, and had a financial arrangement with the head waiter to be seated alone in a discreet corner near the entrance. Yet somehow, and always on the second evening of his visit, his solitude would be disturbed by two or three swaggeringly self-assured individuals entering the dining-room wearing jackets slung across their shoulders like Balkan cloaks. After the head-waiter had surveyed the crowded room he would escort them to Teasdale's table, offer profuse apologies, and request they be permitted to share his table. He would agree politely, without quite concealing his displeasure, then, strangely enough, before long would engage in animated conversation with his apparently unsought companions. As such events only occurred two or three times a year they never became frequent enough to draw a great deal of attention or comment.

This particular weekend went much like the others, but, as only Teasdale knew, it was to be his last. After this weekend he was to be recalled. To be given the royal and ancient order of the boot. Well, they would live to regret it. They had brutally heaved him out of the big chair when he had barely got his backside into it. A rightful reward for all the years of constructive service he had put in. No, not a reward, it was his due, his by right. Then had come that awful mess at Cheltenham. No one is blaming you, old boy, but best we have you out of it. We want you to take the Balkan sector on board for the time being. A little local difficulty has arisen. Needs a spot of discreet liaison to resolve it. Right up your street. We should have you back in office in next to no time when it's all blown over. That had been three years and several months ago. Three years of running a grubby little network producing stale bread – and dry bread at that. At least that glory-grabbing bounder in Vienna had been sorted out. What a mischief he had done. And afterwards it was all – Don't go sniffing round the Ringstrasse, Henry – No more tales from the Vienna Woods for the time being, we are still hearing discordant notes – Leave the Viennese to their coffee and *schlagobers* until we get the fiddle back in tune. Yes, Galahad had stirred up a hornets' nest – and they still buzzed about his head for a time, even down in Trieste. But, gradually, as the smoke signals of compromise were puffed about, things settled down, becoming almost somnolent. Then, during the past six weeks, he had detected signs of a re-awakening and was disturbed by them. The private agreement he had made only concerned Rudolf Abel, head of US/UK Section in Moscow. That had been strictly agreed, yet he was now being harassed by low-level functionaries from satellite departments. Why? Only last week he had spotted Georgy Smisek, a Czech goon from the Rome Embassy, circling round like a shitehawk while he was lunching at Emilio's. A month ago, two Hungars in a Budapest-registered Lada had quite blatantly tailed him from the office all the way to Gorizia, where he had nothing more important to do than have some strong words with Paolo Galatone, who was flooding the home market with fake jeans and plastic leatherwear. Five days later he read in *Il Piccolo* that Galatone had succumbed to an unidentified viral infection, after a progressive illness that must have begun later the same day they had met. He began thinking of umbrellas that fired Ryscin pellets and became greatly concerned. Any more of it and he would complain bitterly. A deal had been made but contracts had not been signed. Any further nonsense and it was all off.

As he registered and surrendered his passport, he cast an appraising eye round the lobby and for once was glad every person he saw wore shorts, T-shirts or beach robes. The staff behind the reception desk were different from his last visit but the barman was the same. The one who looked like a retired middleweight boxer. The one who had presented him with his brandy in a damp glass, who had scowled and shrugged away his protest. That was the trouble with the socialist republics, they ignored history and tradition. Not just the socialist republics – that was the trouble with the world today. Yes, he thought, perhaps it was as well this was to be his last visit to the Grand Hotel. Its architecture might survive but its ambience and style were gone forever. It had only existed in his imagination in any case. The possibility of his dying there never entered his mind.

Rising drowsily at seven the morning after his arrival, sleep having been disturbed by a new horror – a disco throbbing in the cellars until 2 am – he was grimly determined to set himself up for the day with a swim in the brine pool. This marble sanctuary occupied one end of the east wing, its use governed by a set of stringent regulations printed in four languages and enforced by a pair of elderly but muscular Croatian women, whose early years of partisan guerrilla service entitled and fitted them for the job. Although the pool was enclosed, wide glass partitions opened onto a pleasant sun terrace, but a decal showing a brown bottle slashed with a red stripe forbade the use of tanning oils. Another sign, depicting a swimmer plunging into the water, barred such recklessness by cutting his torso into bloody geometric segments. Above the shallow end a face, in expressionless outline, held a finger to its lips demanding a decorous silence.

To his annoyance, for he had three or four at home but always forgot to pack one, Teasdale paid the ex-partisan supervisor twenty-five dinars for yet another plastic bathing cap. Regulation No 1 insisted that bathers, male and female, wear caps; and to this end, those lacking such items could purchase a bi-sexual beret with elasticated edges, fashioned like those worn by women bathers around 1900. Not even Teasdale's almost total baldness excluded him from this rule. But for all that he welcomed the rules, keeping at bay, as they did, the young and boisterous who would otherwise have turned the place into Bedlam.

After taking the obligatory shower before entering the pool, Teasdale surveyed the other early bathers whilst descending the steps at the shallow end. They were six in all. Five of them German, according to the occasional word that reached his ears. This quintet, two stocky and enormously fat middle-aged women, two tall and exuberantly stomached men and another elderly but scrawny lady, stood up to their navels or chests in solemn conclave round the hot-water inlet two feet below the surface. From the little he heard of their discussion the present structure of the Kohl government did not meet with their approval. Ploughing steadily over what he hoped would be twenty lengths, Teasdale observed that from time to time the discussion group would change places in order to give an equal distribution of the voluptuous pleasures to be had close by the hot-water inlet. No danger there, Teasdale grinned inwardly. Nor would there be from the only other bather present, a Finnish woman in her early thirties, pallid to a point where it was difficult to discern where her face ended and the close-fitting cap she wore began. Both had the colour and texture of old ivory. He had seen her there on a previous visit, emotionless, permanently wide-eyed, swimming slowly but remorselessly up and down the length of the pool hour after hour; never faltering, as if intent on setting up an endurance record that could only be recognized by herself. He glanced at her from time to time as they passed, finding neither interest or recognition in her set face. He wondered idly if, during the intervening months between his last visit and now, she had been permanently swimming up and down the pool.

Teasdale himself only completed twelve lengths. Not because he was tired, more because he was bored. At least that was what he told himself, being unwilling to admit to a growing feeling of disquiet almost amounting to anxiety. A sensation not unknown to him, but one he had always previously been able to attribute to a reasonable cause. Needing to find a reasonable cause, for Teasdale considered himself to be a man whose emotions were governed by clear thinking, he concluded that it was due to lack of breakfast. Intent on remedying that he left the pool to take another shower, not that it was obligatory on this occasion, but necessary for bodily comfort to wash away the brine. He had almost completed drying himself, and was working briskly on the area around his crotch when the green canvas curtain hanging at the front of the cubicle was drawn sharply aside. He looked up and saw the man's eyes, the curve of his lips, the exposed teeth, and his earlier anxiety turned to fear. 'It is to be now?' he gasped. The teeth parted and a coarse whisper reached his ears.

'*Hameh kommt. Und mit ihm der Tod.*'

The pitiless ferocity of the blow was so devastating that Teasdale felt no real pain, only a numb awareness that his lungs no longer functioned. But unaware that his heart had been thrust into the final stages of ventricular fibrillation before ultimate cessation. Never to know how, he staggered the few feet from the shower cubicle to the pool, where his fading vision glimpsed the group of Germans in the act of changing places by the hot-water inlet. His brain gave a command to his tongue. '*Hilfe – hilfe,*' he ordered it to call out in German. Henry Teasdale was clear-thinking to the last.

The Germans only saw a man, naked apart from an incongruous plastic bathing cap on his head, staggering to the rim of the pool where he collapsed, rolled over and lay hanging above the water, staring at them with empty, lifeless eyes. They heard nothing of any call for help, but were in fact disturbed by a most peculiar sound echoing distantly down from the vaulted roof of the pool. A sound that Luedke, the naturalist among them, could only, and with some reluctance, later describe as being, '*Wie der Schrei einer tollen Taube.*' Like the cry of a demented dove.

And without missing a stroke, the Finnish woman continued to swim steadily up and down the length of the pool, either oblivious to the death of Henry Teasdale or completely unperturbed by its occurrence.

## POPKISS INTERCEPT

| | |
|---|---|
| *Subject*: | POPKISS Eric Walter – Aged 38 – British subject. |
| *Location*: | 183, Brierley Gardens, Sydenham, London SE 26. |
| *Tel. No*: | Indexed. |
| *Date Commenced*: | 2 August. |
| *Authority*: | HO/1890/79/253 |
| *Registry*: | 781/437/3951GTH 781/635/8677LMT & others. |

*2 Aug. 15.36 hrs. Incoming. Caller identifies self as Terry. Speaks to female (Norah) asks for Eric.*

T.    Hullo, Eric. How's it goin'?

E.    Lousy. Doin' my pieces on the gee-gees on telly.

T.    No luck, eh?

E.    I'm down about a ton.

T.    So that's why I couldn't get through earlier. Never mind, eh. You still got a bit left from the last tickle, ain'tcha?

E.    Schtum on this thing, you stupid prick.

T.    Sorry. I thought you had it dusted.

E.    That don't mean you should rabbit on about private things.

T.  Well, it ain't easy. I mean you said no meets for now.

E.  Just use your loaf, that's all.

T.  Yeah, well. Has the geezer been in touch?

E.  Not since the meet two days ago. He said it would be a few days. He won't get in touch on this, but we arranged another meet for later at the time.

T.  Yeah, well look; I got hold of ... you know ... for makin' the twirls. He says, you know ... the dents ... are good. He wants two up front.

E.  Two? Two ton?

T.  Christ, no. He wants two grand. It's very delicate work, he says. Got to be precise to five thou otherwise they won't work. Then he wants five per cent of the total tickle. Alternatively, he'll take ten per cent of the readies and leave out the tom and other stuff.

E.  He don't want much, does he? I mean, he ain't goin' in, is he? Serve the bastard right if there wasn't no readies.

T.  Christ, don't say that. I'm reckoning on at least half a mil. We'll only get rubbish for the tom and other gear. When can you come up with the two G?

E.  I'm seeing the geezer day after tomorrow. I'll prop it to him then. Shouldn't be no problem. He said he would stand the exes.

T.  The meet at the same place?

E.  No. Somewhere different.

*(there is a pause)*

T.  Look, Eric. I'm a bit sussy about this whole thing. It could be a right old fit-up, couldn't it? I mean, him just wanting that one box. It don't sound right. We could be inside the gaff and down comes the filth. Bang to rights, ain't we?

E.  Don't worry. The geezer's solid.

T.  How can you be sure?

E.  'Cause he put himself on offer and I took him on.

You know that burn-up you sent the bunch of dan-
delions to last week? Nice one that, by the way.

T. That grass Billy...

E. Yeah, him. Down to the geezer, at my request.

T. Jesus Christ! They said it was an accident.

E. Don't you believe it. So it don't pay to mess him
about, do it? Or me neither.

(*another noticeable pause*)

E. You there, Terry?

T. Yeah, if anything I'm more worried. I mean, he's a
mystery, ain't he? We don't know him from
nowhere. Look, where's the meet? I want to be
there.

E. No way, Terry. He was very definite on that.

T. He'll never know. Look, I just want to ready-eye the
geezer, that's all. I'll keep well clear. If he's filth, I'll
know him.

E. You been nicked often enough.

T. It's in both our interests, Eric. I mean, if he's a
wrong 'un, he could be plottin' you for a burn-up,
couldn't he? Wiv nobody around to tell the tale.

(*lengthy pause*)

E. Yeah, well OK. But stay well away. This geezer is
sharp.

T. Don't worry.

E. You're the one that's worried.

T. Yeah, well. Where's the meet?

E. You remember that pussy place we looked at about
five years ago, then gave it the elbow because I
didn't reckon the new wiring?

T. Christ, we must have looked at twenty. Which one?

E. The one with the wild piece of schmutter in the
window, you fancied it for Maisie, if we had it off.

T. Gotcha. Down there, eh? What time?

E. Not quite down there, a left at the end then the

second johnny along. Three o'clock.

T.    You goin' tooled?

E.    Don't be stupid. What's he goin' to do me for?

T.    Well, you won't be dwellin' there, willya? I mean, it's too open, you couldn't stand plottin' things there. You'll be goin' on, won'tcha? Is he bringin' his own wheels?

E.    He didn't say. I expect so. He specifically said I was to come on the plod and do a lot of duckin' and divin' before I got there. What sort of prick do you take me for, I asked him, right out. You don't think I'm stupid enough to go straight to a meet, I said.

T.    What did he say?

E.    Gave me the fish-eye for a time, then sort of laughed. Stout fellow, he says. Can you imagine it? Stout fellow.

T.    Toff, is he?

E.    Hard to put the finger. Could be foreign. Very precise. Polite but precise, know what I mean? Sharp. Very sharp.

T.    That name he put on you. Sounds a right stumer.

E.    It would be, wouldn't it? I'd be more sussy if he showed right out. A right berk we got here, I would say. Wouldn't you?

T.    Yeah, I guess so. What about the ding-dong? Can you manage it all right?

E.    He gave me the complete picture. Amperage and everything. It's a doddle.

T.    Maybe that's why I'm a bit sussy. I mean, how did he get hold of that?

E.    It's a *sauerkraut* system. Maybe he works there. That would explain a lot, wouldn't it?

T.    I think you hit the nail, Eric. But I just can't understand why he only wants that one box. I mean, if he was on top he'd want his corner, wouldn't he?

E.    Maybe there's more juice in that one box of oranges than in the rest of the fruit.

T.    Well, shouldn't we get a drink out of it?

E.    I thought about that. Then I thought about our mate Billy ... Furthermore, it can't be all that much, can it? I mean, from our point of view it could be something for the ... well, the knock-down market. Could be worth millions on that but pure aggravation for us. We don't want no unnecessary aggravation, so why bother. I mean, the rest of the gear. These places ... Aladdin's Cave, ain't it?

T.    Yeah. You're dead right, Eric. Couldn't come at a better time, could it? I'm nearly boracic.

E.    Me too. I've done a grand at the Imperial this month. And what with these fuckin' gluepots I put my pieces on this afternoon...

T.    Yeah, well good luck with the geezer. I'll stay well out of sight.

E.    You do that. And look, if we go on from there, don't try no rub-a-dub. That would only fuck things up. You got me?

T.    Yeah. Yeah. I just want a look at his boat. I'm just being shrewd. You always said, be shrewd Terry.

E.    I did, didn't I. Well, don't come back on this thing. After I've seen the geezer and copped for the keyman, everything should be finalized. So let's say we meet Saturday.

T.    Name a place.

E.    That one down your way. The one with the fat cow behind the bar. Say, eleven-thirty.

T.    The one with the gorgeous tits, you mean?

E.    And fat arse. Yeah, there. In the meantime, you get busy takin' casual sights on the project. Saturday, we'll go across and book in at that hotel opposite and do a more intensive survey over the weekend. If it goes well, we should be in business over the next one.

T.    Great. See you then, Eric.

E.      Be lucky.

         *Call terminated: 16.03*

*2 Aug. 16.15 hrs Subject dials out. (No. indexed.) (Subscriber: John*
         *Gately, Bookmaker, 62 High Road, Sydenham, SE 26.)*
         *Places £30 win bet on Lamplighter 4.30 race at Goodwood.*
         *16.43 hrs Subject dials above, enquires result. Lamplighter*
         *finished third. Subject expresses annoyance.*
         *18.05 hrs Female (Norah Thornton) dials out. (No. indexed.)*
         *(Subscriber: Golden Bowl, Chinese Take Away, Richmond*
         *Road, Penge, SE 20). Orders Menu B for two. Will collect.*

*3 Aug. 11.02 hrs Incoming. Caller (female) identifies as Maisie.*
         *Speaks to Norah. Inconsequential conversation about money*
         *(lack of), clothes (bargains), health (migraine, menstru-*
         *ation), TV programmes, etc.*
         *12.35 hrs Subject dials out. (No. indexed.) Subscriber: Rely-on-*
         *Us, Travel Agents, 9 Station Parade, Sydenham, SE 26.)*
         *Enquires possible late booking for one week holiday Majorca*
         *commencing 13 Aug. Intended travellers Maisie Ackroyd and*
         *Norah Thornton.*
         *14.47 hrs Incoming. Identifies as Mr Bright, Rely-on-Us.*
         *Offers three possible resorts in Majorca to subject. Subject*
         *chooses cheapest at Arenal. Says he will call in 4 Aug. and*
         *pay deposit.*

*3 Aug. 19.17 hrs Incoming call. (Male.) Identifies as Ronnie.*
R.      Eric? Long time no see. Listen, Eric. You got any
         business coming off soon where you could row me
         in? I could do with the work. I'm not worried about
         an equal corner. Flat rate or a third of what anyone
         else is getting. Things are a bit sour lately.
E.      Not with me, Ronnie. I've had a couple of big ones
         off at Goodwood. I'm not lookin' for odd-job men at
         the moment.
R.      Oh. Any chance you could bung me a monkey until
         I get something laid on?
E.      Absolutely no chance whatsoever, Ronnie.

R.      Fuck you too. (*Hangs up abruptly.*)

E.      (*Replacing phone*) Snouting shit-bag.

*Further calls between 4 Aug and 13 Aug. Deemed inconsequential. Not transcribed in accordance with Economy Instruction 156c. No outgoing calls from 13 Aug until 20 Aug, several incoming calls – all unanswered.*

*20 Aug 19.50 hrs Caller (female) dials 999 emergency. Identifies as Norah Thornton. Operator answers.*

O.      Emergency. Which service do you require?

N.      Police for God's sake. Get the police.

O.      What is your number, please?

N.      Number given (*see Index*). For Christ's sake hurry.

O.      Connecting you now. (*Ringing tone heard for six minutes. N. becomes increasingly agitated.*)

P.      Police. Scotland Yard. Can I help you?

N.      Where the bleedin' hell have you been? This phone's been ringing for hours.

P.      Sorry, madam. If you'd just give me your name and address.

N.      There's been a bleedin' murder, you stupid git.

P.      Yes, well we can't do much about it without your name and address, can we?

N.      Norah Thornton, 183 Brierley Gardens, Sydenham.

P.      Has the incident occurred at that address, madam?

N.      He's upstairs in the bedroom. Oh my God, my poor Eric. I'm going to be sick.

P.      Try taking some deep breaths, madam. We will get a car to you shortly.

*Police disconnect. Caller remains with line open. Is heard to say repeatedly, Oh my God, Eric. What am I going to do. Becomes hysterical.*

*20.04 hrs Police siren heard over open line. Voice male. Presumed police officer says, Come on now, let go the phone and tell me all about it. Says Hello – Hello into mouthpiece then replaces phone.*

*21.59 hrs Caller (Identified as Det. Inspr. Worple) dials out. (No. indexed.) (Subscriber: Brian Robert Stanstead, 73 Oakwood Place, Bromley, Kent. Identified as Detective Chief Superintendent, P District, Metropolitan Police.)*

W.    Frank Worple here, Guv. Sorry to bother you at home, but I got a right one on my manor. Thought you ought to know.

S.    What is it?

W.    Suspicious death. Eric Popkiss. Known. A good screwsman. Expert wireman. Found in the bedroom of his gaff here over an hour ago. He's been dead a few days. Phew, the stink.

S.    So what's the problem?

W.    You should see his bedroom, Guv. Jewellery, precious stones, gold coins, objays dah, and readies, bundles of readies, various currencies. It's like Aladdin's Cave. It could be the gear from the Aldwych Safe Deposit job.

S.    Any indications on cause of death?

W.    Nothing apparent, Guv. Post mortem lividity fairly well advanced. A very indelicate shade of blue-green. But no blood or ligature marks. We'll have to wait for the autopsy.

S.    It will be vagal inhibition. Just like the others.

W.    What others, Guv?

S.    If you extended your reading beyond the racing section of that toe-rag newspaper you study each morning and tried police publications and circulations instead, you would know what others. One was Terry Scanlon, found dead in his home at Battersea two days ago when his dear old mum happened to call round. There was also a large proportion of the Aldwych gear inside. Cause of death vagal inhibition. The first was Billy Appleby, a known informer. He had a vagal inhibition on some open ground in East Croydon. That was put down to Larkin. Not now it won't be.

W. Hey, Guv. Popkiss and Scanlon were known associates. And Appleby used to run with them before they sussed him as a grass.

S. Popkiss was a target on your manor. Did you know he was plotting something?

W. Well, not exactly, Guv. My snout, Ronnie the One, blew down my ear well over a week ago that Popkiss had something heavy ready-eyed. I told him to go in on the man direct, but he got the strong rebuff.

S. I think you can look forward to something similar on your next promotion board. Still, I suppose it's some consolation to know we've got most of the Aldwych gear back.

W. Yeah. Funny thing that though, ain't it?

S. I'm not laughing, Mr Worple. I'll be over there shortly.

*In view of intervention by civil police, intercept discontinued in accordance with Standing Orders.*

# Two

......

'Malleable?'

The word fell softly from Quinlan's lips and, lifting his eyes from the pages of the book, he sought an answer among the thin grass on which he was sitting. Finding only the distraction of a stray ant scurrying along under the burden of a dead fly, he spat at the insect with great accuracy, engulfing it in a gob of saliva. For some minutes he watched closely as the ant struggled to free first itself, then its prey, from the clinging mucus. Annoyed by its eventual success, Quinlan allowed the insect to gain six inches of freedom before gathering a more viscous load from the back of his throat. Although he discharged his sputum with great force, he missed by a considerable margin and the ant vanished into a denser clump of grass before he could assemble sufficient ammunition for a third shot.

Angry now, he returned to the pages of his book and again encountered the mysterious word. 'MALLEABLE?' he screamed in frustration.

Dozing nearby on a wooden bench, Lionel Peachtree, QC, awoke with a startled jerk, the brief that had lain on his lap falling to the ground. 'What? What? What?' he exclaimed, then seeing his papers scattered at his feet, eased himself forward to retrieve them.

'Malleable?' Quinlan said again, his tone reduced to one of mere exasperation.

'Well, what about it?' Peachtree asked.

'What does it mean then?' Quinlan demanded; truculent to the point of rudeness. Peachtree, however, appeared to accept the commission gladly.

'Ah, yes,' he replied, scrutinizing the question thoughtfully, then raising his hand he patted the crown of a battered Panama hat as if adjusting a wig. Gathering the pages of his brief together, he drew the thick bundle close to his chest before making a pronouncement.

'Much would depend on the context in which the word is used,' he averred with a lawyer's caution. 'Perhaps you might read out the relevant passage.' A benign smile conveyed his request down to Quinlan.

Obediently, Quinlan picked up the grimy paperback, drawing himself onto his haunches as he did so, as though that position would enhance both perception and understanding. Despite these preparations his diction was faltering and clumsy, but he persevered gamely.

'"As she drew back from him, fear and loathing in her face, he reached out with the speed of a striking serpent. Evil fingers curled round the open neck of her negligée and as he pulled her forward the soft silk was ripped apart exposing her proud bosom. Defiantly she held herself erect, her perfect breasts firm, fair and *malleable* under his hot lustful eyes."'

'Pretty mild stuff for these days, Quinlan.' A voice pleasantly mocking came from over Peachtree's shoulder. Peachtree turned, looking upwards and backwards. 'Oh, good afternoon, Castellain,' he said before the overstretched tendons in his neck recoiled against unnatural tension and pulled his head down into his chest, where it lay twitching in diminishing doll-like nods.

'You can get hold of much more stimulating masturbatory fantasies if you know the right places to look, Quinlan,' Castellain went on. 'The moving pictures seem to be in the forefront at the moment. No sooner were they permitted to raise the foot from the floor when seated on the connubial bed than they jumped in between the sheets in a welter of tits and bums. I've seen some of them, you know. Even on T.V. The shows they won't allow us to watch. Everything graphically and anatomically presented. Each lewd, grunting thrust lustily and lustfully depicted. In current literature, no chapter is complete without at least three or four copulatory pages scoring orgasmic bull's-eyes every time. I can give you several titles, if you wish?'

'I don't read dirty books,' Quinlan mumbled sullenly, without defiance. Castellain was old, at least in his eyes. Yet oddly ageless; worn and craggy, like a rock eroded by time into aggressive and enduring permanence. For all that he had never seen Castellain strike anyone, though his very being seemed to hold an implicit threat that cowed even the Blues: who could be very nasty if the mood took them. Fascinated, Quinlan watched Castellain massaging Peachtree's scrawny neck, his forefingers kneading the stringy muscles.

'As for you, my learned friend,' Castellain was admonishing the lawyer. 'I am, if not shocked, certainly very disappointed in you. Indulging in what appears to be passive perversion. Were you searching for some dimly remembered sexual stimuli by having Quinlan read this rubbish aloud? I have encountered quite a few instances of deviant behaviour in my time, but getting your kicks by proxy is rather out of character, isn't it?'

'Really, it was not like that at all,' Peachtree tried to shake his head in dissent but strong fingers held him still. 'It was a question of semantics. Quinlan sought my opinion on the meaning of the word ... What was the word again, Quinlan?'

'Malleable,' Quinlan obliged.

'Ah, yes,' his neck still imprisoned, Peachtree had no alternative but to address the empty air. 'And in order to assess the intent and purpose of the author, it was necessary to hear the passage verbatim.'

'You could have read it for yourself,' said Castellain sternly.

'I was studying my brief at the time. An opinion on the merit of this case is most urgently sought by my clients.'

'But you've had that brief since I arrived here over three years ago.'

'It is not the same brief. My chambers are constantly sending me fresh briefs. My opinions on chancery cases are highly valued.'

'From the state of it, the one you're holding must be *Jarndyce* versus *Jarndyce*.'

'No, it is not. I am not familiar with that issue.'

'Oh, dear. My poor friend.' Castellain chided. 'And you so learned in law.'

Quinlan beat his heels into the grass in an impatient dance. 'Nobody has told me what *malleable* means,' he cried petulantly, holding up his book.

Without looking at him, Castellain said, 'Doesn't it mention nubile? When describing mammary appendages bad writers always use nubile, under the impression it has erotic meaning.'

Puzzled, Quinlan skimmed through a couple of pages. 'No nubile,' he said regretfully. 'But it does have a nice sound. What's it mean?'

'Simply a woman of marriageable age. It could fit any old hag with tits down to her knees.'

'What about malleable then?'

'Soft, pliable, capable of being moulded. Which makes your author's use of "firm" in conjunction with malleable a gross abuse of language. Wouldn't you agree, Peachtree?'

Peachtree squirmed under the pressure of Castellain's fingers. 'Do please release your grip on my neck, there's a good chap,' he tried to be resolute, but failed. He offered qualified gratitude. 'Initially it was quite pleasant, relaxing really, but I fear you do not realize how strongly you have increased your grip. It could be dangerous.'

'But that is why we're here, isn't it? Because we are dangerous.' Castellain bent over him and the sight of his unnaturally inverted face with its thick iron-grey hair, black arched brows and hooked, slightly twisted nose, induced in Peachtree a weird sensation of giddiness. 'I am only trying to awaken the dormant desires you sought to arouse by listening to putrid prose.' A chuckling whisper sang in Peachtree's ears. 'I want to pleasure you, old chap. Don't you know that partial asphyxiation can bring about an erection; an involuntary orgasm? Look down at yourself.' Castellain leaned into him, pressing his head forward and even as he did so Peachtree felt a stirring in his loins, saw the engorged stiffening underneath the greasy food stains that marred the front of his striped trousers. He closed his eyes and moaned slightly, wanting Castellain to grip tighter. To squeeze harder... Ahead lay the crest of a wave... If only he had the strength.

But Castellain had taken his hands away, leaving him limp and afraid. Not of Castellain, of himself... If only he had the strength. Castellain vaulted over the back of the seat and sat beside him.

'You would never have made it, old man,' he whispered, as if to preserve their secret from the now moodily introspective Quinlan, lying before them pulling at the grass. 'You would never have got there alive,' he emphasized, laying all the blame on Peachtree. 'Another ten seconds and you would have snuffed it. Never mind,' he said, giving Peachtree a consoling pat on the back. 'Try and get some exercise. Give up this vegetarian regime you've imposed on yourself. Get some red meat in your belly.' Castellain laughed deep in his own belly. 'No, maybe not. On second thoughts, forget it. That's what brought you in here, wasn't it?'

Bridling under both implications, Peachtree pulled huffily away. 'It was certainly not *that* which brought me here, Castellain. One does not act as I did because of *that*. Honour certainly, in a personal sense, and decency. Christian duty, if you like, public duty.'

'*Vox populi, vox Dei?*' Castellain suggested.

'*Verbum sat sapienti,*' Peachtree countered.

'Ah, but unfortunately your words did not reach the ears of a wise man,' said Castellain with patently counterfeit consideration. 'Do you think your argument could be advanced to sustain the deliberate but gradual eradication of the female sex entirely? Would there, do you think, assuming we get rid of the lot within, say, a hundred years, be an evolutionary jump, a quantum leap, as people are so fond of saying nowadays, making the remainder of mankind – and I stress the singularity of that term – making them capable of reproducing themselves in a hermaphroditic manner?'

'You are quite mad, Castellain.'

'Oh, indeed. Isn't that why I'm here? Why we are all here? But I am on the rehabilitation course. I'll be leaving you shortly. Therefore, I must be considered no more mad than the rest of humanity.'

'I certainly did not acknowledge insanity in my case.'

'I grant you never acknowledged it. Despite that, what you did offer in your defence was considered so aberrant in a member of the legal profession, the judge had no alternative but to direct the jury to find you potty. I suspect a great deal of method in your madness, Peachtree.'

'That is an instance of the gross over-simplification one so frequently finds in the lay mind. I carried my defence on a logical extension of the law relating to justifiable homicide. Lesbianism in one's wife, in women generally, places procreation in jeopardy and the killing of those deliberately practising it to protect unborn life is justifiable. Unfortunately, my arguments were too complex for a particularly stupid judge and unimaginative jury to comprehend.'

'But you tried to take it all the way to the House of Lords, and they all came to the conclusion you were stone bonkers.'

'You really are enjoying yourself at my expense, aren't you, Castellain? And not for the first time. I keep rising to your bait. Thank God they are throwing you out of here. They deserve you outside.'

'I'm sorry, Peachtree, I really am. I have to relieve the bloody boredom somehow.'

For a time Peachtree cogitated on the apology, considering whether it was sincere enough to purge the contempt. 'I don't know what has come over you these past few months. You used to be such a modest, almost reclusive fellow, yet always ready to stretch out the helping hand. Now, ever since you have been on the rehabilitation course, you have become quite cruelly aggressive.'

'They tell me it's a cruel and aggressive world outside,' Castellain said.

'It is not only myself, you know,' Peachtree finally summed up. 'The others, Talbot, Marsh, Kendigg, even Quinlan, have all complained about the way you rile, yes, even revile them. They want me to draw up a petition to the Whites, to Snow White himself, complaining about your behaviour. If only half the allegations they make against you are true, you would not be on the rehabilitation course, you would be back behind the

Bricks. That is, if I took it upon myself to draw up an indictment based on their evidence.'

'But you won't, will you, old son?' Castellain's hand crept along Peachtree's shoulder until it reached the side of his neck. A wide thumb firmly caressed the side of his throat from jaw to clavicle. 'You won't, will you, old son?' Castellain repeated with threatening amiability.

'Not so long as you behave yourself,' said Peachtree in peevish surrender.

'Oh, I will be good,' Castellain avowed solemnly. 'I'll be very, very good.'

But Peachtree was no longer listening to him. He had half-risen to his feet against the weight of Castellain's arm, and was squinting myopically in the direction of a man some distance away. A man in his forties; broad shoulders hunched as if in anticipation of a blow from behind, one walking with delicate exploratory steps as if doubting the solidity of the ground beneath his feet. Peachtree sank back on the seat. 'Good Lord,' he said in amazement.

'Fresh fish.' Castellain too, watched the man keenly. 'Know him?' he enquired.

'Yes, I do. At least I think I do. It's been several years.'

'I think I know him too. The great avenger. So the bird is back.'

'No. No. His name is Smith. He is a police detective.' Peachtree turned curiously to Castellain. 'Two years ago when we were behind the Bricks, a new man came in. You said he was the great avenger. You remember, the one that fell off the roof trying to get out. His name was Griffiths. A singularly inept fellow who tried to kill his parents with ground glass in their soup.'

'I don't remember,' Castellain replied.

'You must. There was such a to-do about it. We had the police in. We were all questioned.'

'I had forgotten his name. And if you are right, we now have our own policeman. Be no need to get any in from the outside, will there?'

Castellain reached out a long leg and stirred the recumbent form of Quinlan, lying foetally curled and quietly dozing. He snapped out his name. An eye opened reluctantly.

'Whatcha want?'

'Nip across the lawn and catch that fellow walking down towards the Wire. Ask him if he would be good enough to join us. Tell him an old friend wants to meet him.'

'Which one of you is his old friend?'

'That remains to be seen,' Castellain said. 'Now get a move on.'

'Go yourself, I'm sick and tired of running your bloody errands.'

'Quinlan!' Menace and command lay in that single utterance.

Abashed but sullen, Quinlan got to his feet and trotted in the direction of Castellain's pointing finger. They watched as he scuttled up behind the stranger's back, saw him reach out tentatively as if afraid to touch the formidable bulk of the shoulder, saw him withdraw, then, visibly swelling with determination, dance forward again. The slow-moving stranger swung round so quickly the watchers had difficulty in following the sequence of events, knowing only that Quinlan had been projected into the air to land heavily at the side of the path with the stranger standing over him, pinning his right hand against the earth with his foot. They saw the stranger's eyes raking the vicinity as if in search of a dropped weapon.

'So he has come,' Castellain hissed.

'Who has come?' said Peachtree, his curiosity deepening to concern.

'The one who destroyed my soul,' and for the first time Peachtree saw a trace of fear in Castellain's face. Fear mingled with hatred. Hatred conquered.

'I tell you his name is Smith. I remember him well now, Detective Inspector Smith of the Flying Squad at New Scotland Yard. I was against him on several occasions at the Old Bailey.'

Peachtree saw the man he knew as Smith help Quinlan to his feet. The latter, obviously bereft of speech, gesticulated towards himself and Castellain. Smith glowered at them sternly, then placing a hand under Quinlan's armpit, half carried him across the grass to drop the still speechless youth at their feet.

'Next time he comes up to me, tell him to come in from the front,' Smith said brusquely.

'I am afraid the fault was mine, Inspector,' Peachtree offered an apologetic but knowing simper. Smith frowned.

'I know the word is about behind the Bricks, but I didn't think it would follow me through to the Wire so quickly. I should have known better,' he pointed to the now gasping Quinlan. 'Well, I can take care of myself. Particularly against silly little squirts like this one.' He stared squarely into Castellain's face, a face now rigid and impassive. 'Like him or anyone else,' he said, as if aware of the malevolence.

'My dear Inspector, no one means you harm,' protested Peachtree. 'Not here, not beyond the Bricks. We who are within the Wire are not like those on the other side of the wall. Certainly we were all there ourselves for a time, but, well, not to put too fine a point on it, we are special cases. Many of us are professional people, or at least persons of some standing.'

Smith looked down at Quinlan busily easing the aches in his spine and cursing under his breath. 'And what profession is this one a member of?'

'Ah, well, there are also a few like Quinlan whose origins are not quite . . .'

'Top drawer?' Castellain suggested.

Peachtree ignored it. 'The Whites classify them as Responders. Those who have shown a willingness to adapt. We try to use our influence to further their improvement. But . . .' he hesitated, looking woefully at Smith. 'You don't remember me, do you,' he accused.

'I've been trying to place you somewhere among the villains I have dealt with – a con artist – there were not a lot of those – no, you're real enough . . .' He broke off suddenly. 'Peachtree! Lionel Peachtree, QC!' Spreading abject arms a little too expansively, he went on: 'I am sorry, sir. It was the absence of the wig and gown.'

Graciously Peachtree returned the courtesy with a dignified nod. He cross-examined kindly. 'And what, if one may ask, is the nature of the duty that brings you among us, Mr Smith? Not, I trust, another unfortunate falling from the roof in an attempt to escape?'

'No, nothing like that. Like you, Mr Peachtree, I am in here for the good of my health.'

'Ah. Then it is my turn to apologize. We never enquire as to the reasons for which we find ourselves thrown together. No matter how justifiable or excusable they may be.'

'Like serving your wife and her two friends cantharides cocktails because they happen to form a lesbian attachment,' Castellain sneered. Peachtree took it bravely.

'This is Castellain, by the way,' he said stiffly. 'A former civil servant. One, it seems, whose position was so inferior, and whose peccadilloes so trivial, they failed to make even a paragraph in the gutter press. Being aware we know nothing of his background, he chooses to ignore convention. His appearance and speech may be that of a gentleman but recently his manners have been those of a barbarian.' Peachtree slumped wearily against the arm of the seat as though all his strength had been expended. Castellain merely laughed. Quite pleasantly.

'Come to that,' he said to Smith, 'I don't recall seeing your name in the papers. Though with all the bent and brutal coppers that have been in and out of the dock lately it's a job to remember.'

'Take no notice of him, Smith, I beg you,' a weak plea came from Peachtree. 'He will be out of here soon and good riddance. Don't be provoked, you will be back behind the Bricks before you know it.'

'Go on, have a go at him.' On his knees and yelping with excitement, Quinlan pranced about on the grass. 'Go on, belt him one, you're an even match. Have a go.'

'I never step on dog shit,' Smith said. 'Not intentionally at any rate.'

'Oh, good man, Inspector,' applauded Peachtree and turned triumphantly on Castellain. 'You see, in law it is impossible to insult a police officer. That is why your cheap jibes failed to succeed.'

'That's how it is in law,' Smith agreed. 'But,' he gave Castellain a warning finger in the face, 'don't bank on it being that way in fact.'

'I won't, you may rest assured,' Castellain said meekly. 'As a matter of interest, did you ever encounter the great avenger called Hameh?'

'I've never met a great avenger,' Smith replied shortly. 'It always boiled down to nasty, mean spitefulness.'

As he turned to leave them, he swung round again, as if struck by an afterthought, and spoke to Peachtree. 'By the way, my learned friend, the last time I held rank, it was Detective Chief Superintendent. I mention that only to let you know I'm one of the professional people of some standing.'

They watched him resume his progress towards the Wire, his step firmer now, slightly faster. They saw him stop before the lower fence marking the boundary of the Dead Zone. Between it and the Wire no inmate was permitted to stray; to do so meant immediate removal back behind the Bricks – forever, it was said.

'Funny, ain't it?' Quinlan said. 'All the fresh fish do that the minute they get out from behind the Bricks. Go down and have a look at the Wire.'

'It's not the Wire,' Peachtree murmured. 'It is what they see beyond the Wire.'

'Prowlin' up and down like a caged tiger, ain't he?' Quinlan sat up to get a better look. 'I'll bet he's a goer. I'll bet he tries to have it away on his toes before long.'

'Oh, I hope not,' said Peachtree in some alarm. 'After all the fellow is, or was, a senior police officer. I'm sure he has a strong sense of discipline. He will know the importance of obeying the law.'

Disappointed, Quinlan fell back on his haunches. 'I wonder what he did then, to get himself in here?' he asked.

'He killed people,' said Castellain, his eyes closing in repose. 'Just like the rest of us. He killed inconvenient and unnecessary people,' he yawned behind a refined hand. 'Now do be quiet and let a chap get some sleep.'

# Three

•••••••

Rachette removed his half-moon spectacles and placed the intercept file squarely in the middle of his desk, smiling, as if in reminiscent mood.

'An interesting juxtaposition of thought processes, that both criminal and policeman should make the Aladdin's Cave analogy.'

'It must have been a fairly awesome sight,' Protheroe conceded. 'The total value of the haul was nearly three million.'

'Most of it recovered, presumably?'

'As far as they can ascertain,' Hamilton said. 'There are those depositors unwilling to claim or identify moneys and property with the income tax inspector hovering in the background.'

'The Nemesis of the twentieth century. But we public servants who have our hard-earned pelf deducted at source need not fear. Need we?'

For some reason he directed his gaze at Protheroe, who over a year ago had come into a sizeable sum in cash, the savings of a senile parent who distrusted banks. That he had invested the money in a cottage in the Dordogne was, he thought, unknown to anyone. He nodded at Rachette in reluctant assent, shifting uncomfortably in his chair, but saying nothing.

'But it does go to prove we are dealing with highly disciplined people, does it not. Indeed, not only highly disciplined, but remarkably honest. Well, perhaps honest is not quite what I meant, but in no way self-indulgent, shall we say. Unlike some.'

'Unlike who?' Protheroe challenged angrily, and knew he had made a mistake.

'Unlike the policeman Worple, Basil.' Rachette met him with a bland smile. 'His, er, Guv'nor, to use the recent enlargement of my vocabulary,' he pointed at the file, 'sussed him as a wrong 'un and found he had stuffed one and a half grand in, er, readies, under the back seat of his car. Poor Worple, unable to resist the temptation. One could almost say the Aladdin's Cave syndrome is symptomatic of our national disease. Unfortunately, magic lamps are beyond the brief of the National Enterprise Board. But I stray from the serious matters that bring us together.' He reached for the file. 'During my brief sojourn, if such it could be called, as Commissioner of Police, I encountered some of the jargon used in that milieu,' he stabbed at the file with the prongs of his glasses. 'Even where the words are meaningless, they become clear when read in context. However, there are one or two instances... Can either of you assist?'

'Hamilton has done some research,' Protheroe, now noticeably off-hand, spoke as though a descent into the realm of criminal argot was beneath him.

'Was it difficult?' Rachette asked the younger man with unfeigned interest.

'No, sir, I farmed it out to our SB contact,' replied Hamilton. 'To be on the safe side. As a double check ... Not the file, you understand. Just the odd word,' he added hastily.

'How very wise.' The praise was dryly given.

'I take it then, the reference to Popkiss dusting his line did not inconvenience you in any way?'

'Not at all,' said Protheroe, determined not to be entirely left out. 'The fellow trained as a telecommunications engineer and was in honest work for a time until he became criminally involved using his skills to by-pass alarm systems. But naturally he was not abreast of the, ah, technological advances in our, ah, external resources field.'

'I see,' his eyes still on Hamilton, Rachette opened the file.

'Twirls are false keys, am I right?'

'You are, sir.' Hamilton spoke with approval.

'And a burn-up taken in context means a cremation?'

'Right again, sir.'

'And, as is indicated towards the end, the police did not at first treat the death of the informer, Billy Appleby, as suspicious?'

'That is so,' Hamilton leaned forward with a gleam in his eye. 'You see, sir, vagal inhibition as a cause of death is a sort of pathological catch-all in cases where there is no other determinant factor. It can be brought about by a blow, not necessarily severe, in the region of the head, neck, chest or abdomen. In fact, some quite natural respiratory irregularity or muscular spasm may affect the vagus nerve causing death to supervene, either immediately or after a period of coma. Although it need not always be present, a person in a state of fear or terror may suffer, or may be induced to suffer, a vagal inhibition. It has to do with the parasympathetic nervous system, of which the vagus nerve is the largest part, controlling as it does the parasympathetic fibres from the brain to heart. Thus, if one knows where and how to strike or apply pressure, the heart can be stopped. Appleby's body was found near a waist-high fence post and as there was some abdominal bruising it was assumed he had stumbled into the post bringing about an accidental vagal inhibition.'

'Your research has been most thorough indeed, Hamilton. I congratulate you,' speaking warmly, Rachette slowly turned his attention to Protheroe. 'Wasn't that clever of him, Basil? All that medical patter. No reference to notes either, I observe. Most clever, don't you agree?'

Protheroe grunted. 'What he is here for, isn't it?'

'Yes, I suppose so. Well, let us return to the more mundane matters you are here for, Hamilton. "Pussy" is a reference to furs. Am I right?'

'You are, sir.'

'Although I have heard it used in another context, but that need not concern us now. "Johnny" is rhyming slang for "Johnny Horner", meaning a corner.'

It's a damned disgrace, thought Protheroe. Outright

sadism. Having me sit here whilst he exhibits the arse end of his ego.

'But here I am baffled,' Rachette was saying. '"Boracic"?' He lifted an enquiring eyebrow at Hamilton.

'Boracic lint, sir. Skint, meaning broke.'

'Ah, and "boat"?'

'That one had me going too, sir,' Hamilton offered the sympathy of shared ignorance. 'It's for face, you see. Boat race. Face.'

'Are you sure? I mean if there *is* a boat somewhere, it might be important.'

'I am assured it has no other meaning.'

'Very well. The possibilities are endless, are they not? No, never mind,' a quick interjection from Rachette caused Protheroe's opening mouth to close again. Rachette leaned back in his chair, laying gentle contemplative hands on the rotunda of his stomach, allowing his fingers to drum a fleshy but audible tattoo on the surface. Hamilton thought he recognized the beat as Schubert's *Marche Militaire*. He glanced at Protheroe, whose chin rested on a surly fist, while his louring gaze dwelt steadily on a far corner of the room.

'Basil?' The drumming ceased and Rachette eased forward. Protheroe brought his eyes round in slow defiance.

'I am going to have a dickens of a job trying to put all this to the minister in a reasonable light, Basil.' The words were soft, like distant thunder. 'Your surveillance people observe the original encounter between this Bulgarian trade attaché, Slunchev, and a fairly minor home-brewed villain, i.e. Popkiss. As a result...'

'Not my surveillance people, my one man, my single, solitary man.' Protheroe countered viciously. 'The only piece of emaciated flesh left on the broken bones of my surveillance section. Even then it was purely fortuitous, it just happened to be Slunchev's turn to be taken for a walk. That's the only way my man can operate now. He takes them for a walk on a rota basis. Leave, sickness and weather conditions permitting.'

'The economic axe does have a wide blade, Basil. We all get it in the neck, or at least have the occasional limb chopped off. We must hobble along as best we can. It was hardly a shortage of manpower that caused this disaster.'

'I certainly think it was. Those with responsibilities for the Soviets have not been cut to anything like the same extent. I have the entire satellite network, and am chopped forty-five per cent.'

'You are acting as a judge in your own court, Basil. Let us look at it objectively. As a consequence of this meeting you obtain authority to intercept Popkiss's phone ...'

'I wanted his whole place wired for sound.'

'Yes, I know, and you know the policy on that. Not with our own nationals. At least those not bound by the Act. Those whose protests we can stifle, should it, as Mr Popkiss might say, come a tumble.' A raised hand shut out further protest, and words died a writhing but soundless death on Protheroe's lips.

'You got the best we could give you, Basil.' With his chin once more buried in his fist, Protheroe gave a brief snort of contempt. Rachette continued as if he had not heard.

'From what transpires, you assume, and this of course was the cardinal error, that Slunchev has engineered a vastly profitable criminal enterprise and intends to defect on the proceeds without the inconvenience of coming over. You decide to allow matters to take their course and nab Slunchev on his way out with the goods on him. Your reason being that finding himself in such invidious circumstances, he would be obliged to co-operate fully or his plot would be exposed and he would be handed back to the tender mercies of the comrades. Being unable to ascertain the venue, and rightly or wrongly assuming that to follow Popkiss around would not be possible ...'

'Because I did not have the resources. Don't forget that. Because I did not have the resources!'

'Or, as you put it in your report ...' Rachette reached for a red-bound file and wetting the middle finger of his right hand on his lower lip, riffled through the pages. He quoted with due solemnity. '"Our police contacts advise that even multi-stage leap-frogging surveillance would not guarantee detection or evasion by an experienced criminal intent on avoidance ..."' This pessimistic contention makes you decide to break off mobile surveillance, maintaining only static cover on the home of the late and unlamented Popkiss. You predict, wrongly, that Slunchev will call there to collect his loot. Or alternatively, having successfully pulled off his coup and no longer alert, Popkiss will lead you to a prearranged handover point or at least to a drop, where as you so succinctly put it, "In either instance Slunchev will be roped in."''

Gravely, Rachette closed the cover on the file. Things had become so funereal, Hamilton almost expected him to say 'Here endeth the first lesson.'

'But he wasn't, was he, Basil?' he said instead.

'Manpower,' Protheroe barked like a dog demanding to be let in. 'I had to scrape the bottom of the barrel just to cover the Popkiss house. I wanted to bring in Special Branch assistance and was refused. Wasn't I?' He whined at the closed door.

'But you subsequently agreed we could not expect the police, even of the Special Branch, to stand idly by and allow a serious crime to go undetected. We did not want Popkiss making statements to them about approaches from mysterious strangers. Who knows where that sort of thing may lead. We certainly did not want any further public trials with the defendants saying they were really working for the British Secret Service. We've had enough of that nonsense already.'

'Too true,' Hamilton muttered softly, only to find himself under the scrutiny of coldly reproachful looks from both Rachette and Protheroe for his temerity. 'Sorry,' he murmured, not quite abjectly. Rachette sniffed his disapproval. Protheroe merely grunted, and was made once more the subject of Rachette's undivided attention.

'We now know, several days too late, no such handover was made, at least not in the way you so blissfully anticipated. From what the police tell us, in the public media of all places, your tame villains did not immediately return to their respective abodes right away. But each of them, laden with two large suitcases, simply walked across the street and checked into the same hotel they had occupied the previous weekend. No doubt they spent an ecstatic Saturday night sorting out their ill-gotten gains, before leaving next morning. In the meantime, as now seems obvious, Slunchev or someone acting on his behalf, called at the hotel to collect the box, and later visited their homes to send them on an expedition to the undiscovered country from whose bourne etcetera etcetera. And as there was no likelihood of the crimes being discovered before the Monday morning at the earliest, gave himself at least a twenty-four hour start.'

A long hiss of vexation, almost a whistle, fell from Rachette's bared lips. Hamilton looked up in some alarm, at its ferocity. For a Permanent Secretary, Rachette appeared openly disturbed.

'All this was permitted to happen, Basil,' the anger was now unconcealed, 'despite a wealth of evidence in the intercept that Slunchev was only interested in one particular box.'

Turned to stone, Protheroe said nothing. Something akin to pity caused Hamilton to erect a tentative defence. 'We thought the box probably contained negotiable high-value bills of exchange or something similar.' Then, as if seized by sudden inspiration, he added, 'Or that Slunchev intended to double-cross his criminal recruits and abscond with the entire proceeds.' With the air of a gallant loser who has given of his best he stood down, hoping for an honourable mention. It was not forthcoming.

'As to your first contention,' Rachette responded coldly, 'may I enquire how Slunchev knew such purported items were in the box?' Without waiting for an answer, he went on: 'And as for your second, whilst it may be considered possible, the fact remains that he didn't, at least not in any material way. One of the salient features of this mess is that unwarranted optimism based on speculation and conjecture seems to have prevailed over fact and reason. Is that not so?'

'Well, sir . . .' Hamilton floundered.

'Well, sir, the *fact* is, the box belonged to the defunct Teasdale, one of your number. And about which you had no knowledge until the civil police, having lists of renters, made enquiries of his widow, who was equally ignorant of its existence. We know it was Teasdale's box because that was the only one wholly removed from the scene; the others were simply looted and left behind. The question is, what did Teasdale have in his confounded box?'

With some effort, Protheroe broke out of his dull reverie, his lips parting with an audible plop. 'We don't know,' he said wearily. 'It could have been anything and everything. He had top clearance, full access. He ran the division and chaired the liaison committee...'

'Until we put you in over his head, Basil.'

'Are you inferring...?' Protheroe struggled to free himself from the confining depths of the armchair, only to be waved down by a placating hand.

'No, of course not.' Compassion and annoyance strove for dominance in Rachette's voice. 'In that respect I am as much to blame as ... as anyone. I recommended your appointment...' For a while his face mourned the decision, then he continued, 'The horns of our dilemma are, to put it crudely, firmly embedded in our respective backsides. We virtually stood on the sidelines and allowed murder to occur. I mean, your people saw someone enter the Popkiss house after he returned with the loot, and that someone undoubtedly did the man in.'

'But it wasn't Slunchev, we are reasonably certain of that. Besides he wasn't carrying anything when he came out,' Protheroe struggled to enlarge his defence. 'No box, nothing. Just a man of uncertain age in a dark grey coat. We assumed it was one of Popkiss's criminal associates.'

'More assumptions, I see. And no tele-recording? Nothing to give us a picture of this man? This killer?'

'The batteries had given out. Cheap batteries. Everything I have had to do over the past three years has had to be done on the cheap.'

'There should have been spares, or your people could have nipped out and bought some new ones. They would have been reimbursed in due course.'

'It was a Sunday!' Protheroe rammed home his single victory with a triumphant screech.

'So it was,' said Rachette, unperturbed, then frowned. 'Your people would have been on double time. Did you submit for covering approval beforehand? We have still to get over the problem created by giving Teasdale a consular post equivalent to Assistant Secretary. At the time he died his established status was only that of Senior Principal! Pensions and Allowances are in a bit of a fix.'

'Oh, my God.' Protheroe moaned and cupped a hand over his eyes.

'That aside,' Rachette laid *that aside* reluctantly, 'we are faced with what is, after all, the greater problem of Teasdale's box, which, like that of Pandora, may, when opened, as it probably has by now, release untold evil into our little world. But for its existence . . .' Slowly, he drew the Popkiss intercept nearer. 'We could consign this disgusting mess to the flames . . . In the national interest, of course.' Opening the file once again he studied the pages, dismally reflective. 'A right bleeding cock-up,' he finally muttered. 'That's how Mr Popkiss would describe it. "A right bleeding cock-up."'

# Four

**◆◆◆◆◆**

According to the RTR, the Remedial Task Roster, Smith found he was on corridors (polishing). He noted that Castellain was on windows (cleaning), Quinlan was on paths (external) and Peachtree on mail (distribution). So much for being one of the professional people of some standing, he thought. Still, it was only a morning job, the afternoons were free apart from TP&I. The Whites had told him when he was brought into the Wire, they were taking him off P&I – pills and injections; and his T-therapy sessions were reduced to one a month. All treatment is, of course, therapy, but inside the Wire the term was generally used for interview sessions with one or other of the Whites. Behind the Bricks, the field of Smith's particular White had been Psychodiagnostics, and the endeavour of its practitioners had been the discovery of relationships between criminal, paranoid, psychopathic behaviour patterns and external physical characteristics of face, head, speech and gait. To this end he made much use of Smith's experiences as a police officer until, during one session, bored by naive and endless probing, he asked the White if he had ever heard of Bertillon, a French criminologist, who had done it all before nearly two hundred years ago.

'Of course, but he was merely a measurer,' the White had sneered. 'A wielder of calipers and rulers. His only object was to achieve identification by recording the dimensions of a previously known culprit and comparing them with those of an unidentified suspect. He made no attempt, did not even contemplate, relating his findings to behaviourism.'

'Ah,' Smith had said, openly dumbfounded by admiration, and in exercise of a widely-held police principle that bullshit baffles brains. His grading on cognitive functions was increased from satisfactory to excellent as a result.

He had achieved a restful satisfying rhythm, shoving the heavy block backwards and forwards along the floor on the end of its articulated handle, drawing it back steadily to allow the polishing cloth to do its work on the thick brown linoleum without rumpling up and throwing the whole thing off balance. It had taken some time to get the hang of it but now that he had, everything was going smoothly. He stopped for a few moments to ease aching lumbar muscles and admire the gleaming lustre he had re-awakened over eighty feet of corridor, donning a shroud of indifference when a heavy footed Blue came clumping down his impeccable path, but turning a severe glower on the bearded young White pushing a tea-trolley who followed; and who multiplied his offence by slipping on a patch of raw, unburnished wax, allowing the trolley to crash into the wall, and upsetting a jug of hot water over the floor. Ignoring the White as he lay clutching a bruised head, Smith mopped up the water, and with great deliberation squeezed it into the tea-pot whilst the White sat oblivious to everything other than his injured skull. Watching the young man rise unsteadily to his feet, Smith added words to his frown.

'Try and be more careful next time,' he admonished.

'Balls!' cried the youngster angrily, indicating his immaturity and fitness only for menial tasks. 'They make a dammed fine stew,' Smith countered, with airy but malignant mystery. The youngster looked at him fearfully for a moment, then grabbed his trolley and fled towards the Administration offices beyond the steel doors, fumbling for his keys.

The steel door marked the extent of Smith's labours on the ground floor. Inmates were not permitted to enter the Administration section unless escorted. A few yards short of the door lay the ablutions and toilets, entry to which was barred by a broom angled across the opening. A fussy little man, grey-green and wrinkled like an old apple, was shuffling flat-footed towards the opening, waving a mop delicately over the tiles.

'Mind if I come in and wash my hands?' Smith enquired. The small man swung round surprisingly quickly, the mop poised defensively across his chest. 'Take it easy,' Smith said quietly. 'I just want to wash my hands. Exactly that. No euphemism intended.'

His smile brought a lowering of the mop. 'I'm sorry,' the little man replied. 'I'm not long in from behind the Bricks. They used to do things to me in there.'

'They tried it on me too, a couple of times,' Smith smiled sympathetically.

'Because of what you did?'

'No. Because of what I was.'

'I see,' the little man's puzzled face showed that he didn't.

'You'll be Kendigg A.L.' Smith said to change the subject.

'How did you know that?'

'The RTR. Kendigg A.L. Ablutions and toilets. I'm Smith O.J. Corridors. Now can I come in and wash my hands?'

'Can you wait a few minutes for the floor to dry?' Kendigg begged. 'It does mark so if you walk over it while it's still wet.' Seeing him only as another who took pride in his work, Smith readily agreed.

'Very kind of you,' Kendigg said, with the air of one much put upon. 'It's so difficult to make people understand the problem.' He busied himself mopping the last few feet of his domain until he reached the edge of Smith's corridor. Despite himself, Smith saw with disapproval the encroachment of wet rubber boots on his pristine linoleum. As if reading his thoughts, Kendigg said, 'Not to worry,' and, leaning against the tiled wall, removed them. 'There now, all finished. It should dry out nicely.' He turned to gaze fondly at the wet tiles. 'Yes, that should dry out nicely,' he said again approvingly. Then to Smith, 'Fancy a fag?' He pulled out a packet of cigarettes from his overalls. Smith took one, thinking nobody called them fags these days, the imported homosexual connotation was too widespread. Kendigg must have been in a long time. From another pocket Kendigg produced a flat empty tin for use as an ashtray.

'Londoner, are you?' Kendigg enquired as he struck the match.

'For the past twenty-odd years at any rate,' Smith replied.

'How long have you been in?'

'Nearly a year.'

'Did you see anything of Nurse Edith before you came in? How was she looking?'

'Nurse Edith?'

A sad, distraught shadow fell over Kendigg's face. 'You must have seen her,' he implored. 'Nurse Edith Cavell. Shot by the Germans, Dawn-October 12th, 1915. Haven't you seen her standing there? Eternally erect, defiant. Looking straight into the muzzles of the German rifles. Unflinching.'

'You mean the statue? I can't say I've taken much notice of it.'

Kendigg's sadness deepened. He tried a wan smile and failed: and even though his tiles were not quite dry he padded back inside the ablutions, motioning Smith to follow. 'Might as well make ourselves comfortable,' he said, and perched mournfully, like a bedraggled sparrow, on a toilet seat: carefully placing his tin ashtray on the tiled waist-high partition separating each closet. No other privacy was provided. With a gesture that implied the granting of favoured treatment, Kendigg invited Smith to occupy the adjoining throne. He did so. Warily.

'No one is allowed in before lunch,' Kendigg explained his generosity. 'Not unless they've got an incontinency certificate. Peachtree's the worst, he's got prostate trouble. Stands for hours sometimes. I wouldn't mind if he finished in the urinal but he always turns round and shakes it out over the tiles. Dribbles all over the place.'

Kendigg lapsed into bitter silence.

'Nurse Edith, that statue, as you call it,' Kendigg began again. 'More than stone, you know. They say that when Michelangelo finished his carving of Moses, he found it so lifelike, he struck its knee with his mallet and commanded it to speak.'

'What did it say?' Smith asked, interested.

Kendigg considered the question seriously. 'There is no

record of that,' he said at last. 'And not having actually seen the statue, I wouldn't like to commit myself. I often wish I could get to Rome to see it, I'm sure it would speak to me. I have the gift, you see. Nurse Edith spoke to me quite frequently.'

'What did *she* say?' Smith replied, his interest waning.

Kendigg drew deeply on his cigarette. He was smoking it in a most peculiar fashion, Smith observed. The cigarette had been inserted between the middle fingers of his right hand which was formed into a loose fist. He sucked out the smoke by applying his lips to the aperture between the curved forefinger and thumb. Noticing Smith's curiosity, Kendigg brightened a little. 'I learned to smoke this way from some Pakistani friends,' he explained. 'Their religion forbids them to touch tobacco with their lips. This way they can smoke without offending against the letter of the law.'

'But not the spirit?'

'In law, only the letter of it is important. That's one thing I have learned.'

'Apart from speaking to statues.'

'Dear Nurse Edith,' Kendigg murmured, his eyes bright, lower lip trembling. 'I wronged her dreadfully.' He sniffed twice and sucked at his fist for more smoke. 'I first met her a few months after I got out of prison. I got two years even though I was a first offender. My counsel thought I would get a suspended sentence. It was the fifteen cases I had taken into consideration that did the damage.'

'Two years for what?'

'Little girls. I couldn't resist little girls.'

'I thought it might be that.'

'Oh, very clever of you. Does it show that much?'

Smith shrugged a contemptuous apology.

'I suppose you are in for a nice manly rape and murder?' said Kendigg huffily.

'I thought it was considered impolite to discuss why we're in here,' Smith replied.

'You started it!'

'Yes, I did. I'm sorry. I was just being . . . Well, forget it.'

'Oh, I don't mind. You see I can't help it. The last time I

was convicted, three of the biggest Whites in the country all swore I couldn't help it. I'm not like the others. Cold-blooded killers the lot of them, they all put on an act to avoid prison. My urges were compelling and irresistible, they said.' He leant confidingly across the partition. 'It's their flesh, you see – the little girls. There is an area inside the upper thigh where the flesh is so smooth; the skin so silky beneath the stroking finger...' His left hand crept involuntarily from his side, to fondle the wall tiles. 'Tender,' he whispered. 'The touch must be tender, with the lightness of a gossamer wing ... And all the time they look at you with wondering, innocent faces, yet in their eyes ... Oh, what depths of depravity you can see in their eyes.'

He withdrew his hand sharply and glared stonily into its curved fingers, then with great deliberation ground the end of his cigarette into the centre of the palm. With his fingers clenched tightly over the smoking tobacco he rose slowly, and carefully brushed the remains into the bowl, flushing them away; waiting patiently for the storm to subside before resuming the seat. He held up the offending hand for Smith to witness. There was an area of scar tissue two inches in diameter across the middle.

'I always do that,' he said proudly. 'An act of contrition ... for Nurse Edith.'

'Wouldn't she be just as satisfied with lung cancer?'

'Scoff if you wish. I'm used to that. I know I have a rare gift, not given to many. In fact, I am probably unique except for a few holy men in Tibet or Nepal. Ascetics, you know. I reached their degree of suffering and deprivation six months after I was released from the Scrubs twenty years ago. No job, no friends. I had been a political agent,' he boasted proudly. 'Nice constituency. Safe seat. Solidly established member. He could have put something my way when I came out. Wouldn't even speak to me on the phone. Oh, I could have put the black on him – not to mention a few of his right honourable friends, including a cabinet minister. I won't even bother with the judge, the lawyers and the odd policeman. Paedophiles I have known ... Oh, I could tell you tales.' He leaned forward to catch his reflection in the tiles. 'Couldn't I just,' he chuckled at his blurred image. 'They let you go to the dogs, didn't they, Archie Kendigg? Never lifted a finger. Watched you slip downhill all the way. Saw you staggering and slobbering about Waterloo Station trying to cadge the price of a drink from them. "Take yourself out of my sight, you filthy creature, or I'll call the police." They even came over to Charing Cross and Leicester Square to laugh and sneer as you fought off the other hyenas trying to steal your bottle of meth and cider.' He spat into the hazy reflected face then suddenly, realizing the consequences of his impetuous anger, began scrubbing it clean with his stockinged feet.

'I'm sorry,' he murmured to his restored image before turning to Smith. 'I did that to Nurse Edith once. That's how it began.' He relaxed against the low-level cistern.

'Years ago it was. I had established a good doss down under Hungerford Bridge, next to Charing Cross Underground Station...'

'They call it Embankment Station now,' Smith interrupted.

'Call what?'

'Charing Cross Underground. They built a new one at Charing Cross itself and gave it that name. So they had to rename the other one.'

'Are you trying to confuse me?' Kendigg said heatedly.

'No. I was merely explaining.'

'Don't bother. I know London like the back of my hand. Can you tell me where Nurse Edith Cavell stands? Precisely where she stands?'

'Bottom end of Charing Cross Road, a few yards up from Trafalgar Square. There's a pub on the corner...'

'I said precisely!'

'Not to the exact inch.'

'I thought not,' said Kendigg, his triumph strident. 'And you have the audacity to try and confuse me over the location of Charing Cross Underground station.'

'So where does Nurse Edith Cavell stand? Precisely?'

'In St Martin's Place. Where she has always stood. Defiantly facing the German rifles.'

'I was near enough,' Smith protested. 'It's only a small square at the bottom of Charing Cross Road.'

'More a triangle than a square,' Kendigg made three sides out of forefingers and thumbs to demonstrate.

'Whatever shape it is, it was there you spat on Nurse Edith?'

'Not on her, thank God. She is raised on high – above the abominations of men. I spat on the plinth. That was bad enough.' He gave the tiles at his feet another polish with his stockings and leant forward again to communicate with his vague reflection.

'We did it, didn't we, Archibald Kendigg? And we are thoroughly ashamed of ourselves, aren't we? For that and all we said later on?' He and his reflection nodded in agreement. Then, glancing sideways at Smith, he continued.

'It was just after four in the morning. That's when they come round with the hoses to clear the dossers away from their pitches. They say it's to clean the street, but they really want the dossers out of it before they open the station – Charing Cross Station!' He waited expectantly for Smith to take up the challenge but received only an understanding nod. He went on again reluctantly.

'I usually wandered back across the bridge to Waterloo hoping to find someone with a bottle, somebody who might share a drink.' He questioned his image. 'Fat chance, eh, Archie?' he asked it. 'More likely to try and find someone still dead to the world or just plain dead, with some left in his bottle. Might be able to nick it off him, mightn't we, Archie?' He paused to pass an evil grin to the floor, relishing the distorted leer he received in return.

'But on this particular morning,' he said, abandoning his shadowy ego reluctantly. 'I thought I'd try my luck at the warm-air ducts behind the Regent Palace Hotel. That is a highly desirable residential area for dossers. You've got to be able to fight like a bull-terrier to get a pitch up there. I suppose I was feeling particularly reckless or probably more than usually desperate for a drink even to consider it. Anyway, en route, I walked across St Martin's Place. It was deserted at that hour, and it was raining. And there, all alone, except for me, was the proud figure of Nurse Edith. I had seen her before, of course. Like everyone else, never given her a second thought. But that morning I stood below her, feeling her pride, her courage in adversity, being shamed and angered by it; asking myself, what opportunity has life given me to be heroic? Arrogant old bitch, I thought. So I spat on her, or at least towards her. Then I read the words; words dripping with my spittle. "Patriotism is not enough. I must have no hatred or bitterness for anyone."'

A solitary tear trickled down Kendigg's face. His tongue, seemingly without volition, slithered over the ledge of his lips, captured the tear and drew it into his mouth. 'I was so overcome with remorse at the enormity of the injury I had inflicted on this gallant lady, I reached up with my bare hands and scrubbed at the stone, only stopping when blood from my fingers replaced the spittle. I distinctly remember staring despairingly at my bleeding fingers, a despair heightened by incomprehension, for soothing tears were falling on them and I knew there was not a tear left in my body. Then above me, a sad voice, gentle and full of compassion said: "I forgave them, Mr Kendigg. Did you not think I could forgive you?" I could not raise my head, I dare not look up. Then the voice spoke again, firm and reassuring. "I do forgive you, Mr Kendigg." It took some effort of will I can tell you, but I did look up. I swear to you, round her face there was a momentary crimson radiance, nebulous but shining, softening her strong defiant features, radiating infinite kindness. Then it was gone. But in her eyes I could still see traces of her tears.'

As if to confirm his story, Kendigg turned similar eyes on Smith. 'You said it was raining at the time?' Smith enquired patiently.

Kendigg bridled. 'Not to that extent. A light drizzle, that was all. And before you say I was boozed out of my mind on meth and cheap wine, let me tell you I hadn't had a decent drink for two days. I was desperate for a drink. But not after that, not after Nurse Edith spoke to me.'

'An experience like that would put most people off,' Smith agreed.

'We can do without your sarcasm,' replied Kendigg stiffly. 'I take no offence, but I will not have you insult Nurse Edith. Besides, what about the crimson aura?'

'Traffic lights?' Smith suggested, then apologizing hurriedly said, 'I'm sorry,' not wanting Kendigg to spit in his face.

Kendigg however, inclined his head magnanimously. 'I can understand your reluctance to believe me,' he said. 'A genuine psychic experience like that is outside the comprehension of most people, but it was a turning point for me, I can tell you. I was imbued with new life. Inspired. My manhood was restored. I went down to the Salvation Army in Westminster, determined to get back on the rails. They knew me of old and didn't hold me in very high regard, but they were so impressed by the change in me, by the positive way in which I presented my case, by my renewed vigour and sobriety, they welcomed me in. I was given a bath, the use of a razor, a new outfit of clothing. Well, not exactly new, second-hand, but quite presentable. I left there ready to face the world and within five minutes, who should I bump into crossing Westminster Bridge but old Walter, Wally Binbone, chairman of the local party committee, where I used to work. "Amazing," he said. "Been thinking of you all morning," he said. "For some reason, I couldn't get you out of my mind." His conscience was stricken all over his face. "Are you in work?" he asked.

'To cut it short, he offered me a place in his firm, insurance brokers, nothing substantial to start with, you understand. Bottom of the ladder stuff. But it was a new beginning. Within two years I was office manager and during all that time, at least twice a week, I would go up to St Martin's Place before dawn to speak to Nurse Edith. To tell her how eternally grateful I was for her intervention, for her compassion. I could see her eyes welcoming me as I walked towards her past St Martin-in-the-Fields. I could feel the solid stone throbbing with her spiritual presence, I knew she accepted and appreciated my devotion and gratitude. My homage. She never spoke to me though, not again. But I knew she heard me. I could detect subtle changes in her face, the hint of a smile. For more than two years I worshipped at her feet. No religious zealot was more devout than I... Then one day she gave me a sign... No, a warning. A warning I ignored.

'Binbone had opened a large branch office in Caterham, and I was appointed overall manager. There was an additional perquisite, a luxurious flat above the office. When I told Nurse

Edith all this, I was quite exultant and pleased with myself. Rather smug, I suppose. But when I looked to see her reaction, her face had darkened, her hand raised above her head where there is engraved the word "HUMANITY".

'I came away deeply troubled and for a time considered refusing the appointment. But why should I, I told myself! Had I not risen from the gutter and by sheer hard work and endeavour gained this position as a right? Was I not entitled to my just reward? As I walked away, I remembered turning round to look at her for what I thought would be the last time. I knew she was no longer concerned about me. Her eyes, steadfast and true, were fixed firmly on the German rifles.

'I left her feeling quite wretched, yet with a deep sense of grievance. Had I not risen twice a week, hours before dawn, to be with her at the moment of execution? Had I not abjured every temptation to gratify my old urges which had returned as strongly as ever; only subduing them by diligence and long hours of work? Even by self-flagellation! Her rejection of me was unbearable. For a time...'

At that moment a White, portly and balding, entered. Lifting aside the mop Kendigg had laid across the entrance, he tutted as if offended by the attempt to deny him entry. Failing to see either Kendigg or Smith, he stood on the urinal step and addressed himself to the business in hand, studying the flow with bowed concentration. 'Filliphant,' Kendigg whispered in Smith's ear. '"Placebo", we called him. He's harmless. "Placebo" Filliphant.' They saw Filliphant's head turn to one side and an ear lift to the uncertain sound reaching it. 'Staff should use staff toilets,' Kendigg said loudly. 'Inmates aren't allowed to use staff toilets. Inmates aren't allowed near staff toilets.'

Startled, Filliphant swivelled round abruptly from the hips. Seeing them, he gave an embarrassed smile.

'Taking a well-earned rest from your labours, are you?' he said.

'Staff should use staff toilets,' replied Kendigg in a shrill screech that echoed round the tiles like a ricocheting bullet. Filliphant smiled benignly.

'I do apologize, Mr Kendigg. An emergency, we all get

caught short at times,' he brought a benevolent face to bear on Smith. 'I say, you've made a smashing job of the corridor. Never seen it so bright. You must take a great deal of pride in your work?'

'I do,' Smith agreed solemnly.

'That's the spirit. Country wouldn't be in the state it's in today if we all took a pride in our work.'

'You've upset me,' came the dark accusation from a neglected Kendigg. 'Now I'll be under stress for the rest of the day. I'll need some Librium. Are you going to give me some Librium?' he demanded.

'Sorry, Kendigg. We're all out of Librium. Government cuts, you know. Paraldehyde. We've plenty of paraldehyde. If you'd like to come with me to the dispensary, I'll fix you up with some paraldehyde.'

Kendigg made a gruesome face. 'Yeough,' he spat. 'Paraldehyde tastes foul.'

'I could always mainline it for you,' Filliphant produced a disposable hypodermic from the pocket of his white coat, and holding it between finger and thumb, aimed it at Kendigg's face like a dart player. 'How about it,' he said amiably. 'Five hundred and one up?' Kendigg shrank into a corner of the cubicle.

'It hurts,' he whined. 'Not only when it goes in but afterwards. Besides it makes me sick.'

'If you feel under stress, I'm going to have to insist,' said Filliphant, smoothly menacing, the hypodermic still poised.

'I'll be all right in a minute, it was merely a passing storm. I'm sorry to be a bother,' he muttered with more sullenness than contrition.

'No bother,' Filliphant uncapped the needle.

'No, really. I'm all right now. Please. It's not necessary.' Kendigg was now abject.

'Only if you're *really* certain,' Filliphant insisted.

'I am. Most definitely. Thank you for your interest.'

'Not at all, any time you're feeling stressful . . . or aggressive . . . we're here to help, you know.' Filliphant exuded cheerful benevolence. 'Well, keep up the good work,' he patted his flies to reassure himself he had not forgotten the required adjustment in the heat of the moment. Satisfied, he gave an encouraging nod and walked out.

'I thought you said he was harmless?' Smith watched Filliphant's departure admiringly.

'He's all talk,' sneered Kendigg in reply. 'Knows damn well, if he really tried to forcibly sedate me, I'd have the Parliamentary Commissioner on top of him before he could say...' Kendigg broke off and went across to inspect the area of Filliphant's recent occupancy. He returned frowning, but apparently satisfied no remedial measures were required. 'Where was I?' he said, resuming his seat.

'Parliamentary Commissioner. On Filliphant's back before he could say...'

'Yes. Before he could say ... Jack Spratt?'

'Jack Robinson is the more common usage.'

'Proper usage,' said Kendigg loftily. 'My old teacher used to say the English language in general, and proper usage in particular, was invented to confound foreigners and keep the lower orders in their place. I never forgot that,' Kendigg sent his words across Smith like an invitation to dinner.

'It *is* easily forgettable,' Smith declined with thanks. 'What about Nurse Edith?' he continued. 'You left her right up in the air when Filliphant came in.'

Kendigg turned sulkily aside, then began stroking the tiles with the middle finger of his right hand, refusing to be drawn.

'No substitute for the real thing, is it?' Smith enquired.

Kendigg thrust out a petulant chin but remained silent. He continued to stroke the tiles.

Smith put in a sharp goad. 'If you had waited for them to grow up, you wouldn't be here now. The inside of a woman's thigh is still soft and smooth, even when she's thirty.' He considered the strength of his belief. 'That's as old as I've been able to lay my hands on,' he added by way of qualification.

'But the eyes have lost all innocence at that age,' Kendigg responded dreamily, maintaining his light touch on the tiles. 'It was in their eyes, their faces, where the pleasure lay. Full of innocent wonder and yet if you looked close enough you could see all the latent lust and carnal desire hidden under the surface of their innocence. Waiting to be roused.'

Where his fingers stroked, they now began to scratch.

'Paraldehyde,' Smith growled, by way of abuse and warning.

Kendigg stopped abruptly, guiltily, as if suddenly aware he was being observed. Thrusting clasped hands down between his legs, he trapped them between his thighs, and applied pressure. A grunting struggle with himself ensued as he tried to pull free. Succeeding, he brought a scarred palm up to eye level and surveyed the stigma proudly, soothing it with a frigid tuneless whistle.

'Shut it off for Christ's sake,' Smith growled again. Bored. Knowing there was at least another half an hour before lunch and the freedom of the afternoon. He thought of going out to give the corridor a final buffing.

'She sentenced me to a living death,' Kendigg announced tonelessly.

'Nurse Edith?'

'Yes. Nearly two months after I had last seen her – I can do without you, you arrogant woman, I thought. Humility, indeed! Humiliation more likely, I thought. I put her out of my mind and got on with the job of establishing the new branch. Had it running like a Swiss watch, business increasing daily. Binbone was very pleased, talked of a directorship. "You should find yourself a wife," he kept telling me. "Very useful thing a wife when you're in business, not only bedwise but taxwise, things in her namewise." I couldn't tell him I wasn't very good with women.'

'Not very good with little girls either, were you? Or at least not very good *for* them,' Smith snarled.

'Are you going to hit me?' Kendigg enquired resignedly. 'I don't mind. I'm quite used to it.'

'I've seen too many like you before,' Smith felt suddenly tired. 'I hit the first one, but I wasn't used to them at the time.'

'I never hurt them,' protested Kendigg. 'I never even touched their privates. It was only the last one that got hurt.'

'Physically, you mean?'

'She started howling. I could see people looking round towards the bushes where I had taken her to see the baby bunny rabbits. I had to keep her quiet. Afterwards, when I had got to the park gates I heard someone shouting. I turned round and saw the park-keeper running after me. I sprinted for my car and was clear away but I saw him – the park-keeper – in the rear-view mirror. He was writing down the number of my car.'

'Good lad,' Smith loudly rewarded the absent park-keeper.

'I knew I was finished,' Kendigg went on unperturbed. 'I couldn't go back to the office, to my flat, anywhere. I ditched the car at the nearest Underground station and for the rest of the day, and most of the night, I kept going round the system. Out to Stanmore, across to Wimbledon over to Uxbridge, round and round the Circle Line, and all the time cursing myself for a fool.'

'For a child killer, you mean?'

Smith's interjection made no impact on Kendigg. He went maundering on, hypnotized by his own voice. 'Charing Cross! I saw I was at Charing Cross. I was home. Out I got, found an off-licence and spent all the money I had with me on booze. Back I went under the bridge, most of the faces were new, but one or two of the old ones were still around, still alive. Lizzie Fleabag, Sailor Jack, The Hackney Whore, Abie, The Wandering Jew. "Come and have a party," I cried. "Archie The Toff is back. Come and have a drink on Archie The Toff." What a rush there was. The Salvation Army soup kitchen was deserted in no time. What a night we had. Funny though, they couldn't remember me, Lizzie Fleabag, Sailor Jack, none of the others. Only Abie remembered me. They say Jews have good memories. It's true. Abie remembered me. "Good to see you, Archie," he said. "You made it back then, back to the living again?" Then he pulled me close, looked into my eyes for a long time. God, his breath! Finally, he said: "No. You have troubles. Only bad troubles could bring you down here." Also very perceptive people – Jews. "What's happened to you, Archie?" he asks. "Don't tell me," he says. "It was a woman, wasn't it?" "It was, Abie," I replied. "A nurse. Nurse Edith Cavell."

'He raised his hands to his head, then a bottle of vodka to his lips. Then he patted me consolingly on the shoulder and said, "Nowadays, you can't trust anyone. Not even nurses."

'I left them before the rousters came round, and went to St Martin's Place. If Nurse Edith saw me coming, she gave no sign. She was as still and as cold as ... as stone.

'I poured out everything to her, about the girl in the park, how I just wanted her to be quiet, that I didn't mean to hurt her. It made no difference, she stood aloof, her eyes fixed on that damned German firing squad, far away in Belgium. I pounded at the plinth with my fists, my head even. It made no difference, she ignored me completely.

'The next thing I knew, two policemen had me by the arms. This should make you laugh. All the time I was there pouring my soul out to Nurse Edith, they were sitting behind the plinth having a quiet smoke. They heard every word I said.'

'Maybe I'll laugh about it later. Right now I don't find it funny,' Smith said.

'Neither did my solicitor, when I told him,' mourned Kendigg. "Very far-sighted of you, Mr Kendigg," he said, with that knowing little smirk solicitors are so fond of. He thought I had gone there deliberately, to put on a show, knowing it was all up with me. Knowing the police were there. But the Whites believed me, that's what matters. Three of the top men in the country all said I was mad; despite being harangued and ridiculed by the judge and prosecutor. So did the jury. Not that I have anything to be grateful for. "Well," said the judge. "If you suffer these irresistible urges to the peril of young children, you must be kept in a secure institution until they are destroyed by the irresistible decay of age."

'That was twelve years ago. Every time I come forward for review, they look at me and they look at the judge's comments and I am finished. Written in red they are. Written in fire.'

Outside in the corridor they heard the stamp and march of many feet, a Blue shouting: 'Get a move on then,' and they knew the results of their morning's work would soon be blighted and soiled. But tomorrow would be another brightly shining day, no matter what the weather. Kendigg rose to his feet and shuffled out, mumbling more to himself than to Smith, 'To destroy my urges is all very fine. But he never said anything about destroying me.'

Smith called to him sadly. 'It's terrible I agree. These days they don't even give you a blessing. Twenty-five years ago you would have got a "May God have mercy on your soul" thrown in without asking.'

As he strode down *his* highly polished corridor, accepting the primitive sway of his fiefdom with despotic presumption, Smith observed another inmate stroking a duster down the oak-panelled walls, the rag wielded with an air of languid indolence. Jenkins R., walls and skirting boards (dusting) he said to himself, recalling the Remedial Task Rota, and critically eyeing the lack of effort. Another new boy from behind the Bricks. Fresher fish than himself. An artist, Quinlan had reported to the assembly at the bench of Peachtree QC. Adding with ambiguous, but evident relish, 'a right bleeding carver.' As Smith passed the new man they exchanged the cold, ungracious glances of rivals to a disputed throne, but neither uttered a word.

# Five

••••••

Even though it was a soft and gentle afternoon Protheroe had his shoulders hunched and head down as he butted his way through Admiralty Arch and across Horse Guards Parade, rolling like a battle cruiser in an Atlantic gale. Hamilton scuttled alongside in the role of destroyer escort. Ascending the King Charles Street steps in silence, they went through the Clive entrance in a flurry of passes and vague salutes and clattered along marble corridors to Rachette's office.

'Do find yourselves some chairs,' Rachette said without looking up. He sat, pen poised above a sheaf of papers, his half-moon spectacles perched on the end of a snub nose. The pen circled a few times above the documents, then speared towards the surface, making slashing deletions, quick cuts of emphasis and thrusting marginal notations. That done, he pressed a button on the desk, and all waited in glum silence until his secretary entered. Rachette thrust the untidy sheaf of papers into her hand. 'Retype, with copies to the Secretary and Minister of State, the PPS and Cabinet Office.'

'And JIC Secretariat, Sir Desmond?' she enquired, gathering the papers together.

'I would have said so, would I not?'

The secretary offered no reply and turned towards the door. 'And by not later than seven this evening,' Rachette barked, hurling the words at her retreating back. The woman faltered slightly in her stride, regained momentum, and slammed the door behind her. Hamilton watched the brief interlude with interest. No wonder it had taken all the weight of the Head of Service to make Rachette use female staff. No wonder they had made him Cabinet Office hit man on the SIS. Still, was it not all a bit too blatant? He speculated on the possibility of Rachette having her over. She was no longer young, but decidedly interesting. Full-bodied. Wouldn't mind tasting it himself. He saw the object of his speculation direct a bland smile at Protheroe.

'Basil, my dear friend . . .'

'Don't bother going on, Desmond,' Protheroe sighed, wearily omniscient. 'That smile and the dear friend opening is all I need. They have accepted it?'

'But with regret, Basil. With profound regret. You will get it in writing. In the most glowing terms. I dictated it myself,' Rachette paused to allow Protheroe an opportunity to express his appreciation. Seeing none forthcoming, he went on briskly. 'As to the immediate future, I have arranged a little something for you on the Arts Council. Only as deputy administrator, I'm afraid, but there will be all those free tickets . . .' Protheroe rose to his feet without a word. Rachette no longer smiling, enquired haughtily, 'Are you leaving, Basil?' Protheroe nodded, his eyes distant.

'I think I'll go and get drunk,' he said. 'It's what one does in the circumstances, isn't it?' He swung round slowly and halted, squinting towards the door as if it lay on the far side of a burning desert. Hamilton made to join him but was waved back into his seat by Rachette.

'You will see my secretary on the way out, Basil,' he said, as Protheroe lurched forward. 'She has the usual forms for you to sign. The Act and that sort of thing.' Protheroe had reached the door. 'What about the Arts Council vacancy?' Rachette's voice shrilled down the length of the room. 'Can I say you are interested?'

Protheroe swung the door wide, holding it open to admit the sound of busy typewriters. He drew himself proudly erect.

'Stuff it up your fucking jumper,' he declaimed loudly. The typewriter noises ceased abruptly. Protheroe turned again. 'As Mr Popkiss might say,' he added with sardonic dignity; and the door slammed for a second time.

Rachette vented an amazed 'Pah' directly at Hamilton. 'Had he been drinking before he came here?' he asked in outrage.

'Not as far as I am aware, sir.' Uncertain of his own fate, Hamilton dithered between obsequiousness and truculence. 'I have never seen the Chief take a drink. At least not until the end of the day.'

'His day ended months ago,' said Rachette, flatly final, and ignoring Hamilton completely, withdrew a Stationery Office note-book from his desk drawer and began making copious notes. Hamilton could not quite understand why such seemingly ordinary behaviour should send a chilly claw clutching at his heart. He fell to wondering what it would be like working for the Arts Council? Would there *really* be all those free tickets? Covent Garden, the Royal Shakespeare, the National Theatre, Festival Hall? It might not be half bad, especially if they made it doubles. His heart warmed again at the thought. Dreams of pre-performance canapés and drinkies, of introducing impressionable female companions to Luciano, Trevor, Peter and André – and of post-performance sexual gratitude – were disturbed by the intercom on Rachette's desk. It was of antique design, fitted with an earpiece which Rachette applied to the side of his face. He listened for a moment, then said: 'Yes, send him in immediately.'

The man who entered was approaching middle age, tall and thin to a degree beyond leanness. Skinny was the word that came to Hamilton's mind. Yet he noted the quiet strength in the fellow's determined chin and the calmness apparent in the lofty brow, albeit a rueful calm, furrowed by more than a trace of anger. The face was familiar, but Hamilton was at a loss as to his actual identity. In his hand, Hamilton was horrified to observe, he held the file on the Popkiss Intercept.

'Take a pew, Fairchild, if you will.' Rachette returned briefly to his notes before looking up. 'You've read it then?' He nodded at the file.

'I have,' Fairchild's reply was sombre. 'And I am seriously concerned. 'I've had sixty men fully engaged on these killings for over a week and all the time you have been sitting on the only reliable lead. In addition, your people allowed a heavy burglary to take place. Had we had foreknowledge of this intercept, we might well have averted it and saved at least two lives.'

'Oh, come now, Fairchild,' Rachette protested. 'That's the policeman in you still talking. You must realize that in the national interest certain legal niceties must of necessity be put aside. Nevertheless, one of the reasons you were approached to take over the Division was because of our concern that police interests were becoming increasingly tied to our own. And not only in this particular case. That being said, now that your, er, manor – I believe is the constabulary term – extends from Gdansk on the Baltic to Varna on the Black Sea, you will need to develop a broader view. However, you may be assured that, other than on those rare occasions where the national interest must prevail, you will not be called upon to do anything you cannot square with your conscience.'

'How does one define the national interest?'

'I will do that for you,' Rachette extended a cautionary finger. 'The law on that will be laid down according to circumstances as they arise; by myself ... and the minister, of course.' He paused to allow space for the importance of the subject. 'The minister is, as we know, a businessman, or at least he was until obliged to divest himself of his interests on taking office. But he remains a businessman. Between you and I, Fairchild, good businessmen make rotten politicians. Just as good – and I use *good* merely to indicate ability, not as a standard of probity – just as good politicians make rotten businessmen. Lawyers now? They are different. Since the nature of their calling requires them to ignore the obvious truth and argue the contrary case, lawyers usually make excellent politicians.' He nodded in confirmation of his own opinion. 'So,' he went on, 'in those cases where you may feel that natural justice, fair play, conscience, call it what you will, are in conflict with the national interest, you must refer to me. It is a burden I am accustomed to bearing.'

Hamilton saw in Fairchild's glum face, particularly in his tightening lips, the look of a man who has made an important career decision he deeply regretted. But having made it, was stuck with it, and determined to make the best of a bad job. 'It would have been helpful if we – the police, I mean – could have had words with Slunchev. Diplomatic privilege or not.' He spoke wistfully, as if recalling pleasant memories of happier times. 'You've burned your boats, me old shipmate,' Hamilton said to himself.

'Slunchev is no longer relevant,' Rachette said firmly. 'He had a tiger by the tail and the tiger has gobbled him up. Slunchev is a dead duck.'

'But what..!' A startled and mystified Hamilton came to sudden life.

Rachette rose from behind his desk on a flurry of apologetic arms, directed at Fairchild. 'My dear fellow, most remiss of me,' he cried. 'I haven't introduced Hamilton. Hamilton will be your staff officer. Meet your new Head of Division, Hamilton. Cyril Fairchild, until recently Assistant Commissioner, Crime, at Scotland Yard.' The name and face clicked together in Hamilton's mind. The name he had heard frequently, the face he had seen infrequently, and then only discreetly at the rear of some police panel on the box, always allowing others to do the talking.

'I hope you will consider retaining me in post, sir?' he said, with what he hoped was becoming modesty.

'That will be up to you, won't it.' The threat was baldly implicit as Fairchild released his hand.

'Now then, Hamilton,' Rachette was *too* pleasantly encouraging. 'Let's see what you are made of. Give us an outline of Teasdale's operating function.'

But Slunchev? I want to know what happened to Slunchev? The thoughts held his mouth silently agape.

'We are waiting, Hamilton,' Rachette prompted.

'He had consular cover in Trieste.' Hamilton drove his mind back slowly, undecided how far to go. Wouldn't do to offend Fairchild by trying to teach him to suck eggs. Yet the man was green to the game . . . Better to give him the full treatment.

'Geographically, it was a reasonably central point from where he could have oversight and control of incoming intelligence from the satellites. A base in Austria would have been

better, but their non-aligned status made it somewhat...'
The thread snapped. What the hell had happened to
Slunchev?

'Dodgy?' Fairchild was saying in a helpful way.

'Dodgy is excellent,' said Rachette approvingly. 'Indeed, I
will make a note of it.' He repeated the word slowly, seeming to
watch it float in the air before snatching it into some mental
recess with his eyes. 'Do go on, Hamilton,' he ordered sharply.

'Teasdale had a courier relay bringing in the items from
Hungary, Romania and Bulgaria into Yugoslavia. Sometimes,
even though he had an extension direct to his doorstep, he
would go over to Marovic himself, especially when he was
paying out. He didn't quite trust the Trieste–Marovic relay
where money was concerned. As we now know, he was cashed
in on his last trip.'

'We accepted the Yugoslav medics' opinion that it was a
heart attack,' Rachette intervened smoothly. 'There was no
autopsy as such, and it seemed perfectly reasonable at his age.
The body was brought home and cremated. We knew nothing
of vagal inhibitions at the time.' He laid a condescending hand
in Hamilton's direction, giving him the floor once again.

'He had an independent field man operating in Vienna, controlling and collecting from Czecho, Poland, the DDR, and
dabbling on his own in Hungary. Teasdale didn't like that.'

'Because it was dodgy?' Fairchild queried.

'No. The cover was foolproof. The field man in Vienna was
married to an Austrian woman. She...'

'Not an arranged marriage. Don't go leaping to unpleasant
conclusions.' Pious and solemn, Rachette deplored the
knowing smile on Fairchild's lips. 'We wouldn't countenance
such a thing,' he huffed.

'Not that I got to know much about him, he was before my
time,' said Hamilton, as if speaking of a dead ancestor of
dubious repute. 'He was allowed to go into business on his own
account. An independent. All we did was quartermaster him
through Teasdale...'

'I'll take it from here!' Hamilton subsided into his chair,
forcibly shoved there on the end of Rachette's verbal arm.

'The files on the Vienna end are open to top echelon only,'

he explained for Fairchild's benefit. 'That will include you, of course, but it will save a great deal of reading if I outline the story – nay, saga would be more appropriate.' Removing his spectacles, Rachette delicately massaged his brow to aid recollection.

'It began before my time also,' he said. 'With our hero, a newly commissioned subaltern, going out to join his regiment in Austria a few years after the war, when it was part of our occupying forces. Regimental HQ was in a requisitioned hotel in Graz. The hotelier had a beautiful seventeen-year-old daughter, and she and our hero fell deeply in love. Thus smitten, the lad applied to his colonel for permission to marry. Colonel furious. It was what they used to call a good regiment. Good; appertaining to the birth and social status of its officers. Our hero was something of a misfit in that direction.'

Rachette briefly consulted a thin blue file, as if to satisfy himself that what was already in his mind was factually correct. Closing the covers on the solitary sheet it contained, he confidently resumed his narrative.

'The mother was a west-country Liberal, which may account for something. His father, an Oxford Arabist, more scholarly and reticent than the nationally renowned in that field, such as Burton, Storrs and Lawrence. Shortly before the war, he took his son with him on an expedition to the northern Hadramaut. The boy was then fourteen. During a field trip, the father and his guide were murdered and robbed by bandit Bedouin. Our future hero had been left at base camp. It is said, but not confirmed, that he organized the remaining guides and retainers into a hunting party and they tracked the bandits through some of the worst desert in the world for three weeks, until they found them somewhere near Wadi Rasha in the Yemen and slaughtered them on the spot. Well, there *were* only four of them. And in any case, by the time the boy and his party managed to get back to Aden, war had broken out and there were more important matters to think about.'

Returning the file to his desk drawer, Rachette turned the key in the lock with studied finality.

'So, against this family background,' he continued, 'and an intention to marry into trade, little wonder he was not exactly the pride of the regiment. Worse. His intended's *lieber papa* had tainted blood. He'd served briefly with the 11th Reinhard Heyrich SS Gebirgsjäger, until a partisan booby-trap took the old boy out late in 'forty-one, leaving him *sans* one arm and half a leg. Being discharged medically unfit, before the SS really got nasty with the peasantry and others, he escaped retribution. Nevertheless, it was all too much for our hero's colonel. He had the lad bounced back to the holding battalion in the UK.

'But our lovesick swain was not to be deterred. His ageing mama still had some political clout, even though Labour was in power, and he was eased out of the Army. Our hero promptly returns to Austria and marries his heart's desire. By this time the hotel has been de-requisitioned, and under the expert tutelage of *der Schwiegervater*, our hero and his *gnädige Frau* take over the running of it. Shortly afterwards, *der Schwiegervater* succumbs to the effect of his wounds. He snuffs it, as Mr Popkiss might say; leaving our young lovers with the business. Regrettably, it does not prosper. Now, about this time, the occupying Powers agree to withdraw, with Austria assuming a completely neutral posture. Quite naturally, we, and the French, Americans and Russians, begin looking for air pockets in what would otherwise be an intelligence vacuum. We approach our young hero, now battling bravely against financial adversity, and offer to put up the capital so he can sell up in Graz and take over another hotel in Vienna. Nothing ostentatious naturally, we could not afford the Bristol, could we, Hamilton?'

Still engrossed by the mystery of Slunchev's fate, Hamilton had not been attending closely. Knowing only that an answer was required of him, he followed his natural inclination and said, 'Yes, sir.'

The look on Rachette's face told him he had got it wrong. He began thinking of life on the Arts Council once more as Rachette's lingering glare slowly drifted away to resume his tale.

'The hotel was discreetly, but conveniently located near the Volkstheater, and it greatly pleased our hero's wife, who could now flaunt her beauty in a more sophisticated *milieu*. Not that

Vienna in the immediate post-war years had much going in the way of *Wein, Weib und Gesang*, but the seeds were beginning to root once more. And our hero was pleased; not only because his wife was pleased, but also because in return for our generosity, a price had to be paid. One that our hero was glad to accept, for I do not call him *our hero* cynically. He was a thwarted warrior born too late to fight, and when given the opportunity to redeem a patriotic duty he had pawned for the – dare I say it – the love of a woman?' Rachette smiled in unrepentant apology. 'Well, suffice it to say, he did us proud. Didn't he, Hamilton?'

Alerted by the pause in Rachette's speech, Hamilton met the challenge. 'Plunder is top tier access only, sir. I have never read the Plunder Files.'

'They have turned to dust, Hamilton. But I do assure you, Fairchild, he did us proud. When Hungary kicked against the pricks in 'fifty-six he went into Budapest like Blackbeard boarding a Spanish treasure ship, rescued an ARVIN colonel from the mob, turned him round, brought him and some absolutely priceless material out. Sapphires and rubies straight from the KGB mines. In the Prague spring of 'sixty-eight he butchered his way into the Czech Intelligence meat safe and came away with the choicest cuts. Fillet steak, two inches thick. No fat, no gristle. All this despite Philby. All laid on the plate of old Crombie-Nicholls. You wouldn't remember him either, Hamilton. Long before your time. You would never have heard of him. No names, no pack drill in those days. Well loved was our hero! Given an unlisted OBE, a you name it, you've got it, contract. And constantly, a supply of bread and butter was coming through. Sliced bread, dairy-fresh butter. Even the hotel was showing a profit. Our hero ran the slickest team the service has ever *not* known about. Direct access to Crombie-Nicholls. Nothing went downstairs. The great thing was, he had no high-powered commissars, no party secretaries, no politburo princes on the pay-roll. Only low- and middle-echelon functionaries, the people who take it all down, write it all up, who file it all away in the archives. He called them his gold miners . . .'

Rachette paused reflectively, as if in envy of predecessors

who had the great good fortune to have such a paragon serving them. Whilst Hamilton, wondering where on earth it was all leading, thought only of Henry Ford's aphorism that history was bunk. If that had any truth it was in the field of intelligence work. Yesterday's secrets, tomorrow's revelations. But today?

'It lasted almost twenty-five years,' Rachette was musing now, slumped in his chair, his eyes half-closed. Far off, but persistent, the strains of a Sousa march penetrated the room from the band-stand in the park. Rachette's fingers went tapping in time to the music on the muffled drum of his belly while continuing to enlarge his story. Hamilton marvelled at such mental dexterity.

'Naturally it couldn't go on forever. The Czechs nabbed a miner with gold dust in his pockets, put the screws on, and back-tracked him through all the cut-outs and diversions, right into our hero's hotel. It took them quite a few months, but in the end they got there.'

'Then they put the boot in,' said Hamilton, intervening recklessly.

'As Mr Popkiss might say?' Rachette queried coldly, his fingers stopping in mid-beat, the forefinger poised threateningly. Hamilton retreated into his chair, casting an appeal for help in Fairchild's direction, seeing only a face, attentively inclined. And slightly open-mouthed, either in amazement . . . or horror.

'They tried to put something into our hero, not however with the boot,' Rachette sniped contemptuously at Hamilton over the rim of his glasses. 'But with a gun. A person or persons unknown belonging to, or hired by the opposition, entered the domestic suite during the early hours and pumped several bullets into the couple who were in bed. One of them was our hero's wife, the other a rather mediocre tenor from the Opera. Our hero, you see, when leaving on some clandestine mission, as he had done several hours earlier, always sagaciously left the hotel from a fire-escape at the rear, having previously made his usual obvious entrance. Yet, it would appear he suffered from that defect of vision, common to the dedicated and far-sighted. An inability to see what was going on under his nose.'

'I seem to remember an Interpol circular on the case.' Fairchild murmured, as if intent on clinging to his former profession for as long as possible. 'It was put down to an unidentified hotel thief. No one heard anything and it was believed a silenced revolver had been used.'

Seeing Rachette nod in agreement, Hamilton seized an opportunity to go out with a flourish. 'It wasn't a revolver actually. You can't effectively silence a revolver, too much gas escapes from the space between the cylinder and the barrel. That's what makes the bang, you know. The rapid expansion of gas. It was a nine-millimetre self-loading pistol that was used, make unknown. An automatic, as most people erroneously call them.' Hamilton gathered his resolve, prepared to stand his ground and faced Rachette with a challenging eye. Rachette however, did not even look in his direction and spoke only to Fairchild.

'What a knowledgeable fellow you have at your right hand, Fairchild. That handsome head of his is crammed full of completely irrelevant facts with which he can illumine the darkness of our ignorance at the turn of a switch,' he sighed gravely. 'If only he could recognize the simple fact that no one has yet pressed his button.' Only then did his eyes swing towards Hamilton. Likening them to a pair of homing torpedoes, Hamilton half rose to his feet and prepared to dive overboard. 'I must protest, sir,' he spluttered. 'What on earth am I doing here, if I'm not allowed to speak?'

'The lad *was* only trying to be helpful,' Fairchild murmured.

Hamilton clutched gratefully at the thrown lifebelt. 'Exactly, sir.' He was gasping now, finding himself in freezing waters. 'Only trying to be helpful. I mean the Division does pride itself on accuracy. Technical and historical.'

Wearily, Rachette quelled the troubled seas. 'Oh, do sit down, Hamilton, there's a good fellow. Just wait for the button. That is what you are here for. Should the need arise, I'll press it quickly enough. Damnation, where was I?'

'You have just murdered the hero's wife and her lover. Anecdotally speaking,' said Fairchild dryly.

'Ah, yes. Now whether it was the death of his wife or her

treachery that caused it, or a combination of both, the upshot was; our hero ran amok. Out came the naked *kris*, so to speak, and there was carnage in the streets. First to go was a Czecho courier named Koutsky, who had journalistic cover. He was pitched out of a seventh-floor window into the middle of Wahringer Strasse; yards too far out to be written off as accident or suicide. That was still in Vienna, two days after the wife's death. Five days later, a trade attaché called Voda from the Polish section, who ran their West German network, was found floating in the Worthersee, near Klagenfurt, where he had been doing some business. He hadn't drowned. Death was due to a boat-hook in the belly. Had been pretty roughed up before he was finished off.' Rachette gave Hamilton a wintry smile. 'Are there any technical details about the lethal effects of boat-hooks through the abdomen I might have overlooked?'

'I don't think so, sir,' Hamilton replied miserably.

'Good. So pleased to hear it,' Rachette thawed to a sleety simper. 'Now, with all this happening just after our hero's domestic tragedy, plus the fact he had broken contact, and was deliberately ignoring recall signals going up all over the place, the horrible realization dawned that he was well and truly on the rampage. A Hungarian and another Czech, both with opposition intelligence connections, were found mangled on a railway-line south of Ljubljana in Yugoslavia and barely a hundred miles from Klagenfurt, where the boat-hook had been employed two days previously. Anticipating that our hero was moving east, we felt obliged to notify the opposition in Belgrade, Sofia and Bucharest that one of ours had unilaterally declared war. I mean, we had to, there was enough ill-natured reciprocity going on as it was. We did not want an escalation, an unrestricted open season. I mean that sort of thing can destroy carefully built organizational structures on both sides. Careers would be placed in peril.' He sought a glimmer of appreciative comprehension in Fairchild's face but met only an impassive mask. One drained of colour, apart from a livid patch of scarlet under each cheekbone.

'Was he addicted to silent movies, your hero?' A hoarsely uttered query came in response.

'The railway-line business? Melodramatic, I agree,'

Rachette conceded. 'And it was too blatant ... and personal. Uncontrolled. Neither side want their people going around uncontrolled. There has to be control. You can see that?'

'Very clearly,' Fairchild coughed into a handkerchief. 'Did it work? Did you get him under control?'

'Unfortunately not. At least not in the way we anticipated. After the Ljubljana mess, a State Security Kapo, one Ernst Frenzel, was found in a side street off Lenin Allee in East Berlin. At first they thought he was dead, no need to go into details, enough to say that in his condition even St Sebastian would have confessed to devil worship. At the *Krankenhaus* they found he was still alive. Just. He regained a few moments of consciousness and made some fearfully demented statements recorded as:

*"Wer ist Hammel?"*

*"Ich sage ihnen, Ich kenne niemand, der Hammel heisst."*

*"Mein Gott! Bitte, glauben sie mir, Ich kenne diesen Hammel nicht! Wer ist Hammel?"*

'Having uttered these words, he lapsed into coma and died two hours later. Translation please, Hamilton.'

At first Hamilton thought it was a test, but quickly changed his mind and decided it was to be a demonstration for Fairchild's benefit. Had the man no German? Perhaps it was not meant to be either, merely one of Rachette's neat little put-downs to show Fairchild who was boss. In either case his resentment of Rachette was temporarily drowned in a surge of gratitude. He spoke with confidence. 'Who is Hammel? I tell you, I know no man named Hammel. My God, please believe me, I do not know this Hammel. Who is Hammel?'

There was a moment of anxious silence before Rachette rewarded him with an approving nod.

Things are looking up, Hamilton thought. Perhaps it will not be the Arts Council after all.

'Who *is* Hammel?' Rachette was repeating the question. 'An answer must be found, for Hammel looms large and black on our horizon. Odd though, the name means "mutton" in German.'

'Before we go into that,' Fairchild interrupted, doggedly determined to do it the police way, chronologically, sequentially.

'What happened to your hero in East Berlin?'

Rachette frowned at the demand to alter his route, but gave way to an insistent thrust from Fairchild's jaw. 'He was disturbed in the act of dumping Frenzel's body. A night watchman heard someone howling like a banshee and alerted the Volkspolizei. A chase ensued, developing into a runaway, bang bang, cops-and-robbers hue and cry. Police sirens, searchlights, bursts of automatic gunfire. They could hear it across the Wall. For a time it was thought another uprising was in progress. But it quietened down shortly before dawn. Later that morning, our hero marches in to our sub-station in West Berlin. God knows how he got across.'

'With one mighty bound?' Fairchild suggested ironically.

Rachette ignored it completely. 'He wanted money, a new cover and an armoury large enough for an infantry platoon. "I've got to get Hammel," he kept urging the resident. "I've got to go back and find Hammel." Now the resident had little knowledge of our hero as such, and no idea he had been running round with the naked *kris* over in the East. But his responses fitted key questions asked by the resident and he was clearly one of ours, so to speak. Nevertheless, the resident, bright boy that he was' – a glance in Hamilton's direction excluded him from that category – 'realized all was not as it should be, insofar as our hero's thought processes were concerned. On the pretext of going to the bank for the funds demanded, he left the premises to return with a handful of heavies and a medic. It was assumed that sight of them, plus a little cajolery and coaxing, would induce our hero to go quietly. Not a bit of it. He singled out one of the heavies and crying, "Hammel, you bastard," went for him like a mad buffalo. Putting it briefly, two heavies were hospitalized, and the office reduced to a shambles before he was sufficiently restrained for the medic to shoot a quick-acting barbiturate into him. He was reduced to a whimpering hulk, reverting to a childlike state, uttering repeated babyish moans sounding, according to the doctor, like . . .' Rachette wrinkled his nose in disgust at the prospect of repeating babyish moans. 'Iss-coo'ee,' he uttered in distinct unbabylike syllables. 'We can find no nominal or geographic base for the sound, so it is probably as the medics say, a reversion to child memory. From there on it was the usual fast car to Gatow and RAF transport back to Blighty double-quick.'

As his narrative reached British shores, Rachette's mood lightened. Easing himself more comfortably into his cushioned chair, he allowed it to swing from side to side, as thrumming fingers marched on the spot above the robustly distended stomach.

'Is he still alive?' Fairchild was asking, with, thought Hamilton, some anxiety.

'My dear fellow, of course he is. What do you think we are?' Mock outrage heightened Rachette's voice. 'No Lubianka solutions here, you know.'

'I thought you might have handed him back. In the national interest, as it were.'

'Not once we had him. Not a chance. If they got him whilst he was on the rampage, well and good. We were satisfied they wouldn't take him alive. Not our hero. But now we had him, albeit in defective condition, we were hanging on to him.' Rachette tapped his forehead significantly. 'Especially with all he had in there, however scrambled it might have been.'

'I was merely wondering,' Fairchild said.

'Hardly justifiable,' Rachette chewed on the wound. 'But something obviously had to be done, and his condition dictated the solution. He was quite mad. Psychopathic paranoia, the shrinks said. Most reputable people. An institution, a secure institution was the answer.'

'Which one?' Fairchild tried to make his enquiry sound casual.

'Wyldwood. Where else?' A sly smile dimpled one side of Rachette's face. 'Same place you deposited one of your own a year or so ago. Wasn't it?'

'Mine was only suffering a transient situation disturbance,' Fairchild countered.

'If we are discussing the degree to which we have driven our respective operatives mad, then your man Smith created a much more serious problem than our chap. He at least retained sufficient wit to stay within the trade. And the casualty list was nowhere near as high. Your chap was catastrophic.'

'But not deliberately so.'

'Oh, come now, Fairchild. Let us avoid invidious comparisons at all costs. They are largely irrelevant now. I repeat our problem is to find the answer to Frenzel's dying question, "Who is Hammel?"'

'I fail to see his immediate significance.'

'The significance is that he has Teasdale's box.'

Despite all previous warnings, Hamilton was compelled to ask, 'How do we know, sir?'

'Because he told me, you silly boy!' Rachette's snarl was venomous. He leant over and pulled out the bottom drawer of his desk. There was a sudden click.

The voice that filled the room made Hamilton shudder. It had resonance, yet was not loud. It had the mutilated sonority of a cracked bell. If the devil could talk, Hamilton thought, his voice would sound like this. It had no accent. It was universal. It said, 'Good morning, Sir Desmond. My name is Hammel.'

He sat in admiration at Rachette's coolness under fire. His hesitation only momentary before he had haughtily replied:

'I am afraid you have a wrong number.'

The answer was preceded by a dry chuckle. 'Then so must your Minister and Secretary of State, and your two Heads of Division. But I, Hammel, I have your number, Sir Desmond. I also have Teasdale's box.' But was he actually saying 'Hammel?' To Hamilton's ear, it sounded more like 'Hamme'.

Rachette's hesitation was longer, but his reply still cool ...

'Easy for you to say. How do I know that?'

'The mere fact I mention it should be enough.'

'I need more proof. What does it contain?'

'Documents, Sir Desmond. Sensitive documents. So raw and tender they scream at the slightest touch. Screams so penetrating as to bring down governments and those who serve them. So anguished as to cause nations to shun and vilify those whose thoughts and actions have been so meticulously recorded within them. So dreadful as to make the heavens weep.'

What followed changed Hamilton's admiration into awe.

'Now look here,' Rachette's recorded voice was saying dismissively, 'I find your speech opulent, verbose and objectionable. Whatever you have, assuming you have anything at all, are bound to be forgeries and will be declared as such. Her Majesty's ministers do not surrender to blackmail. That aside, if you have a point to make, some accommodation you wish to enter into, I will see it is directed to the proper quarter.'

There was, before a reply came, what Hamilton likened to the whine of a rain-laden wind among high trees. He thought it might have been a chuckle.

'No deals, Rachette. Is that blunt enough for you? Goodbye, for now. And, by the way, give my regards to Galahad!'

Rachette leaned into his desk drawer once again and switched off.

'Galahad?' Fairchild enquired.

'Operational work name for our hero,' Rachette answered.

'Then, ignoring Teasdale's box for the moment, we have been deeply penetrated. He has code names, your secure phone number and God knows what else.'

'It is possible he got that from Teasdale's box. I'll have the phone number changed, of course.'

'Don't do that, he may come back. Did you try to get a trace on it?'

For the first time signs of panic crossed Rachette's face, he tried to conceal them amongst furrows of exasperation.

'I am a senior civil servant. One not given to yelping – "trace this call" – at staff who would have no idea how to go about it, even if they understood what I was talking about. We have two unknown quantities facing us: Hammel, and the contents of Teasdale's box. I have no doubt the former is in possession of the latter. I also have no doubt these contents, whatever they may be, could be extremely hurtful if disclosed.'

'Would Teasdale have had access to the sort of stuff Hammel mentioned?'

'He undertook a lengthy vetting and investigative exercise into Cabinet Office leaks about six months ago. We brought him back temporarily from Trieste for the purpose. He was the only one with acceptable seniority. He would not have access to Cabinet papers of course.' Rachette stuck out his lower lip before going on. 'At least, not within his terms of reference.'

'But he may have gone over the top?' Fairchild suggested. Rachette viewed the prospect uneasily.

'It would have required an act of burglary, of safe-breaking,' he protested.

'We saw an excellent example of that at the Aldwych Safety Deposit,' said Fairchild.

'This is pure speculation. In any case, there are darker areas of policy ... No, no, this is pointless. Gets us nowhere. Whatever Hammel has got hold of, whatever its importance may or may not be, even if it's only the PM's laundry list, it must be recovered and Hammel must be found. We don't know what he's got, so that makes him doubly dangerous. Besides ...' he hesitated and, pulling his spectacles down to the tip of his nose, squinted at Hamilton across the rims. 'Would you be so kind as to instruct my secretary to prepare tea. Please remain with her until I ring – a few minutes only.'

Hamilton rose without a word. The unaccustomed courtesy, and the chance of dalliance with the full-bodied secretary, ameliorated the meniality of his task and deliberate exclusion from further counsel. When the door had closed behind him, Rachette spoke again. 'You see, I have told our masters nothing of Teasdale's box. Nothing of this ... Hammel development.'

'That could be dangerous for you, couldn't it? Careerwise, I mean.'

'If there was a premature explosion before I could get deep trenches dug, the end would be abrupt. Now that I have told you, you may feel an imperative desire to protect your newly acquired skin and go speeding off to tell them the tale. It is a matter for you to consider. I will bear no ill will.'

'Why haven't you told them?' Fairchild demanded bluntly.

'They are political animals, the herd instinct is too strong. They would stampede. Start bellowing alarm signals. Be heard all over the plain. Media poachers alerted. Poisoned arrows would fall like rain. Indiscriminate slaughter. I wouldn't survive either way.'

Fairchild grinned wryly at the suddenly succinct explanation ... And at himself. 'I suppose we *could* say it was in the national interest.'

Rounding his desk, Rachette went over to Fairchild and placed a grateful hand on his shoulder. Fairchild noticed he was blinking rapidly. 'My dear chap,' Rachette said, 'I knew your appointment was the wisest choice.'

'Then I think we must look to the future,' Fairchild replied. 'For the present, Hammel merely wants us to know he has the contents of Teasdale's box. He wants us worried. But sooner or later the demand will come in. Obviously, having spurned the Aldwych loot, it will not be for money.'

'No, it was Slunchev that spurned the Aldwych loot,' a testy interjection came from Rachette.

'But Hammel is Slunchev's man, surely? What he is doing, he's doing for Slunchev.'

'I wish I could be certain of that,' Rachette pondered the imponderable. 'Slunchev has vanished from the scene. His own people say he has returned to Sofia. We know they are lying. They are as puzzled about him as we are. They have no knowledge of his true whereabouts.'

'Or are pretending to have none? Is that not how they would act, if they were on the verge of some momentous coup?'

Fairchild met a dismissive shrug, but no answer.

'It may be,' he persisted. 'Once he, or they, have sweated us long enough the contents will be released without a demand. Politically we should be prepared to deny authenticity. Just as you told him we would.'

'A denial would be taken as a certificate of provenance. It would keep the issue, whatever it may turn out to be, alive even longer. The fat cats in Fleet Street much prefer a clock-work mouse to play with. The real ones either bite back, or die too quickly.'

'It's going to be difficult. We know nothing of this ... Hammel.' Fairchild, who had reached the same conclusion as Hamilton, hesitated over the name. 'By the way,' he said firmly. 'I do not accept Hammel. It sounded more like Hamme. With a faint stress on the "e". Hammel would only exist in a game of Happy Families, the equivalent of Mr Mutton, the Butcher.'

'*Herr Hammel, der Fleischer*? Not inappropriate though.'

'Neither is Sir Galahad, the Gravedigger,' Fairchild retorted, annoyed by the sly, lopsided smile, growing again on the side of Rachette's face. 'Am I privileged to be present at the birth of inspiration?' he enquired coldly.

'We could bring our hero into play,' suggested Rachette softly.

'Release a homicidal maniac!' Horror brought Fairchild to his feet. 'Is this a joke?'

'I have been known to indulge in the occasional witty aside, but to joke? Never.' Rachette stalked to the fortress of his desk and issued a command. 'Do sit down, Fairchild. It isn't as bad as all that.' Leading by example, he lowered himself behind the bastion. 'Let's look at this logically,' he became placatory and fulsome as Fairchild reluctantly returned to his own seat. 'Hammel ... or Hamme. Yes, I'll go along with your Hamme. Let's stay with Hamme, unless or until evidence arises to the contrary. Whoever he is, he is clearly connected with Warsaw Pact intelligence in the widest sense. We can particularize when we know more about him. The probability – it seems to me the fact – is, he was the one who murdered Galahad's wife and lover in Vienna. We know now, he's not a figment of our hero's distorted mind. He exists. And Galahad knows of his existence.'

'Does he?' Fairchild interrupted savagely. 'He has killed four different Hammes and tried to do in another who was on our side. It seems to me the fellow sees Hammes lurking in every shadow, but he doesn't *know him* from a bull's foot. The man is mad.'

'Not any longer,' Rachette said strongly. 'He's been under treatment for several years and made excellent progress. He is well into the rehabilitation programme. He's even been released on short parole a few times. The odd long weekend. There's a married sister whose husband farms in Kent; they've proved wonderfully supportive. He has stayed with them. Behaved impeccably. At the present moment he is back in Wyldwood for final observation pending release. The shrinks are very happy with him. Something of a triumph for them.'

'And what's going to happen when you pull the Hamme trigger on him?' Fairchild muttered sullenly.

'Oh, we won't be involved in anything like that.' Rachette pressed the intercom button on his desk and said, 'Hamilton? You may bring in the tea now.'

When Hamilton had laid out the cups and poured the tea, he carefully presented the plate of biscuits to Rachette, who picked them over fastidiously, selecting the only two with chocolate coating. As he laid them in his saucer he looked up at Hamilton, removing his glasses as he did so, with a flourish that forgave all past sins. 'My boy,' he said, 'I have a task for you. A case officer's job. One that requires great tact and discretion . . .'

Fairchild, nibbling on a soggy wholemeal, began to think of geese and ganders.

# Six

◆◆◆◆

Smith started running two days after he had passed beyond
the Bricks and was admitted inside the Wire. The Whites
observed him with discreet analytical interest; the Blues
watching with dour suspicion, for his track took him round the
perimeter of the Wire, the padding of his feet heard by the sensitive ears of its ever-listening geophones, his loping stride seen
by the pole-perched eyes on close circuit TV as he passed
under the pylons holding the massed array of security lights.
He ran, hoping to quench the day-dormant flames that night
after night rose to sear and sever his sleep. To silence the voice
that came as he lay awake, occasionally argumentative and
complaining, sometimes agreeable, even congenial; but
always persistent.

At first he could only manage two circuits, for the fence was
nearly a mile in circumference, but as he went at it day after
day his lungs, heart and legs responded to the strain. After
three months he could comfortably complete fifteen laps in an
hour and forty minutes. He never went beyond fifteen laps,
concentrating only on time, not distance. His aim, a target of
one hour thirty. Now, several nights would pass before the
flames returned and then, only briefly and without heat. The
voice was rarely heard, and when it came, was only a faint
whisper. He was sure that once he could manage the distance
in an hour and thirty, it would go forever.

It took nearly another month to accomplish, for he was tall

and well built, and the weight was not easily shed. Besides he was forty-three years of age. On the day he did it, breaking his target time by two minutes, it left him feeling peculiarly empty. He knew he was going to do it that day, for the day was right and he was right. And afterwards he knew he would never see the flames or hear the persistent voice again.

He had showered and changed into normal working drab, intending to ease his muscles by giving the corridors another polish. Smith on floors, Kendigg on washrooms, Castellain on windows. The long hinged pole holding down the heavy weight on the polishing felt was running smoothly as a piston and the pad slithered across the thick brown linoleum with unerring certainty as he guided it deep into awkward corners and under the overhang of ancient radiators, without damaging or marking the green paint on the skirting boards. *Jenkins on walls and skirting boards.*

He was almost at the end of the main corridor when the blissful emptiness in his mind was shattered by the voice of a Blue coming from behind.

'You got a visitor.'

'Who . . . ?' he turned to enquire.

'A Special,' the Blue cut him short. 'Not in the visitors' parlour. In the Medical Superintendent's office. Come on now, get your gear put away.'

'Who is it?' he managed to complete the sentence.

'Don't ask me,' the Blue replied. 'They don't tell the likes of me the identity of Specials. A Special you got, so get a shift on. Peachtree gets Specials all the time. People with pull outside gets Specials. Last week Castellain gets a Special. Now you got a Special. Soon every bleeder in the place will be gettin' Specials. Seems like everybody in here has people with pull outside. All except the bleedin' staff who has to round them up and who never gets to know who the bleedin' Specials are or what's so bleedin' special about them. Some nosey bleeder from Mencap prob'ly. Or from Amnesty International. Maybe even Lord Longford. Maybe it's your lawyer. You appealing to the Court of Human Rights? Well, you ain't appealing to me. None of you is.'

Having delivered his views with amiable truculence, the

Blue unlocked the steel door and passed Smith on to a Serge Suit waiting behind the steel door. One who was neither a Blue or a White, but an admin clerk. It was rumoured they also had Skirts and Dresses working in the admin section but hid them away on the rare occasions when any of the Inmates had to be taken beyond the steel door. Guiding him between empty desks, thereby confirming the rumour as fact in Smith's mind, the Serge Suit led him into another corridor. Smith noted the carpeted floor with some resentment, had it been linoleum its surface might have been within his mandate. He might have made contact with a Skirt or a Dress, for he had been taken off the capsules some time ago and the insides of Skirts and Dresses had been much on his mind of late. Maybe he should aim to get his time down to an hour and fifteen.

Leaving Smith outside an oak door with an escutcheon bearing the words Medical Superintendent, the Serge Suit retreated backwards along the corridor as if practising withdrawal from a royal presence, or fearful of displaying an unprotected rear. Smith knocked once on the door and entered.

He found only one man in the room and the sight of him induced surprise and a shiver of fear. He put the latter emotion down to the old impending-doom syndrome, an occupational disease among those who were active in *the* Job. But he was no longer in *the* Job. Nevertheless he said, quietly cautious, 'Hello, Guv'nor. You're a bit off your manor, aren't you?'

'My old manor, perhaps,' Fairchild answered with that quirky smile he knew so well. 'My new one is a lot wider.'

'Oh, yeah, I forgot. I read about it in the papers a few weeks ago. You've taken up a Home Office appointment. Gone to join that gallant band, Her Majesty's Inspectors of Constabulary, have you?'

'You've lost a bit of weight, Owen, but I'm glad to see you're otherwise your old cynical self.'

'Ever since I came off the tabs six months ago, I've been as cynical as hell.'

'Are you still on drugs?' The question was casually neutral.

'Not even aspirin.' The answer was defiantly proud.

'They tell me you're getting plenty of exercise, your EEGs

are excellent and your Rorschach and other projection tests quite normal.'

'I also have a good bowel movement at least once a day. Didn't they mention that?'

'No, I'm afraid they didn't. Is it important?'

'Important? I should say it is. One of the clearest indications of sanity is a well-controlled shit. A failure to master the sphincter is a failure to master the mind.'

'You always had plenty of bottle, Owen. Everybody said you had the tightest bottle in the Job.'

'Everybody said, everybody said. But nobody had the bottle to come down and ask, "How's *your* bottle holding out these days, Owen? Must be twitching a bit. All those people dead in the States. How did you manage to row out that one, Owen? Got yourself quietly binned away on the funny farm, eh? Nice one that, you always had plenty of bottle, Owen." But it's not like that. My bottle goes in and out just like everybody else's. Is that why you're here? To admire my bottle?'

'No, not really. They're considering discharging you in the near future. I was wondering if you had anything lined up? If not, I might be able to put something your way.'

'You're the only one in the Job who has come to visit me.'

'No need to get maudlin about it. You know what it's like, once you're in bother, no one wants to know. He who touches pitch...'

'But you're different, above all that? At your rank you get the dirt-resistant white gloves.'

'Not in the rank I hold at present.'

'You're not HMI?'

'I am the director of a Division of the Secret Intelligence Service. And *you* are still under the Act, Owen. So don't repeat it or you'll be transferred to Dartmoor.'

Breaking his silent astonishment, Smith said, dolefully, 'I sigh because I know you are not kidding. Cyril Fairchild, how could you be such a prize prick? You don't mind if I call you Cyril? You're not in the Job any more. I'm not in the Job any more. We're a right pair of prize pricks together. But I've got an excuse, I'm a nutter. What's yours?'

'The country called. It was in the national interest.'

'Oh, yes? And you've come to recruit me as your intrepid secret agent? Now let me see, would it be to recover the Nazi gold from the depths of a Bavarian lake, before the Neos get their filthy hands on it? Or find the looted art treasures of Europe that Goering stashed away in a hidden mine? I know! I am to rescue the eccentric old scientist who is in the hands of a terrorist organization. The one who has discovered a deadly virus that will wipe out the Western world.'

He smothered an incipient protest from Fairchild with further sarcasm. 'You see I've had plenty of time to catch up on my reading. I know all the plots. Is it something simple; like penetrating the Kremlin, parcelling up the head of the KGB and smuggling him out to the West? No problem, Cyril. Put it down to me; Owen Smith, licensed to kill, beer, wines and spirits.'

'I *would* like to put a little job down to you.'

'You really are serious, aren't you? I always know when you're serious.'

'The job specification doesn't measure up to the standards you describe, but should be right up your alley.'

'What, no mad scientist? I was hoping for a mad scientist. There'd be a beautiful daughter I could have over in no time at all.'

'It's a matter of murder and theft, but as far as you are concerned it's primarily the recovery of stolen property. Let me tell you about it.'

'If you must, but it's rather a mouldy old plot. I've heard it before.'

'So the only people who have seen this Hamme are the Funnies who were watching the Popkiss drum? Assuming he was Hamme.'

'They didn't see much of him. It was dark. No pictures. Their equipment went down. The best we have is a mature male, six-two, proportionately built, wearing a dark grey raincoat. Probably clean-shaven; at least no beard. All other features vague.'

'It's not only the features. What the hell is a mature male? Anyone between nineteen and ninety?'

'Not less than thirty-five, not more than fifty-five.'

'Very precise people you've got working for you.'

'They were new to the job. Pulled out from behind desks.'

'Or from under them. Does the name Hamme have a meaning in any other language?'

'The name was first thought to be Hammel. It could still be. That means mutton in German. However, we have agreed on Hamme. Expert opinion on our recording thinks Hamme the more probable. But it has no specific meaning.'

'Spell it.'

'H-A-M-M-E. That's phonetically, of course. Do you have any German?'

'A smattering. The odd word and phrase.'

'People who have a smattering ask the way to the toilet and wind up in shit creek.'

'I've been there several times in pure English.'

'In English maybe; I doubt the purity.'

'Let's change the subject. Has Hamme been in touch again?'

'Twice. The second time was just to put the frighteners on again. The last time he gave us a small sample.'

'Such as?'

'No comment.'

'As bad as that, is it?'

'No comment.'

'Any demand made? What's his price?'

'Nothing yet. He's keeping us sweating. He's enjoying it.'

'If I take this on, what are the going rates?'

'I thought the current monthly pay and allowances for a Detective Chief Superintendent might appeal to you. Plus reasonable and proven expenses.'

'Do I have access to an informant's fund or whatever they call it in your new game?'

'Provided it's not exorbitant. Provided it's worth it.'

'Nothing changes. Do I get rank or position in your outfit?'

'You're not in my outfit, Owen. I'm sorry, you're strictly casual labour. Your salary will be paid in cash for as long as the job lasts. Maybe a small bonus if you get results. But otherwise you're a member of the black economy. You will not be on record. I have never been here.'

'It was silly of me to ask. I should have known. It's in all the books. So how do I keep in touch; have you got a direct line?'

'Look up the Home Office number in the book, ask for BARKER. Speak distinctly. This will switch you to a computerized scrambler. Leave a message. Your call will be monitored. If a reply is needed, leave a number.'

'It's all so bloody dismal, Cyril. I can't understand you. You were never a chancer. Smart, shrewd, but never a chancer. And look what you wind up doing.'

'Like the man said, it was an offer I couldn't refuse.'

'A "K"? Is that it? *Sir* Cyril Fairchild? I don't like it. Makes you sound like a Tory politician . . . Lord Fairchild now, Lord Fairchild of New Scotland Yard! Yes, that has a ring to it. I hope you held out for a peerage?'

'It wasn't anything like that. Can we get back to business?'

'OK, m'lord. What about this box; the usual safety deposit thing?'

'Pressed steel, green-painted, eighteen by ten by six inches.'

'And the contents? I'll need some idea of what I'm looking for.'

'Documents. They'll be photo-copies, or on microfilm. Possibly both. Prints and negatives. There are no original papers missing; at least nothing we can establish. There may be a tape. Teasdale may have made a tape. Excuses, justification. I'm told they do things like that. The ones that go over. If you come across anything, please do not read or playback; it could seriously damage your health. That is an official Government warning.'

'I'm down to ten a day and I don't inhale. What if I get a lead that points due east. Do I follow it up?'

'You don't. You are strictly the London end. Someone else is handling the East.'

'Oh, yes?'

'If that cryptic remark and the knowing smirk on your face means you have something up your sleeve, I suggest you pull back your cuffs. I repeat you are not to leave the country. The East is being handled by someone else.'

'Like Castellain?'

'How the hell do you know about Castellain? This is out-rageous. Who else has been to see you about this?'

'You're the first.'

'Then I repeat, how the hell did you manage to tie Castellain into this?'

'When I was dumped inside the Wire for being a good boy, Castellain found out I was from the Yard. He asked me if I'd ever known a great avenger called Hameh. That's how I heard it. H-A-M-E-H. Hameh. Anyway, I put it down to the sort of question one nutter asks another, and told him I didn't mix with great avengers. Then you come here and start talking about Hamme. If it is any consolation, Castellain never mentioned what's his name again.'

'It's no consolation. None at all. And the brief mention of a name six months ago by, as you say, one nutter to another, is a tenuous basis on which to make a connection.'

'It was strengthened by events of last Thursday. I was doing my floors ...'

'Doing your floors?'

'Polishing them. I'm on floors, Kendigg is on washrooms, Castellain was on windows. Cleaning them.'

'What has that got to do with anything?'

'It has to do with manual therapy – or slave labour – depending whether you're outside or inside. But in this particular instance it's merely scene-setting. I was doing my floors on the upper corridor, when out of one of Castellain's highly polished windows overlooking the staff car park, I see a young Sloane Ranger ride up in his yellow Morgan sports. He gets out, all matching sweater, leather patches, twill trousers and cheese-cutter cap. Castellain emerges from the side door and gets the dark blue plastic ID flashed at him. He also gets the fawning smile, the doffed cap and the friendly but respectful mit – which he ignores. Anxiety reigns high with the Sloane Ranger, he does some slow hand washing and a lot of fast talking. Eventually, he and Castellain begin a funeral march up and down the car park, with the Sloanie pulling out all the stops; the big clutch at the heart, the despairing grab at the forelock. At one stage something is said that doesn't go down well with Castellain. He hauls in the Sloanie by his coat collar and gives him a bad case of strangulation with his own lapels. It was nicely done. The Sloanie's toes were at least three inches off the deck. Surprised me somewhat.'

'Why?'

'I always reckoned Castellain had a strong head of steam in his boiler, but his throttle control was good.'

'What happened? What did you do?'

'Nothing I could do! The windows here are shatterproof. In any case, Castellain drops him after a few seconds, dusts him down, and gives him something that under a strong microscope, might be seen as an apologetic smile. They continue walking up and down, this time the Sloanie keeping well out of Castellain's reach. Castellain was now doing most of the talking and clearly laying down terms and conditions. The chat goes on for another twenty minutes or so, then Castellain comes back inside. No parting handshake by the way, but plenty of nodding and bobbing by the Sloanie and obviously a definite understanding had been reached. I didn't see Castellain leave here on the Saturday, but I'll lay odds he was picked up in a yellow Morgan sports. Do you want the licence number?'

'It won't be necessary. I am familiar with both car and driver. Did you see anything more of Castellain before he was discharged. Did he say anything ... about anything?'

'He did not. And I didn't ask him. I didn't fancy having my lapels twisted around my throat. I'll tell you this though; that one is good. And I don't just mean with the rough stuff. If you've got a few more like him around, perhaps you're not as daft as I thought.'

'I wish I could be sure, Owen. I wish I could be sure.'

'Cheer up, Cyril. Now you've got two right nutters working for you on this one, we'll get the job done. Don't worry! I mean, think of all the other nutters you've got working for you. Can any of them prove they are sane, like Castellain and me?'

Fairchild drove slowly away from Wyldwood, carefully easing the car out of the turreted gate, seeing the studded doors and the great red brick wall fade from the rear-view mirror as he negotiated the first of many tight bends along the narrow lanes. He had used official cars with official drivers for so long now, he was out of practice. It was a hired car; small, sensitive and Japanese. Liable to oversteer at anything more than the slightest twitch of the wheel, the horn giving a high-pitched, penetrating yelp when pressed on approaching every blind corner. He did not want an accident while still close to the institution.

'I have never been here!' Aloud, he reasserted the disclaimer he had given Smith. He was glad Smith was all right. They had all said so – the psychiatrists, the psychologists; the shrinks. Provably sane. Fully aware of the consequences of his actions. McNaghten Rules? Did they still apply in the courts today? Probably not. They had taken Smith in with mixed emotions, the shrinks. 'Strong evidence of transient situation disturbance and accompanying melancholia. An interesting case considering the history, but hardly one for custodial treatment.' It had taken words from on high at the Home Office to convince them, custodial treatment was not only necessary, but politic. 'Certainly in the best interests of the patient if you follow our meaning.' They had followed, the shrinks. Now he would have to convince the Home Office it was time to rescind the order. The dust had settled, the smoke had cleared; the heat was off. He allowed himself a shallow chuckle at the aptness of the simile.

'But why do you want to use me, Cyril?' Smith had asked as they parted, suddenly and querulously suspicious. 'You could get a Chief Inspector out of C1 or Special Branch to punt this around.'

'Could I, Owen?' he had replied, daring him to face the facts. Smith had turned on that sardonic sneer of his and accepted the challenge. 'Yes, I know,' he had said. 'Anything goes boss-eyed, and it's down to another of those rampaging nutters they've let out too soon.'

Rachette had meant exactly that, in respect of Castellain, although in more subtly euphemistic parlance. But there had been another reason why Fairchild wanted Smith to do the job. A reason he had not mentioned to anyone. Smith was one of those rare people who had a peculiarly catalytic effect on events. One that brought about a speedy reaction in the elements involved ... Although sometimes with ... catastrophic results. Rachette's words. He shivered involuntarily, nearly swerving into a ditch to avoid the remorseless approach of a farm tractor. Yes, if anything goes wrong, Smith would definitely have to be another of those nutters they let out too soon. He hoped it would never come to that. The motorway was visible ahead, he could get his foot down. Fast driving from now on.

# Seven

❖❖❖❖❖❖

Smith paid off the cab outside his Kennington flat and surveyed the street. Nothing had changed. Somehow he felt it should have changed; as he had changed. Been changed? They could have brought in the developers and made changes. Changed its character as they had ... 'Try and avoid the influence of morbid thoughts,' Snow White had stressed at their final session. 'Do not dwell in the past. The past is ancient legend, it holds little in the way of truth. The past recedes at the speed of light. So, also, does what we choose to call truth, at least in the visual sense. In less than six seconds truth is a million miles away. It is a memory, subject to all the exaggerations and omissions of the human mind. Its form altered and mis-shapen by our fears and prejudices. Oh, the consequences of truth in action may remain as inert reminders of its presence, but they are mere objects for argument and debate as to causation; one wherein a preponderance of artificial facts may lead to a logical conclusion as to what the truth *was*. But logic at best is no more than a reasonable guess, a two-dimensional version of truth; lacking solidity. Should you endeavour to chase after the past, you will never catch it in its real form, and such a pointless pursuit will only lead you to the lair of a repulsive monster which will inevitably drive you back in here.'

The street had not changed. Though it was only late September, the same dead leaves swirled about his feet. Even in midsummer there were dead leaves. Lead and carbon monoxide slowly poisoning the trees. Jalal, the Pakistani who ran the corner shop, was still in business, and he was pleased to see his plate-glass windows looked as if they had remained intact for a time. That was good. He looked up at the windows of his own place.

The Force Welfare officer had agreed to find a tenant to take the place furnished whilst he was inside. As far as the Welfare officer was concerned, Smith was another unfortunate who had succumbed to the pressures of the job. A mentally sick man, medically retired. The sort of case Force Welfare officers were there to assist – within limits of course. He had written asking for the existing tenant to be given notice to quit. And now there were frilly lace curtains between the glass and the velvet drapes he had spent so much time, effort and money in fitting. Dammit, were they still in there? Well, they could bloody well get themselves out of it – double quick – and take their frilly lace curtains with them. He marched grimly up the stairs, letting his feet kick ominously against the risers. As he reached the landing, the door opened.

'Hello, Owen,' she said. 'Come on in.' The suitcase fell from his grasp, rocked and slid over on its side.

'Elstow!' Her name barely escaped a constricting throat. 'Detective Inspector Marion Elstow! It's been a long time.'

'It need not have been,' she answered softly, yet with a hint of recrimination. 'I went down to Wyldwood three times to visit you. Each time you refused to see me. George O'Brien and several others tried at different times and got the same answer.'

Suddenly, he was lost. *No one in the job had been to see him.* That was what he had told Fairchild; and he had believed it. Still believed it. And yet . . . He tried to re-enter the dark swamp of the depression in which he had lain behind the Bricks. He could recall his listless acceptance of the capsules, the tablets and the brooding sessions with the White, Ludovic, and his Psychodiagnosticians. The electroconvulsive therapy. He could not remember any of that, only the call to its electrodes. 'Come along, Mr Smith, it's ECT time.' But visitors? Rejecting visitors. Rejection? But he would, wouldn't he? He would not have wanted anyone to see him that way. Especially Elstow. He had forced her into the hidden recesses of his mind long ago. Something precious he had once possessed, then lost to the greater demand of the job. A demand they both recognized and were bound by. A loss. A mutual loss? Where the emptiness was filled by something so overwhelmingly intangible they would never call it duty. Simply the Job.

Now she was back, standing in front of him, her neat, pert beauty unchanged. She had tried to see him in Wyldwood? 'I can't remember,' he said helplessly, feeling a hot wetness on his cheeks.

She must have noticed, for she quickly turned away, saying cheerily, 'Well, don't just stand there, come on in. It's your flat. I'll put the kettle on.' He took the opportunity to wipe his face. The apartment still held its familiar warmth. His books and record albums lay neatly on the shelves, the big leather chair, the sheepskin in front of the gas-fire with its imitation logs. Nothing had been changed except those fancy lace curtains ... And flowers, fresh flowers on the table. Another suitcase, a large leather suitcase, in the middle of the room.

'You are looking very fit, I must say,' Elstow called from the kitchen.

'I can run nearly fifteen miles in less than ninety minutes,' he boasted absently, studying the suitcase.

'Without stopping?' she enquired above the strident whistle of the kettle.

'Of course. There would be no point if you had to stop and rest every five minutes. You couldn't make the time. There would be no achievement.' The whistle stopped abruptly and he felt the silence. He filled it quickly. 'Have you been staying here?'

'Uh huh. I heard it was available. It's very handy for the Yard, I can walk there in twenty minutes ... Without stopping,' her laugh tinkled among the coffee cups. 'Besides, I know the place of old,' she added, bringing in the tray. She looked at him. 'Why are you standing in the middle of the room? Why don't you sit down, Owen? You're home *now*.' Taking backward steps away from the suitcase he eased himself slowly into the leather chair. Passing him a cup, she settled catlike on the rug.

'Are you over it?' Her enquiry was tender, yet he felt her unease.

'No,' he said. 'I don't think I'll ever get over it.'

'I was speaking of Wyldwood ... and whatever it was that made them put you in there.'

'I'm over that. Are you moving out?' he nodded at the suitcase.

'I got notice to quit. Very official.'

'Tear it up. Please stay.'

'I've already booked a room in the women's section house. *Pro tem*. Until I find another place.'

'Cancel it.'

She peered up at him, a loose strand of hair falling over one eye. 'It died, didn't it, Owen?' It was a question, not a statement of fact.

'No. It went dormant. We didn't nurture it, neither of us. We let the job smother it. But it never died.'

'It could spoil things for me. In the Job, I mean. I like being in the Job.'

'Still got ideas on being the first woman Commissioner?'

She smiled ruefully. 'No. You knocked those ideas out of me long ago.' Her resolute little jaw tightened. 'But I still intend to get on. I am good, you know,' she claimed defiantly.

'The best,' he acknowledged. 'One of the very best.'

'They might not think so, if I take up with you again.' He recalled that she had always been painfully blunt.

'He who touches pitch is defiled,' he said. 'Somebody mentioned that a few weeks ago. He was wrong. I know that now. But you must do what you think is best. I had no right to ask you to stay.'

'We're talking in clichés, aren't we?' she enquired doubtfully. 'It's more serious than that.'

He tried to laugh at her fears, for that used to be his way, but now the confidence had gone. At least as far as she was concerned. She was still in the Job. But the sight of her, the nearness of her, made him realize how precious she was to him. Memories! How often behind the Bricks he had thirsted for memories. Had tried to revive a mind lying dead as a bleached bone in a remote desert. Had tried to get back, even beyond her, into a warm, placid meadow, where bright-eyed children played along the banks of a shallow stream. Never reaching beyond the old ruined house; a forbidden place, where deep in an overgrown garden stood the broken stones, the dank mildew, of a poisoned well. Under a surface scum, it was full of tar-black, impenetrable muck. No place to slake his thirst. There had been times when he had been tempted to hazard death by drowning in that unrepentant slough. If only he dared risk it, he might plunge down through the slime to find some hidden cavern where there would be a cold clear underground river that would carry him out under the hill, to emerge in that sunshiny meadow he had known as a boy. There had been the night when he took the chance. No longer afraid of drowning in all that mud and muck, only afraid of what he might find beneath. And when he made it, he was outside the Bricks, but still inside the Wire. But he could see beyond the Wire, though he never saw as far as Marion Elstow.

'Did you hear what I said?' she was enquiring, albeit tenderly.

'Yes,' he said at last. 'It could be serious for you, for your career. Though they say they're more broadminded now. I even know a couple of Inspectors who got divorced and still made Superintendent.'

'We're not even married,' she said primly.

'Not an insurmountable problem.'

'Clichés again? But thanks anyway. I know you mean it. I know ... Oh, hell. I don't know what I know.'

She laid her head sideways on open knees, pulling gently at the sheepskin, trying to straighten out the fleece, watching it spring back into a tight curl. Doing it again and again with greater force as if hoping it would snap loudly, breaking the silence.

'All right,' she said at last. 'I'll stay.'

Smith turned his head to the ceiling, eyes closed in gratitude, then snapped forward in a seizure of pride and fear. 'Not out of pity?' he meant it to be a plea, but it emerged as a rasping interrogative. 'Not out of pity?' he repeated softly.

She considered her emotions for a time. 'No, not out of pity,' she said. 'I'm certain of that.' Rising from the rug she kissed him, sisterly fashion, on the cheek.

'I never felt sorry for you when they put you away,' she said matter of factly. 'I knew whatever had happened you walked into it with your eyes open. That you would accept the consequences.'

'Right in the first instance,' he said, seeking refuge in ambiguity. 'Wrong in the second. I guess that's what drove me round the twist.'

'But it's over now,' she snuggled into his lap.

Comfortingly? Or was it pity? The fear came back but he turned aside the knife that might open the wound. You must learn to accept things as they are, he told himself. She's here in your arms, be thankful for that, it's a great mercy.

'Have you anything in mind as to what you are going to do?' she was asking.

'I certainly have,' he laid a hand on her thigh.

'I meant in the way of a job.'

'I've had an offer. A bit of private enquiry work. Trace and recover some stolen property.'

'That's a matter for the police!'

'You're not very good at it these days.'

'Ever since the great Owen Smith left the Job, you mean? So who are you working for?'

He hesitated. 'A firm called National Security,' he improvised.

'I've never heard of that one, but there are so many about these days. Are they reputable?'

He smiled inwardly. Never in her wildest dreams would she imagine him working for the funnies. Not the way they all thought of the funnies.

'They have a former Assistant Commissioner on the board,' he said solemnly.

'They all have,' she picked up the cups and went through to the kitchen. 'They like to spice up their letter headings with a sprinkling of OBEs and QPMs. What sort of gear have they hired you to find?'

'Part proceeds of the Aldwych Safety Deposit job.'

She returned slowly, a cup in one hand, a dish cloth in the other. 'What kind of proceeds?'

'Documents. Valuable documents and company records.'

'Owen. I'm on the squad investigating the Popkiss, Scanlon and Appleby murders. The killings are tied in with the Aldwych job. No one has reported any missing documents.'

'The owners don't want it known. They don't want business rivals putting in offers to the villains.'

'The villains were Popkiss and Scanlon, and they are dead. As far as we know, we've recovered all the gear with the exception of a box belonging to a civil servant named Teasdale, and he died two weeks before the job was pulled. His wife thinks it could only have been family papers in the box. From his side – he was very proud of his side of the family – Owen ...' He could almost hear the thought processes going click click click inside her head. He went over and took her in his arms.

'Don't ask any more ... I can't lie to you. Better you don't ask, for both our sakes.'

'Oh, Owen, you bloody fool. Did you *have* to go across the street? Couldn't you have found something decent!'

'They invoked the Old Pals Act. You can't resist the power of the Old Pals Act.'

'Can that be why I agreed to stay here?' she countered stiffly.

'No. Look, you mustn't let it affect us. Never again. It's no more than a job for a reasonably competent detective sergeant. No James Bond stuff. They've got someone else handling that side. All they want me to do is to get among the associates, second-class villains. Find out if they know what happened to the gear.'

'I can save you the trouble. We've been among the associates. They know nothing about nothing.'

'Fine. You can see how easy it is. But don't deprive me of the chance to earn a few quid. Hit or miss, I still get paid,' he allowed the irony to creep in. 'Just like I was back in the Job.'

'You're not short of money, Owen,' she said accusingly. 'You've got a bit put by, you told me, that time when ...' she snapped the reminiscence like a dry stick before continuing:

'And you've got a sick pension – index-linked.'

She felt him slide down the length of her body until he was on his knees before her, his arms encircling her, his head nuzzling between her thighs. 'Elstow,' he begged of her. 'I've got to do this. You must understand. I've got to get in amongst it again. I've crawled out of the pit, but I'm still on the edge. I've got to get away from the edge. This is the only way I know.'

She dug her hand into his thick iron-grey hair and pulled his head back. 'I need you, Elstow,' he whispered. 'Mind, body and soul. I need you.'

'Then you had better take me to bed, Owen,' she said simply. 'Just take me to bed.'

Afterwards when she had showered and put on her street clothes, she came into the bedroom telling him she had to get back to the Yard. The enquiry was getting nowhere slowly and as with all enquiries getting nowhere, was generating more and more work. It was at the straw-clutching stage and everyone was diving into the haystack. Each random stalk would have to be examined for signs of a needle before it could be asserted that no needle existed. Commander Joe Potch was in charge.

He knew the score and he knew Joe Potch. No one, least of all Joe Potch, running a major investigation would submit a negative report without being able to say he had been down every avenue, up every street and round every corner. But to him it was academic. He was not greatly interested. Only Elstow mattered to him, now. Elstow and his little tuppeny-ha'penny enquiry on behalf of the intelligence service. It was a small beginning on the journey away from the pit. Elstow came in and kissed him adieu. He called her back from the door and pointed at the windows. 'I love your frilly curtains,' he said.

Five minutes later the phone rang.

## SMITH INTERCEPT

| | |
|---|---|
| *Subject*: | SMITH Owen John – Aged 43 – British subject. |
| *Location*: | Flat 7, 96 Bishops Terrace, Kennington, London, SE11. |
| *Tel. No*: | Indexed. |
| *Date Commenced*: | 21 September. |
| *Authority*: | JIC333629/85/281. |
| *Registry*: | 781/437/3951GTH 781/635/8677LMT & others. |

*21 Sept. 17.23 hrs. Incoming. Caller identifies self as Julian Rice, Producer's Assistant, BBC-TV.*

J.    Good afternoon, sir, am I speaking to Mr Owen Smith?

S.    Who wants him?

J.    Oh, I'm Julian Rice, Producer's Assistant, BBC-TV. Please call me Julian. May I call you Owen?

S.    No.

J.    As you wish, Mr Smith...

S.    Who said I was Mr Smith? But as it happens I am. What do you want?

J.    Mr Smith, we have been told that...

S.    Told by whom?

J.    Ah, by a little bird, Mr Smith. As an ex-detective

you will be familiar with the chirrupings of little
birds?

S:     And the croaking of vultures.

J.     I am sure your ornithological repertoire is very
extensive, Mr Smith, but the bird song we are
interested in concerns the mystery surrounding the
fate of the Space Temple just over a year ago in
America. Where all those people died – or did they?
Our little bird tells us you were somehow involved
in that. Were somehow responsible for what
happened. We are thinking of doing a programme
based on the incident and we would like to . . .

S.     What other little perversions do you people get up
to? I'll bet you get a helluva kick pulling the wings
off butterflies.

J.     Really, Mr Smith. We are talking of a matter of
great public concern.

S.     You know as much about what concerns the public
as an organ-grinder's monkey.

J.     How dare . . . I'll have you know, Mr Smith, this
call is being recorded.

S.     So what do you want from me? An aria from *La
Bohème?*

J.     Oh, this is too much. Will you hold the line, please,
(*pause*) Morpeth, will you please speak to this
dreadful person? (*prolonged pause*).

*New caller, female, authoritative, identifies self as Morpeth
Anatole.*

M.     Mr Smith, my name is Morpeth Anatole. You may
have heard of me.

S.     Morpeth Anatole? No, I don't think so. Wait a
minute though. Morphy Annie, of course! You used
to do a bit of business up behind the Greek restaurant in Dean Street, Soho. The punters used to
call you Morbid Anatomy. I remember you now.

How are you, Morphy, it's been years? You must be getting a bit past it these days.

M.    Mr Smith, I'll have you know I present the Spotlight Tonight show . . .

S.    Oh, you've gone in for the exhibish, have you, Morphy? Not a bad idea. At your age you're right to let others do the donkey work. Making a crust, are you?

M.    More than you'll ever make, Mr Smith. We've been told you've just been released from Wyldwood and we will attribute your eccentric manner to the fact your treatment did not quite succeed. I don't wish to be unkind, but I too can lash out if driven to it.

S.    I know you can, Morphy. They always said you had a good strong arm for the fladger.

M.    You have been told this call is being recorded. We will not hesitate to play it over the air if you force us to.

S.    *(Singing – badly) Che gelida manina* . . .
*Caller disconnects – 17.29 hrs.*

# Eight

❖❖❖❖❖

He decided to begin with Maisie Ackroyd. She was the nearest, having lived with Terry Scanlon in one of the small side streets between Battersea Park Road and Lavender Hill. An area of what once would have been called working-class respectability. A social delineation more severe and rigid than the degree of rank or the protocol of nobility. Postmen, railwaymen, minor civil servants and the occasional policeman lived in the streets; and all knew and jealously preserved their place in the scheme of things. But that was before the war when regularity of work and income assured ability to pay the rent, to hire-purchase a three-piece suite in uncut moquette, a gramophone, possibly a three-wave-band wireless set, and the aspiration to one day acquire a second-hand Austin Seven. Afterwards, when the days of full employment came along, the postmen, railwaymen, minor civil servants and policemen found themselves at the bottom of the pay scales and all the new plastic furniture, TV sets, Ford Prefects and the occasional flashy Zephyr, were being bought by formerly despised bricklayers, plumbers, mechanics and the unskilled labourers... And the spivs and villains. Especially the villains. For, from the 'fifties onwards, villainy, petty and grand, became the most progressive and burgeoning enterprise in the country, growing as the rewards became richer and the risks and punishments lessened.

Even from the top of the street, Smith knew it had to be

Terry Scanlon's house. Its former red-brick exterior had been faced with an artificial York stone that could not quite subdue the lividity of its yellow pigment, or come to terms with the asymmetrical black cement pointing that held it in place. Smith grinned inwardly. Terry Scanlon, the late Terry Scanlon, like his late father, a travelling post-office sorter, clearly knew his place. Not for him investment of his ill-gotten gains in some detached suburban mansion as was the practice of his more enterprising peers. Those who had quickly learned there was as much to be gained from the legal villains in the property market as there was in a full-blooded blag on any so-called security company's armoured truck, whose so-called guards would hand over fifty grand and upwards at first sight of a sawn-off.

Pausing by the gate of the semi-detached house, Smith took sights. The walls of the small front garden had been removed and the garden itself paved in red and green stone slabs to allow a once-prized, metallic silver Jaguar off-street parking, the space between the houses being too narrow for a garage. The Jag was gathering dust, and one of the tyres sagged from lack of air. Yes, Smith thought, Terry at least had the *nous* to reckon he would never fit in around the stockbroker belt. But no reason not to let the neighbours know this was the home of a geezer who had a few quid to bung about. Even if he did get nicked now and again and had done a bit of bird.

He saw movement among the waterfall of curtaining, frothier by far than anything Elstow had hung in his own place; went in through the gate, pressing the bell by the side of a tacked-on porch extension in Canadian red cedar and bottle-green glass. The head that eventually came round the door frame was armoured in pink hair-curlers, the face bleary-eyed, blotched by decaying and mouldering cosmetics. On a pert, but angrily red nose, hung little nodules of sunburned skin.

'Miz Maisie Ackroyd?' Smith smiled invitingly. 'My name is Smith. I'm from the insurance assessors.'

'Don't want none,' the door rammed hard against his foot.

'I am not selling, Miz Ackroyd, I am giving. Your name has been selected as qualifying for our star prize.'

The pressure eased. 'What sort of prize?'

'A cash gift of fifty pounds. All you have to do is correctly answer a few simple questions.'

The door opened wider disclosing a plump and sagging frame enclosed in a purple dressing-gown. Podgy little toes, tipped by nails encased in chipped red varnish, leered obscenely beneath the hem of the garment. Maisie Ackroyd had known better days. 'I've spent fifty quid on a round of drinks before now,' she said contemptuously. 'What's fifty quid these days.'

'The price of six bottles of vodka, a carton of tomato juice, with possibly enough left for a few packets of potato crisps, bacon and egg flavour.'

Maisie frowned and simpered in a confusion of puzzled pleasure. ''Ere, how do you know I'm a Bloody Mary lady, an' that about the bacon and egg flavour? If you must know, it's cheese and onion. An' what's it to do with insurance anyhow?' she demanded.

'We have an interest in the Aldwych Safety Deposit tickle,' Smith eased himself inside the door. 'The one Terry and Eric had off. Or nearly had off.' He smothered Maisie's flow of startled but half-hearted abuse under a stream of placatory words, gently using his weight to force her gradually into the living-room. An elderly woman seated by the gas fire looked up from a newspaper.

'Good morning, Mrs Scanlon,' Smith said respectfully. 'You'll be poor Terry's dear old mum?'

'What's he want, Maisie?' the old woman asked querulously.

'Bleedin' law, ain't he,' Maisie announced with intuitive certainty. 'Said he was from the insurance, but I know the bleedin' law when I sees it. As if they ain't been pestering us enough. Why didn't you say you was the bleedin' law? We've told you everything we know.'

Smith sat himself at the table and laid out a row of ten five-pound notes. 'Now when has the law come round and done that, Maisie?' he challenged.

She looked at the money wistfully. 'I've seen that table a foot deep in fivers,' she said even more wistfully.

'But not any more, Maisie. Not now Terry's gone. Now

you'll have to start knocking out the car, the video recorder, and that lot over there, that looks like the control panel for a space ship, but is, I presume, the latest thing in hi-fi.' He pinned her on the end of a knowing stare. 'You and Terry did it in as fast as he made it. Before long you will be down to Uncle with the mink coat and the fox stole. Fifty quid, it's not much I know, but it should keep you in Bloody Marys for a week.'

'But we told the law all we know,' Maisie wailed disconsolately. 'Didn't we, Ma?' she turned to the old woman for support.

'And a lot of good it did,' the old woman confirmed. 'They still 'aven't found them what did for my Terry.'

'There *was* something you didn't tell the law,' Smith said, gathering the notes together. 'You didn't tell them about the time Terry ready-eyed a meet between Eric Popkiss and the guy who set the job up.'

For a time Maisie's gaze wandered speculatively between the notes and Smith's face. 'How did you know *we* covered the meet?' she asked slowly. Smith held his voice steady.

'I know it happened, let's leave it at that.'

With her eyes, Maisie consulted Terry's mother. Brows lifted, lips twitched and pouted, but no word was spoken. Finally, Maisie pointed to the small collection of fivers under Smith's fingers. 'Double that up and I'll see what I can remember,' she said.

'I can put another score on top,' Smith said after due consideration. 'And that'll have to come from my own pocket. It's the best I can do.'

'I'll go and make us a cup of tea.' The old woman rose and went through into the hall. Smith knew a deal had been struck. He offered Maisie a cigarette. She accepted without thanks and seated herself opposite. Her hand reached out for the money and Smith let her take it. He was with people to whom a deal was a deal. He removed another twenty from his wallet and slid the notes across. A deal was a deal.

'You went with Terry?' he opened for half the pot.

She nodded. 'He thought it'd be less conspicuous, the two of us together. And he was shit scared. I don't know why he was shit scared. Neither did he. But he was . . . Shit scared!'

'Had he ever actually met the geezer. The one who set the caper up?'

'No. That was down to Eric. The geezer would only deal with Eric. Eric felt he was being ready-eyed all the time and made Terry stay clear. He wouldn't even make a meet for Terry to pick up the key moulds. He had to fetch them from halfway up a tree in Battersea Park. Have you ever heard the likes? Fourth tree on the left from inside the gate, on a branch halfway up. Have you ever heard the likes? I wonder how Eric came to think of it?'

'It's the class of people who're setting jobs up these days,' Smith said sympathetically.

Maisie continued, sadly reminiscent, 'It should have been a doddle. They had all the main keys; the wiring system for the alarms. It should have been a doddle. Like going out on the hoist.' Smith nodded sagely; Maisie had two cons for shoplifting in her younger days. 'Well, it was a doddle,' Maisie was saying. 'One of the biggest tickles of all time. Just the two of them, my Terry and that Eric. Straight in and out. No bothers, no aggro. Made them train robbers look like a bunch of slags doing the offertory boxes in a Methodist chapel.'

Maisie sniffed noisily. 'All the bothers came afterwards, didn't they?' She went in search of paper tissues.

'Who did Terry get to make the twirls?' Smith asked idly. Maisie stopped abruptly, halfway through blowing her nose. 'That ain't in the deal,' she said, flatly adamant. Raising complaisant and apologetic hands, Smith acknowledged the fine print. 'Where did they make the meet,' he enquired instead. 'Eric and the geezer? Did he put a name about, by the way, the geezer?'

'There was more than one.'

'More than one name?'

'More than one geezer. The one Eric did the business with said his name was Trench. Mr Trench. But Eric said he clocked another geezer in the background. He always stood a good distance away with his back to them, but Mr Trench kept looking round at him. Sort of nervous like. Eric was good at spotting things like that. Eric could always suss out a minder.'

'How did they first contact Eric?'

'Outside the Leather Glove. You know the Leather Glove?'
Smith knew the Leather Glove.

'Mr Trench pulled Eric in the car park, propped it to him
there and then. No actual details. Just that it would be a big
one, and it would all be down to Eric and whoever he wanted
to row in. Naturally Eric thought it was sussy. Thought it was
all a fit-up. He tells Trench this, and Trench says what can he
do to show good faith. More for a giggle than anything else,
Eric tells him there is a snouting bastard named Billy Appleby
who is a menace to society and should be cut off at the throat.
You see, Eric had the notion that the filth had propped
Appleby to fit Eric up, and Appleby was putting this Trench
geezer in to front the frame. He thought he was being clever,
working one right back, letting Appleby know he knew sort of
thing.'

Absently, Maisie's hand strayed into the box of tissues.
Dragging out a thick bundle, she chewed at the edges. Smith
waited patiently.

'Next thing that Eric hears is that Appleby has met with an
accident. Same day Mr Trench fronts him in his local betting
shop. They take a walk over to the park at Crystal Palace
where he fills Eric in on the caper.'

They could hear the old woman singing in the kitchen. A
dirge about Red Sails in the Sunset. She knew little of the lyrics
making *la la* noises in time to the melody. It was as if she
wanted it known she was not listening at the door. Ignoring
the row, Maisie went on with her story.

'All the time Eric is aware of the minder sort of hovering in
the distance. Well afterwards, Eric steams over here and props
the scheme to Terry. Terry gets a strong suss as well, but Eric
is convinced the geezer is a hundred per cent. He says nothing
about Billy Appleby though, at least not then. Personally, I
think he was scared to, or maybe he was sorry for the poor sod.
I mean he only meant it as a giggle.' Maisie spat a ball of wet
tissue into the ashtray and spent some time removing the
residue from her lips and teeth.

'But he soon got over that. Started boasting about it. He
liked to think himself a right hard nut, did that Eric. Not so

bleedin' hard now, is he? Nor my Terry either.' Tears began to stream down her face. 'It wouldn't be so bad,' she sobbed, 'if it hadn't all began as a bit of a giggle.' As if on cue, the old woman brought in the tea.

'How much of this did you tell the police?' Smith asked when the desiccative effect of the tea leaves had dried Maisie's tears.

'What d'you take me for?' Maisie howled indignantly. 'A bleedin' idiot! They'd do me for conspiracy, wouldn't they? Why do you think me and my friend always go for a holiday when Eric and Terry have a bit of business to do? So's the filth can't roll us in for conspiracy or receiving. So's they can't use us to pressure them.'

'A wise investment,' Smith said. 'And good for the health as well.'

'Not this time, it wasn't. Was it?' She came close to a scream.

'I'm sorry. I meant it as a compliment to Terry and Eric. To their far-sighted desire for your welfare.'

Puzzled but mollified, Maisie regained some composure. Smith thought of taking advantage of it by asking after her friend, but quickly realized that area would also be excluded by the fine print. Better stay within the terms of the deal, he concluded. He went back to the beginning. What he had got so far had been bunce. A nice piece of bunce; above and beyond the terms of the contract, but the time had come to extract the juice.

'So you and Terry took sights on the meet,' he squeezed gently. 'Where was that?'

The old woman slurped her tea noisily as if in warning. 'Got another cigarette?' Maisie sought a delay to interpret the meaning of the sound. Silently, Smith passed her the packet. She lit one hesitantly, still in a quandary.

'You straight up?' she asked. 'You definitely ain't the law?' She tried to remove the cigarette from her lips but it clung to a morsel of flesh like a white leech. She eased it away with her tongue, cursing inaudibly.

'If I was the law, Maisie,' Smith said, in a voice that was not quite a threat, 'you'd be on your way to the nick right now, just on what you mentioned earlier. Now don't try and stiff me, Maisie. That which is given can be taken away.'

'Go on, gel,' the old woman said encouragingly. 'It don't make no difference. I'm your witness. You never said a bleedin' word. Even if he is the law, he can't do much. An' if he is, we might want a bit of help ourselves sometime. I mean we might 'ave to get back at the hoist, now Terry's gorn.' She uttered a brief, shrill cackle into her tea cup. A deal was a deal.

Reassured, Maisie pulled the top of her dressing-gown apart and displayed a generous expanse of breast, as if offering Smith recognition of her mistake.

'It was up West,' she said wetting her lips with a provocative tongue. 'Corner of Albemarle Street and Piccadilly. Me and Terry were doing a slow plod past the Ritz on the opposite side. We see Eric arrive, and he's no sooner on the corner when this car swings round out of St James's Street and stops. Well, we see the back door open and Eric gets in, then this other geezer appears out of nowhere and climbs in behind Eric. Then a bus comes along on the off-side and blocks the view. By the time it clears, the motor has gone. Must have moved on with the bus. Probably turned up Sackville Street; Tony went over the other side of the street but he said there was no sign of it further down the 'dilly.'

'The one who followed Eric into the motor, that would be the one he and Terry put down as a minder?' It was a question Smith put to himself rather than Maisie. But she obliged with an answer.

'Prob'ly,' she said.

'Did you get a look at him?'

'He came out of the blue. Above average height, but not really tall, bit like yourself. There was a face, a flash of a face, handsome, but not soppy. Strong. That's what I said to myself at the time, that's a strong 'un, I said to myself. A strong mover.' Memory of it made her pull the top of the dressing-gown wider. She placed a hand inside and fondled her breast.

'And the driver?' Smith pursued her, undistracted.

'Nuffink. I was too busy watchin' Eric.'

'And the strong mover?'

'Him as well.'

'What about the motor?'

'A Merc. A dark blue Merc. I kept saying to Terry, we ought to get a Merc. Touch of class is a Merc.' The reminiscence brought more tears. Smith turned to the old woman.

'That time, Ma, when you came in and found Terry. You didn't accidentally put a bit of gear out of the way? A tin box, a bundle of papers, anything like that?'

'You rotten bastard,' Maisie was on her feet, holding the top of her dressing gown tightly clutched together. All promises as to the future cancelled. 'That's just like you lot,' she choked out the words. 'Think the likes of us got no finer feelings. She walks in, a poor old woman, and finds her son lying dead on the floor. And you imagine all she thinks about is nicking some of the gear?'

'What do you say, Ma?' said Smith, calmly riding out the storm. There was malice in the old woman's face that was not directed at him.

'Wish I 'ad done,' the old woman screeched spitefully. 'Cor, stone the bleedin' crows, wish I 'ad done.' She looked up at Smith, her eyes sparkling. 'Trouble was, it was gettin' dark when I come in. No sign of Terry, so I goes upstairs, thinkin' he might be havin' a kip. I open the bedroom door, and in the light from the landing, there he is stretched out on the floor. I knew he was dead all right. I've buried two in me time. 'Usbands, I mean.' She paused to allow the significance of her marital misfortunes to sink in. Smith allowed his head to drop in condolence.

'I didn't go inside the room, silly old cow that I was. Went back downstairs and phoned the law, silly old cow that I was. Then when they comes along, I go up wiv them and they puts on the lights, an' there is poor Terry an' all that gear. Cor, I'd never seen the likes. The coppers neither. One of them, 'e says to me later on – know what 'e says?' Smith professed his ignorance.

'"Ma,"'e says to me, "I don't know what my face was like at the sight of all that gear, but by Christ you should have seen yours." "I know exactly what yours was like," I says to 'im, "a picture of bleedin' greed an' avarice," I says to 'im. "That wasn't me, Ma," he says, all hoity toity. "You was lookin' in a mirror at the time."'

'And what about the copper?' Smith intervened, coldly impartial. 'Could he have nicked anything?'

'Never give 'im the chance,' the old woman cackled merrily. 'Watched 'im like an 'awk, I did. "Why don't you wait downstairs, Ma," 'e says. "Can't be very pleasant for you in 'ere, wiv your poor son lying dead in front of you." "I'm keepin' an eye on Terry," I says. "An' I'm keepin' an eye on Terry's gear. Don't you worry your 'ead about me," I says. "I've laid out two 'usbands in me time an' I can lay out me own son."' Her hard, wizened face attempted to depict remorse, and failed.

Course, I never got the chance,' she wailed in simulated grief. 'In no time the 'ouse was swarming wiv coppers. All shapes an' sizes. Poor Terry is whipped orf inside a plastic sheet. I still ain't got 'im back. They've cut 'im into pieces and put 'im in a freezer. What's left of 'im. Coroner won't release 'im yet, they keep tellin' me.' She pinched the side of her cheek to adjust the set of her porcelain teeth and regained her malice. 'Bleedin' sods,' she snapped crisply. 'Wished I 'ad got the chance to put a bit of that gear out of the way. I wouldn't 'arf 'ave 'ad a fair codgel of that lot.' She questioned Smith indignantly. 'I mean I owed it to Terry, didden I?'

'It would have been a fine tribute to his memory,' Smith replied, not hiding the irony in his voice.

'I got the number of that Merc!' Maisie glared defiantly at Terry's mother. 'Never knew that, did you?' she sneered. 'All your bleedin' talk about layin' out poor Terry and the gear you didn't manage to nick. That's all I've had night and bleedin' day. Nothing about layin' out them that did Terry. You left that down to me. You wasn't even interested in doing them that did for Terry. All you've ever done is mump about what you could have done with the gear Terry nicked.' She turned aggressively on Smith.

'How much is that worth?' she demanded. 'The number of that Merc? And I can save you the trouble of tracing it. Unlike some,' she shot a withering look at the old woman, who retreated into the fragility of her years. 'Unlike some, I've been trying to sort out them that did Terry. I've got six good lads waiting to go.'

Smith emptied his wallet. 'Twenty-four quid is the best I can do, Maisie,' he said simply. 'Take it or leave it.'

'Hand it over,' she said, and taking the money, gave him the number. The notes disappeared inside the neck of her dressing-gown. 'Won't do you much good,' her words were carelessly triumphant. 'The Merc is down to a car hire firm, Emperor Motors in South Kensington. They don't know from nothin'. The boys have tried. A load of snot-nosed gits, they are. They got straight on to the law, before my friends could ask them the time of day.'

The sign above the plateglass windows of the showroom read Emperor Motors Ltd, Suppliers and Hirers of Superior Vehicles since 1806 (Incorporating Emperor Hackney Carriages Ltd). That was good, Smith thought. Carriages were carriages, it was the horses that pulled them that were called hackneys. A long time ago, when young and keen and still in uniform, he had worked a beat in the North London borough of Hackney. Being curious about its origins, he had assumed the place got its name from the making of hackney carriages. But when he looked it up, he could find no reference to that trade. Hackney the borough, was simply Hackney. Hackneyed. Like this enquiry he had taken on. Find the Papers! The Plans? Hackneyed. Like the plot, Fairchild's plot. Hackneyed. And he was the hack. A hired horse. What was that cockney song they used to sing? How did it go? 'Wiv a ladder and some glarsses – you could see to 'Ackney Marshes, If it wasn't for the 'ouses in between.'

That was the trouble with most plots, the bleedin' 'ouses in between. A snot-nosed git strolled over to him and enquired archly: 'May I be of assistance?' He turned on him with the eye of an eagle. 'I am Detective Inspector Strang from Scotland Yard,' he snapped, quelling any incipient impudence over identification. 'I phoned earlier about a Mercedes that was hired from you and used to commit a particularly serious crime. Have you found the relevant documents for me?'

# Nine

**◆◆◆◆◆**

'They say you ducked out of serious bothers yourself?' Frank Worple was defensively aggressive.

'I never ducked them, Frank, they just didn't come in my direction. So there was no need.'

'Lucky you,' Worple sneered.

'That's the way it goes in the job, Frank. You know that. Sometimes it doesn't even come close, sometimes it bounces off, sometimes it hits you right between the eyes.'

'They planted it on me, Owen. Twoomey's mob. The South London villains have been trying to fit me up for years. They knew I was right on top of the bastards.'

'It lacks originality, Frank, but good luck with it at your trial. That said, don't try it on me, old son. We've both heard the same fairy story too often.'

Worple surrendered to a pale, sweaty grin.

'Yeah. I don't know whether it's the prospect of running that line, or the sheer stupidity of weeding out the gear in the first place that makes me so miserable. Don't be surprised if you hear I've topped myself.'

His words drew a long hard look from Smith. Behind his back the barman was shouting for whoever had ordered the ploughman's lunch. Smith raised his hand and went over to collect the bread, cheese and pickles.

'You're sure you won't have something to eat?' he asked Worple before sitting down.

'It would stick in my throat. You can get me another large G and T, if you like.' Smith returned to the bar. When he got back, Worple had eaten the half tomato from his plate.

'You shouldn't talk such bollocks about doing yourself in,' he admonished.

'Ways and means, that's the only problem,' Worple raised his glass in a mock toast, searching the bubbles for a solution. 'Throat-cutting is messy. Hanging is undignified, in any case I'm already suspended. And that means I can't lay my hands on a shooter. You can't slip me about ten grains of heroin can you, Owen? Twice the fatal dose!'

Smith shook his head.

'It's ironic really,' Worple replaced his glass and twisted his lips to demonstrate the fact. 'A couple of months ago, I went in on eight kilos of smack, Moby Dix's stash; uncut. The biggest trafficker in the country. He should go down for ten. Now he'll walk out of it because I'm a tainted witness. So they'll put me away in his place. Funny how powerless and naked you feel when you're in schtuk. You noticed that?'

'There were times when I felt it even when I was still in the job.'

'Yeah. But you've come out clean, haven't you? At least on the surface. You didn't get caught nicking anything. The word is you snuffed out some people over in the States. These days snuffing out people is respectable. Not like nicking. Nicking is shameful. I feel shameful, Owen. It is a bloody awful feeling, I've thrown shit all over my wife and kids. How do you feel, Owen? Killing those people? Respectable?'

'Where I've been it was considered impolite to discuss the past.'

'But I'll bet you all did. That's something I've learned. Once you are inside – even if like me, you are only inside yourself – you can't help talking about it. Trying to justify it. Everything, anything, can be justified.'

The cheese felt dry and rancid inside his mouth. Smith gulped at his beer. It tasted sour.

'Look, Frank,' he said. 'I know you've got severe aggravations. Nothing I can say or do will help you. It'll not make the slightest difference to your troubles if I slaughtered half the world's population. I'm trying to do a job, trying to get back on my feet. It's selfish of me, I know, coming to you when you're in bother. But you're the only one who can help me. I need to know if you weeded anything from Popkiss's room besides the cash they found in your motor.'

'Who said I weeded anything? I told you, it was a fit-up. The big villains have been out to get me for years.'

'Then why all the bullshit about topping yourself?'

'For anyone else there is a presumption of innocence. For coppers nowadays you're guilty even if you are acquitted. It sticks like shit to a blanket. In and out of the Job.'

'Listen, Frank,' Smith held out a persuasive, pleading hand. 'I'm not wired for sound. I'm strictly on my own. I swear to God this won't go any further.'

Worple finished his gin, gazing speculatively at Smith over the rim of his glass. Smith saw something approaching pity in his eyes, detesting him – and himself – for its presence.

'You sound desperate, Owen. Not like you to be desperate. Almost makes *me* feel better. Maybe it's the gin. I'll have another. Put it down to incidentals: Purchased Refreshment for Informant. Bump it up. I should be good for fifteen quid.'

Smith bought him another, glad to know it was not pity. Worple was enjoying himself; enjoying having an ex-Detective Chief Superintendent running around buying drinks for a crooked DI on suspension. That did not matter. Worple was entitled to have his fun.

'Ice and lemon this time, Owen,' Worple called loudly, rubbing it in.

Carefully, deliberately, Smith set the glass down in front of Worple. 'So how about it, Frank?' he asked softly.

There would be long moments of sullen silence, Smith knew that. That was the way it always went. There would either be a crack or the silence would become heavier, deeper. It all depended on the strength of the maker of the silence. The silence belonged to him and Smith knew that to intrude upon it with persuasive cajolery or threats would only increase its strength. He had taken it as far as he could go – at least, in the saloon bar of a crowded pub. He saw Worple making indecisive circles with the base of his glass on the table-top, staring at them intently as though trying to give them form and substance ... and failing. Smith knew he had won. He waited patiently for the trickle that would grow into a flood.

Eventually Worple raised his head, his face set, a picture of honest candour. Authentic? Smith wondered.

'At the front of the Popkiss house,' Worple began in a whisper, the sibilants hissing like a suppressed scream. 'There's a low wall, right behind it a privet hedge. In the space between the wall and the hedge, about five feet from the front gate, you should find a charm bracelet.'

Smith failed to conceal his chagrin and Worple saw the tightening lips. 'A real good 'un,' he reassured him. 'You know the sort of thing, a linked chain hung with gold miniatures. Twenty-two carats.' Smith now presented an impassive mask.

'It was something special, that *fucking* bracelet.' Worple made the point with deliberate coarseness, and it seemed to Smith, he did so in order to conceal a trace of apprehension ... Of fear?

'I was alone in the room, just me and Popkiss – him stinking to high heaven. I had sent the uniform out to radio for the Divisional Surgeon. There was just me and Popkiss – and all that tomfoolery and bundles of readies. Honestly, Owen, no thought of doing a weeding job entered my mind. Not then,' he paused to lament the passing of his honour.

'I remember looking down at Popkiss, I could see the watch-strap on the inside of his wrist, white platinum, expensive. It stood out against the post-mortem lividity like a – a tombstone! Thinking it might be an old-fashioned wind-up job, I thought I ought to note the time it had stopped. Routine stuff. I didn't want to hold his bare wrist so I grabbed his sleeve halfway down the forearm to turn the wrist over. I felt something concealed underneath. I rolled the sleeve back and there was this *fucking* charm bracelet dangling there. Not round his arm you understand, he had a rubber band holding it in position. Dangling there, between his shirt and the sleeve of his jacket.'

Worple reached into his thick black hair and dragged his head forward into the depths of his breast, then quickly, seeming to realize the weakness of the gesture, released his grip and made a puzzled parody of scratching his scalp.

'I don't know what the hell made me do it,' he continued. 'There was something about that *fucking* bracelet. Somehow I had to possess it.'

Smith had noted the emphatic oath which accompanied every mention of the bracelet but otherwise, his interest was merely academic. Charm bracelets! What the hell did a man want with a charm bracelet?

Flat and toneless now, Worple went on, reminding Smith of Kendigg. 'Anyway, I pulled it clear, the *fucking* bracelet, leaving the rubber band. That would be put down to Popkiss using it to conceal a set of twirls, a blade, anything small but dodgy, to beat the chance spin he might get from some DC trying to make a name for himself. So there I was with this *fucking* bracelet in my hand. The odd thing was, I was thinking clear as a bell, but like in a nightmare, one of those nightmares where everything is so real you wake up sweating. You know what I mean?'

'I know exactly what you mean,' Smith said.

Gratified by the answer, Worple made an appreciative grimace. 'I thought you would, Owen, I mean you and I ...' He left the conclusion undrawn, perhaps aware of the smouldering coals in Smith's eyes. 'Well, I knew what I was doing, I can't deny that,' he muttered nervously. 'But at the same time I was under some irresistible compulsion. I slipped the *Thing* ...' It was as if Worple realized the barren monotony of his adjectives and sought more respectable speech. Why not the *frigging Thing?* Smith wondered. Years ago when he worked with him, Worple had been a 'frigger'. A user of what he thought to be the acceptable euphemism; somehow always making it sound more obscene than the full-blooded oath. Worple had continued, 'I slipped the *Thing* in my pocket and as I stepped back from the bed – Popkiss was lying half across the bed – did I mention that?'

'No.'

'Well, he was, like that was the way he finished up when he got it.'

'So what happened when you stepped back from the bed?'

'I brushed off a bundle of readies. Twenties, not that many.

Again, like in a dream, I am slipping them inside my pocket. Nice. No bulge. You know how much I weeded out, Owen? One and a half thou. Know how much I could have weeded? Three hundred grand. If I was going to weed, why didn't I weed the entire bundle?'

'Too rich for your blood, Frank. For anyone's blood.'

'No way. I know some big punters. I've seen fifty grand go over on a bet at Epsom on Derby day,' Worple boasted.

'Not on outsiders, Frank. Like you and me. Suppose you get back on the rails.'

'Yeah. You're right. Both of us, we're not even in with a chance.'

Worple returned to the fence where he had fallen. 'I went downstairs and posted the uniform inside while I waited for Stanstead. I needed the fresh air.'

Of its own volition, this time, Worple's head slumped down on his chest; Smith could see in the thick curly hair of which Worple was so proud, a rich seed-bed of dandruff. Worry. A sure sign of worry. The head raised slowly and frightened eyes sought refuge in his stern face.

'This is strictly between us, isn't it, Owen? You promise?' Worple pleaded, anxiety making him piteous.

For a time Smith gave no answer. The moist eyes collapsed into fawning submission. Then he said with angry impatience, 'That goes without saying, Frank.' He knew he was dealing with a conscience ulcerated by discovery, not by guilt; with a confession induced by professional respect. Worple could not sustain the lie; not in front of a hard case like himself. Worple was not only bent, he was broken. Needing to embroider the sackcloth of his repentance with a thin thread of mitigation.

*A hard case?*

Me? he thought. That was yesterday, before he went down the strange street and got lost. But he had found a way out, the landmarks were familiar once more. Maybe tomorrow he would be a hard case once again.

'How did it come a tumble, Frank?' his tongue processed a syrup of synthetic sympathy. Worple pondered the question, puzzled by it, as though it had never previously entered his mind. Then he arrived at a conclusion, inspired; seemingly invigorated by the discovery.

'Because I wasn't a good enough villain,' he announced boldly. 'I bottled out completely when Stanstead fronted me.' He said it, managing to make his lack of criminal resolution sound praiseworthy.

'Brian Stanstead fronted you with it? Right out of the blue? No cause?'

Worple had to give the matter further thought.

'Funny,' he said at last. 'He didn't actually front me. Not directly. We were up in the bedroom, him and I – and Popkiss – and all that gear. Stanstead is giving the scene the preliminary scrutiny. All of a sudden he looks at me and says: "Have you taken possession of any exhibits yet, Mr Worple?" Thinking back on it, it was quite a casual question, almost to be expected, and all I could do was stand and gape at him. There was I, with that *fucking* bracelet burning a hole in my pocket, and all I could do was stand and gape at him.'

Smith noted the return of the adjective.

'I had bunged the readies down the back seat of my motor while I was waiting for him outside. Somehow, I forgot that . . . that *Thing*.'

Would Worple ever be able to mention the bracelet at his trial without cursing it, Smith wondered. Or would it eventually and finally be reduced to that *Thing*?

'I stood there dumbfounded,' Worple was saying. 'I kept asking myself, does he really know something? Is he offering me an outer? Or is he sussing me on spec? I try to say: "Look, Guv, I'm an experienced DI. I wouldn't interfere with a crime scene, not one like this, not until you got here." I can hear the words hammering inside my head, loud and indignant. But nothing is coming out of my mouth. I keep thinking; is he giving me an outer? Maybe if I show out and say, "Yeah, I put this and that aside, because it was lying loose on the landing . . ." Some bollocks like that . . . He wouldn't believe it, of course, but he might just swallow it to avoid the aggravation.

'All this is going through my mind, but I couldn't get the words out. I see Stanstead's face stiffen and harden, like the crust on cowshit. He comes right in on me. "You idiot," he says, giving it to me from between his teeth. "You stupid big idiot," he spits it right in my face.

'I'm ordered downstairs and right in front of all the uniforms he spins my motor. Even when he finds the thin codgel of readies he doesn't stop. He goes crazy. Seats thrown out, leather slashed open, the fascia, radio, everything. He's in a muck sweat by the time he's finished. Does it all on his own, orders a uniform Inspector out of it who wants to get into the act. Everybody is watching him, fascinated like... Well, at least it gives me the chance to ditch ... the *Thing* ... behind the wall. When it's all over, and my car, inside and out, is strewn all over the pavement, Stanstead comes over to me, blue in the face, his eyes popping out of his head, breathing like a busted boiler. Know what he does then, Owen? Know what he does?'

Smith shook a disinterested head.

'He smacks me across the chops with the bundle of readies. "How dare you pollute my Department," he says. *My* Department, if you please. From him, too old to make Commander, let alone Assistant Commissioner Crime." Worple begged Smith to share his incomprehension. Rebuffed, he gave him another sight of his dandruff.

'I was degraded, Owen,' the brief euphoric interlude had vanished. His shoulders heaved beneath his soiled curls. 'I was humiliated, Owen,' a sob choked into noisy silence. 'I had to endure all that humiliation.'

'There's been a lot of it about lately,' Smith replied, not without real sympathy.

Worple made another brave attempt to regain his composure. Surfacing, shiny-eyed and smiling with pathetic levity, he held his glass aloft. 'Gin,' he said. 'Gin for melancholy, scotch for merriment. I got on the wrong tipple,' he drained the glass.

'Another?' Smith enquired.

'No, sod it. I'm not going to hide in a bottle. You can't find your bottle in a bottle,' he gave a brave, but jangled laugh. 'Good that,' he said, repeating it like a prayer.

Smith steered him back to reality.

'Did you notice any documents amongst the gear?' he

enquired bluntly. 'Any official papers?' Then he cursed himself for an impulsive fool.

'What the hell . . . Why should there be official papers in the drum?' Worple queried, suddenly the alert, suspicious detective once again.

'A stupid question.' It was Smith's turn to cavil.

'What kind of official papers?' Worple persisted.

'Insurance policies, title deeds, Popkiss's will, stuff like that,' Smith said, inspired.

'So you are working for the wife then, Mrs Popkiss?' Pleased with his acumen, disappointed with the meagreness of its findings, Worple made his conclusions known in a sneering laugh.

'I am not supposed to divulge that, Frank,' said Smith, almost humbly.

'Norah Thornton is the one I feel sorry for,' Worple spread his concern generously. 'She sticks by Eric for five years, then when he gets it, back comes his legal wife and takes possession of the house. Poor old Norah gets sod-all.'

'Is she still about, Norah Thornton?' Smith asked offhandedly, trying to disguise his interest.

'Got a room over Blackheath way, near the railway station,' Worple confided with the air of one prepared to give advice based on secret knowledge. 'Don't waste your time trying to get anything out of Norah. It's been tried by experts.'

'Like you?' said Smith with a smile.

Worple shrugged an awkward disclaimer. 'Don't waste your time,' he repeated sourly.

Smith went elsewhere. 'The Aldwych job, the keyman. I'd put it down to Lomax. Bernie Lomax, the keymaker. What do you reckon?'

'Him by a mile,' Worple agreed. 'He did work for Terry Scanlon before. Terry would go to him. He's expensive, but the best.'

'Have they had him in?'

'I doubt it. Another waste of time.'

'Not even for appearances sake? To show it'd been done?'

'Why bother? You know Lomax. He has lawyers hanging on hooks inside his front door. They're on the step before you can hit the knocker. It would be another complaint. Harassment. Who wants the aggravation.'

'We are letting them win all round, the villains,' Smith said sadly.

'Not you and me, Owen. Not any more. You and me – we've been middled. The squeeze is on from both sides.'

Smith rose from the table. 'Got things to do, Frank. Good luck with the gardening. I hope your plant turns out to be a prize orchid.'

Worple laid a restraining hand on his wrist. 'Before you go, Owen,' he said beseechingly. 'As a favour – one for one. Tell me how you managed it? The funny farm caper? If I could get myself lodged in the funny farm they might decide to stick on that, not go for the full house. No trial, no bad things in the papers. It's for my wife and kids. I'm only thinking of my wife and kids. How can I work it, Owen? What sort of act do I have to put on?'

Smith shook himself free. 'Just act like your normal self, Frank,' he cried hoarsely, fury burning in his voice. 'Exactly the way you did when you cut yourself a corner of the Aldwych gear. Only a nutter would do it that way.'

Three days later, a skin-diver searching for antique wine bottles in the Thames mud beneath Putney Bridge found Frank Worple lying on the bottom of the river. The River Police had difficulty hauling him into their launch, for he had a fifty-six-pound weight tied to his ankles and his hands were bound together at the front of his body. Smith was not surprised, knowing that people who talk of suicide quite frequently act it out. Neither was he particularly sorry for Frank Worple. His feelings, if any, were of admiration. Shrewdly done, he thought, when he read the press report. "Detective found Drowned" ran the headline. "Gangland Revenge Motive?"

Well done, Frank, he acknowledged. Even if they do say at the inquest you could have tied yourself together like that, it won't be easy to prove. Should get you an open verdict at least. Removes the shame from the wife and kids. And old Brian Stanstead will be happy; rubs out the stain on *his* Department.

They'll pay out on your life insurance, your wife might even get a police widow's pension. 'Shrewdly done, Frank,' saying it aloud this time, by way of a requiem.

Unlocking the drawer in his desk, he brought out the bracelet and for the first time had a close look at the dangling trinkets. A little gold trumpet and a little gold drum, a heart-shaped padlock with a tiny key, a cross bearing a homuncular Saviour crucified by microscopic nails. The puny baubles slid through his fingers in ostentatious motley: a pistol, a pair of scissors, a psalter, a sword, all were superior to their common kind; the workmanship exquisite, the detail meticulous. Most striking of all was a gold skull, slightly larger than the rest, about the size of a cob nut. Small rubies lurked redly in the eye sockets, diamonds glinted in place of bared teeth. Almost instinctively, he stroked the crown of the skull with his thumb; it responded, warm and comforting to his touch. Sensual. Reluctantly, he held the bracelet out at arm's length. It was an eyecatcher all right. It had tempted Frank Worple beyond the theft of easily disposable cash, into the dangers of nicking something traceable and identifiable. Why? Again his thumb stole across the gold skull. Maybe Worple had sensed its virgin purity; been seduced by it – had sat fondling it? As Smith himself was doing now! He tried to crush the bracelet inside his fist but the point of the tiny sword pierced the puffy flesh of his palm. With a curse he hurled it into a corner of the room, angered by his own maudlin imaginings.

He had only recovered the bracelet in the first place because it gave him an objective to strive for. He had not run since leaving Wyldwood and besides the *Thing* had now been mentally inserted into his personal remnant of the System, the Scotland Yard Indexing and Cross Reference System for Major Investigations that rigidly demanded every item entered must be checked; and either eliminated or resolved. He was not sure which imperative drove him to run through the early-morning streets of South London and on out to Sydenham. The distance was right, about fifteen miles there and back. But the streets were harder than the soft fields of Wyldwood, where the occasional hills he faced did not exist. There was some consolation in the fact that even though he knew the streets well, they were not so monotonous as the endless confines of the Wire. And when he raised his leg onto the low wall outside the Popkiss house to retie a loosened shoe-lace, his fingers made almost immediate contact with the bracelet as he discreetly slipped a hand down between wall and hedge. I'll give you this, Frank, he had thought to himself as he trotted away, you didn't lose your sense of judgement altogether.

He returned to his flat disappointed. His time, nearly two hours, was well outside his best. He should have gone to Hyde Park where there were grass and trees, the Serpentine at dawn. Yes, he could even have rendered Kendigg's fond remembrances to Nurse Edith Cavell en route. Now he was stuck with this *fucking* bracelet, the bauble of some rich overdressed bitch, a flashy accessory to set off expensive rings on fat fingers. He had thrown it into the drawer without a second glance, thinking only of the trouble it would take to work it back to the Aldwych Safety Deposit. Through Fairchild! He would have to do it through Fairchild. *But discreetly, Owen. Everything you do must be discreet. Promise me you will try and be discreet.*

It had taken the report of Worple's death to bring the bracelet back into his memory. Slowly he went over and retrieved the *Thing*. A single red eye winked accusingly at him from the skull. He laughed at it – and himself.

'There's a little one-eyed idol, or is it a one-eyed little idol? Whatever it is, mate, Mad Carew has got you in his clutches once again.'

On hands and knees he scoured the floor for the missing ruby. It took an irritatingly long time but at last he found it embedded in the pile of the carpet. Fitting it back in the socket was difficult, for he was not naturally nimble-fingered. He fiddled about with it, becoming more and more annoyed as several times it rolled to the floor and on each occasion proved elusive and hard to recover. Only when an idea came to him and, struck him by its cleverness and originality of thought, did he recover his good humour. Retracting his ball point, he found the housing fitted almost completely over the small gem. By this means he could lift it securely and work it back into the socket. As he forced the ruby home, the top of the skull flew open.

For long moments he stared into the open skull, then he began to laugh – softly at first. 'Oh, my Christ, Smith,' he chuckled. 'They really do it. They actually do things like this!' Unable to restrain himself further, he threw back his head and roared.

He was still chuckling to himself a few minutes later when Marion Elstow returned home. She looked at the silent radio, the blank TV screen, and barely concealing her anxiety, asked, 'Was that you hee-hawing like a drunken donkey? I could hear you out in the street. What's got into you?'

'I suddenly remembered an old joke, my darling,' he said, rising to greet her. Now tightly in control, he showed nothing more than a welcoming smile. 'I was giving it a new twist,' he added.

'At least let me in on it. Lord knows I could do with a laugh myself,' she replied with a derisive snort.

'Not one for your tender ears, my darling,' he said soothingly, giving her a light kiss.

'One of those, was it? I've been told dirty jokes before, you know.'

'Not by me. And this must be the dirtiest of them all. Besides I don't know what the punchline is yet.'

'The lead-in must be terrific.'

'Forget it. I'll take you out to dinner.'

She had brought in lamb chops and all the other ingredients for a home-cooked meal, but he insisted they go out. It had been a long lonely afternoon, he explained. Claustrophobic. The walls were closing in. He had to get out.

'So you pass the time inventing new versions of dirty stories,' she said without sympathy. 'And what is worse, laughing at them.' The benevolence of her intentions spurned, the warmth of her desires stifled; she complained bitterly. 'It's bad enough having you creep out of my bed at five in the morning to run through the town! Who do you think you are – Wee Willie Winkie? Much more of it and they'll revoke your licence.'

'My bed in fact. Our bed in truth. Further, I wore a tracksuit, not a nightgown. Revoke my licence! My God, what a case-hardened little bitch you have become since you served with me at Cobb Common.'

'Since I served under you at Cobb Common, you mean. And you know what I *mean*,' she lashed out wickedly.

In pain, he struck back. 'So, now we have role-reversal. Is that it? Promoted, therefore I dominate this rankless ex-copper. The feminist rampant rides tonight. Copulation followed by capitulation. Is that what you're after?' He bit his lip until he tasted blood. No more, he thought, anguish and fear merging in his breast; expanding under the pressure of panic. He fought against his pride. I mustn't lose her, not now. Not ever. His broad shoulders slumped helplessly.

'I am very sorry, Elstow,' he muttered sullenly, not looking at her. The chilly silence that followed washed over him and was somehow refreshing. He raised his eyes and faced her squarely. 'I suppose I do resent the fact you are still in the Job. And I resent the fact that I'm out of it. But I don't resent you. I'll never resent you.'

He went over to her and took her in his arms. Her rigidity was unyielding. He thrust her away, holding her at arms' length. 'You must make allowances,' he pleaded. Her gaze was unflinching. 'Can't you see,' he explained, 'I've still got withdrawal sickness. From the Job, I mean. Twenty-four years is a long time.'

'Becoming a cheap tout for the funny people is no cure,' she replied scathingly. 'You are only changing your habit from cocaine to acid. What you need is cold turkey. Get thee to a monastery, Owen. Or at least find an honest job. You may be running well, but you are running in the wrong direction.'

'I tried to tell you the first day I came home. It is the only way out I've got.'

He felt the stiffness in her relax a little, but still she stood apart, contemplating him, seeming to examine him for signs of sincerity or – he wondered gloomily – madness? He summoned up a solemn little smile.

'The running proves one thing,' he said. 'The *corpore sano* is there. The *mens sana* part might need a bit more exercise. I'll keep working on it.'

She pondered his convoluted construction for a time, and as the meaning dawned, gave way to a reluctant sigh. Slowly she slid into his arms and he buried his face in her rich brown hair, relishing its sweet perfume.

Forcibly, but without malice, she thumped his chest with a small hard fist. 'You have more than the running to prove your *corpore* is perfectly *sano*,' she murmured. 'So take me out and feed me sensual and voluptuous dishes. Intoxicate me with wanton wines. Then bring me home and show me what a mad, bad bastard you are.'

Reaching for his jacket, he swung her into his arms and carried her to the door. 'Two hamburgers, french fries and a strawberry milk shake coming up,' he called out merrily. They exited laughing. Both of them.

They were still laughing when they returned nearly four hours later. Both were a little drunk and in them was a relaxed contentment, made more pleasurable by avid anticipation. It was perhaps fortunate Marion decided to make Irish coffee before they settled down on the sheepskin rug in front of the fire, for, as she was thus engaged, the phone rang.

Smith took the call, and even though only a mechanical voice spoke to him, it sounded vaguely petulant, as if it had been trying to reach him for some time. The tinny voice said: 'Mr Barker has a message for you. Please repeat his name clearly – Barker!'

Involuntarily, Smith obeyed. A subdued hiss followed until the voice spoke again. 'Mr Barker requires you to meet him tomorrow morning at ten. If fine, by the north terrace in Victoria Embankment Gardens. If raining, in the upper reading room, Westminster Reference Library. Please acknowledge receipt of this message by clearly enunciating the name Barker once more – otherwise the call will be repeated in fifteen minutes.'

'BARKER.' He raged against the inhuman voice. 'BARKER! BARKER!' he roared again before he could place a clamp on his anger.

'What was that all about?' Marion Elstow stood by the kitchen door making no secret of her amazement and concern.

Breathing deeply, Smith replaced the phone, watching it settle in its cradle through narrowed eyelids. 'A weather forecast,' he replied shortly.

She placed the glasses carefully on the coffee table. 'You reacted to it like a Pavlovian dog,' she said, her voice trembling slightly.

He nodded dully. 'Better be careful what you say on this phone in future.'

She stared at him in awe. 'My God, has it gone that far? Are you in *that* deep?' She sank down slowly on the rug.

'No. It's nothing like that. I think they are just being cautious. They can't afford to trust me.'

'Can I?' she asked helplessly.

'You can, Elstow. My darling Elstow, you can with your life.' He turned bitterly to the telephone, a pointed finger giving it sinister credence. 'But not *them*,' he spat at the instrument. 'Not now. Not any more.' He knelt beside her, still watching the phone, feeling for her hand, only to meet a shudder at his touch. 'It could still be monitoring us,' she whispered in his ear. 'Voice-activated, on or off the line.'

'I'll rip the damned thing out!' He had half risen before she pulled him back. 'No, you mustn't,' she spoke strongly, outraged professionalism dominating her fears. 'I get called out too, you know. I'm still in the Job. Besides you are only playing a hunch, aren't you? Despite her bravado, she sought comfort and he sacrificed himself unstintingly. 'I guess I am still a little paranoid,' he admitted. 'They told me I must be constantly on the alert for regressive symptoms, now I'm no longer on drugs. Not to draw irrational conclusions from natural or even unnatural occurrences. After all, when you weigh it up, it's perfectly natural, in this day and age, for some unnatural bastard to invent a machine that will ring your phone every fifteen minutes until you answer. But it is a complete lunacy to expect the recipient to stand like a prize prick, shouting a meaningless codeword to shut the thing off... Without doing his nut as a result.'

'That is rational and logical,' she agreed, now quite cool and calm. 'But it rather puts the mockers on things, doesn't it? I mean even the possibility that they *might* be listening, puts the mockers on things.'

'*Denn alle Schuld rächt sich auf Erden –* ' Smith muttered savagely into the perpetual flame of the gas-fired logs.

'It sounds as though you are trying to convey some great and portentous thought,' Elstow said, her sarcasm leavened by a smile.

'It's only a smattering,' Smith replied. 'I picked up a lot of smatterings in Wyldwood. A smattering of Goethe, for instance. It means "For all guilt is punished on earth."'

# Ten

Next morning low cloud and a desultory wind promised rain but, as it was still dry, he made for Embankment Gardens. Waiting by the traffic lights on the far side of the road for a favourable colour, he saw Fairchild emerge from Whitehall Place and walk towards the rendezvous. For reasons beyond mere cussedness, he withdrew into the shadows of Hungerford Bridge until he had ready-eyed the minder; the back-up man. Watching him as he overtook Fairchild to make a preliminary recce inside the gate. Noticing the negative shrug he offered his master as he turned about and passed him at the entrance. This time purely out of cussedness, he allowed five minutes to pass before strolling casually across the road and into the Gardens.

Sardonically, he offered Fairchild a droll salute and the time-honoured greeting required of a junior to a senior police officer. 'All correct, Sir.'

'Is it?' The reply was humourless.

'Not really. Some mouthy cow from the BBC rang me. She wanted to talk about what happened in the States.'

'What did you say?'

'This and that. Nothing relevant. But that's not the point, is it?'

'The point being?'

'Don't play the civil servant with me, Cyril. You're not good enough at it. Not yet. The point is, I've been blown. Haven't I?'

'Obviously.'

'By your department. Or at least by one of your fucking cowboys.'

'Not necessarily. There are a few of our former colleagues at the Yard who might wish to do you down. You've upset quite a few over there in your time.' A thumb jerked vaguely westwards.

'Not good enough. I got the call the evening of the same day I was discharged from Wyldwood. My coming-out ball wasn't announced in the social column of *The Times*. And Con Circs are always a week behind notifying the release of nutters. Nobody knew at the Yard.'

'Except your friend Detective-Inspector Marion Elstow.'

'So you've got me ready-eyed as well?'

'As well as what?'

'As well as putting an intercept on my phone.'

'Ah. I was pretty sure you were in one of your moods. Despite the graven image you generally present to the world at large, you cannot avoid a distinct, an almost primitive, flaring of the nostrils when about to grind your axe.'

'I need it to chop down the bats in my belfry.'

'The aptness of the metaphor is yours. Remember that. I assure you – no I cannot assure you, you know the form – we never confirm or deny interceptions.'

'The form also says warrants will only be granted in cases of serious crime when all other investigative measures have failed.'

'Or where the security of the state is at risk.'

'In which category am I?'

'Owen, I do not wish to be at odds with you over this. Let me simply refer to your own professional experience. We both know the special measures you have in mind are extremely limited, politically and materially. That state of affairs applies as much to my present work as it formerly did. Is it likely we would expend them on a casual part-time employee engaged on a trivial assignment?'

'That's rational and logical,' he said, echoing Elstow's words. 'I'll give you that.'

'I think you had better, don't you? Have you anything concrete to report?'

'Only negative stuff. I saw Maisie Ackroyd and her mother-in-law . . . Little to help there. It's all in here, together with my expenses. She wasn't cheap.' He passed an envelope to Fairchild before going on, 'Frank Worple,' he began . . .

'The late Detective Inspector? Why him?'

'On the off-chance he might have nicked something in addition to the money.'

'And had he?'

'He said he hadn't.'

He saw Fairchild's minder seated on a park bench fifty feet away, face hidden behind the *Daily Telegraph*, one eye boring into him through a fifty-calibre hole in the title. Malice made the lie easy. If they didn't trust him, why should he trust them. Nothing against you personally, Cyril, he wanted to say. It is *them* I don't trust.

'Don't look so glum, Owen,' Fairchild was saying. 'We did not expect results overnight. Anything I can do to help things along?'

'Norah Thornton. She's moved out Blackheath way. Somewhere near the station. Can you get her housed for me? I don't want to show out more than I have to.'

'Surely you have an old pal at the local station who could locate her?'

'You told me to be discreet.'

'Yes, I did,' Fairchild said ruefully. 'Very well. Any further bees in your bonnet?'

'There was an intercept on Eric Popkiss!'

'Are we back on that tack again? I don't want to repeat myself . . .'

'Look, Cyril, remember me? Owen Smith. I know the score. What you told me about the caper when you came to Wyldwood could only have come off the tinkle. I would like to look at the transcript.'

'Why?'

'Nuances.'

'Nuances?'

'When the villains speak on the phone, it's not so much what they say that's important. It's what they don't say – or the way they say what they say. Nuances.'

'I see. Or at least I think I do. All right. I'll have someone bring it to you in the reading room. The one you were notified about. Be there in an hour. The messenger will wait. Naturally we cannot let the material out of our possession.'

'Fair enough. Anything else?'

'Yes, I would like to get round to the reason I brought you here.'

'Feel free.'

'Thank you.' It was Fairchild's turn to pass an envelope. 'I am going beyond permitted limits, Owen. But my concern for your personal safety is such I am prepared to take a chance.'

'I am duly grateful,' Smith said. Fairchild searched for sarcasm before continuing. 'Inside is a photograph of Slunchev. He has gone AWOL from the Bulgarian Trade Mission. I want you to be aware of him in case he crosses your path. Should that happen, inform our electronic friend, Barker. Slunchev is a very frightened man, but no physical intervention is required from you. I stress that. He is a run and tell target. Not to be hit. Is that clear?'

'Not really. If he is running scared, why doesn't he run in our direction?'

'I have no idea.'

'Maybe he's gone over to the Yanks? They pay better.'

'They would have told us.'

'Eventually.'

'Immediately. There is still an alliance in being whatever you may think. Bearing in mind your last escapade you should be grateful. You would not be here otherwise.'

'I lost my gratitude in Wyldwood. You brought me out on the prod, so let me prod. If Slunchev can't turn to his own, or run to us or the Americans, there can only be one reason.'

'And that is?'

'Hamme. If you insist on Hamme. Anyway, his hired minder has obviously gone bent on him. If that is the case, it must be he believes whichever way he goes Hamme has the means to get at him. That is not good. THAT is very nasty.'

'Hamme is not your concern, Owen. Hands off. You have been told – official. Theorize by all means, I will provide a willing ear. But do not let your feet get tangled in your mouth.

It is a bad habit of yours.'

'I've lost many of my bad habits lately.'

'Glad to hear it. Now are you certain there is nothing further? You are not keeping any little surprise packets up your sleeve...? Your nostrils are flaring again. Why?'

'You reminded me of that dirty joke. The one about the Irishman who always kept a French letter up his sleeve... Didn't you ask me once before if I had anything up my sleeve? No matter. There was this Irishman—'

'Spare me, please. I must get back to the office, I have a two-foot mound of files to plough through.'

'Just one thing, if that electronic idiot of yours is going to ring my bell every fifteen minutes, why do I have to say Barker to shut him off?'

'The word contains a combination of consonants and vowels easily recognized by the computer.'

'Couldn't you come up with something less Pavlovian?'

'Like what?'

'Bollocks. For instance?'

He went directly to the library, a brisk five-minute walk up Villiers Street, across the Strand into Duncannon Street and along past the Church of St Martin-in-the-Fields, to come directly and unexpectedly under the stony glare of Nurse Edith Cavell. Momentarily robbed of will, he paused, looking for a sign, finding only lifeless disdain and imperious rigidity. Not for him the clemency she had shown Kendigg. Ah, well, he never had been one for nurses. He ran the ball of his thumb over the smooth golden skull in his pocket, allowing himself a secret smile in response to the pleasure of its touch. He hoped they were into microfiche at the library. If they were, it might be possible to feed the roll of microfilm into the reader. Discover exactly what *they* had got him into.

It was not to be. 'We did have plans,' the assistant librarian sighed. 'But cuts in public expenditure, you know.'

He took a magazine from the rack and waited. 'Funny how naked and powerless you feel when you are out of a job,' Frank Worple had said. Once he could have gone to the Yard. Everything there was either on microfiche or computer now. But it was no longer open to him to walk in flourishing the warrant and authority of Detective Chief Superintendent Owen Smith to act as a constable anywhere within England and Wales. At the Yard, and everywhere else within the Metropolitan Police District, he was under a cloud. Nothing official. No listing on the keep off the grass sheet, but he was distinctly *persona non grata*. Lucky to get away with *it*, they were saying. No one knowing exactly what *it* was, but the rumours were about. He had wet-jobbed some people in the States. Unofficial. Lucky to get away with *it*. And double lucky to have Marion Elstow standing by him. She could get it done! Get the Photographic Section to run off half a dozen copies. No problem. But that would involve her with whatever was in this *Thing*. He felt the skull again. It no longer comforted. It could blind. It could kill.

The man who entered carrying a black leather briefcase, marked with the Royal Cypher, was the same young Sloanie Castellain had hoisted by the lapels in the car-park at Wyldwood. The sheepskin coat and twill slacks had given way to a dark blue three-piece. The yellow sweater, exactly matching the paint job on the Morgan, had been replaced by a blue and pink vertically striped shirt with a plain white collar. But it was the same young Sloanie.

He had caught the fellow's eye as soon as he entered, but the man chose to make a circuit of the bookshelves, casually inspecting a volume here, perusing another there; and all the time his eyes constantly skittered round the room like a pair of demented bluebottles trapped behind a window pane. Eventually, and expressing a solemn profundity, the fellow settled in a seat opposite Smith and buried his head in a volume of Russell's *Logical Atomism*.

'You can get a bad case of astigmatism doing that,' Smith said quietly. The young man's head rose, frowning.

'I beg your pardon?'

'Rolling your eyes about like a sideways slot machine. Keep on like that, and you will wind up with a melon and a lemon instead of two grapes.'

The eyes steadied and considered Smith soulfully.

'Barker sent you to deliver a typescript,' Smith insisted.

'OK, deliver. I have other things to do.'

The young man crooked a finger over his lips and made another survey of his surroundings. This time he actually turned his head. 'Keep your voice down,' he admonished haughtily. 'Have you no sense of security!' Fumbling in his briefcase, he withdrew a brown envelope with OHMS in large letters across the top. He glanced around the room once more before sliding it across the table to Smith. 'I am not to let it out of my sight. You understand that?'

'Keep your hair on, Sunshine,' Smith answered in a low growl. Taking out the file and spreading it flat on the table, he commenced reading. He had barely reached the middle of the first page when he was interrupted by a warning hiss. He looked up.

'What's the trouble this time, Sunshine?' he asked.

'My name is Hamilton,' came the stiff reply. 'Please stop calling me Sunshine.'

'I thought you might prefer a code name in your line of work. All right, what's the trouble, Hamilton?'

'Can you not be a little more secure and read that below the table, in your lap as it were. Someone may see it over your shoulder.'

'No one is looking over my shoulder. Besides, isn't that where you are supposed to be, looking over my shoulder?'

'Oh, please get on with it,' Hamilton said, looking baffled and cross. He broke away from a sneer that drenched him in cold contempt, and presented instead his smoothly sculpted profile, loftily inclined. As soon as he considered it safe, he slid his eyes to the left in order to maintain discreet surveillance on this untutored lout his new chief had brought in, this uncouth clown whom he had seen as a rival for his job. New men nearly always brought in their own professional siblings, but this ... mentally defective hulk? He dismissed his fears and gave vent to a soundless 'Pah' in the best tradition of Sir Desmond Rachette. Astigmatism indeed ... Peripheral vision! He had the best peripheral vision in the service. He had lectured on peripheral vision at the Training College. 'Nothing is more helpful to the field officer than peripheral vision. The ability to observe what is happening at least ninety degrees to one's right or left, without displaying an obvious or direct interest in the object of one's attentions, is an art that can only be acquired by constant practice and ocular exercise.'

And, quite clearly, by the exercise of peripheral vision at one hundred and twenty degrees, he saw Smith reach into his pocket and bring out a notebook and pen. Aha!

He swung round triumphantly.

'No notes,' he hissed across the table in a fierce whisper. 'Barker specifically said, you were not to be permitted to make notes of the transcript.'

'I did not intend making notes of the transcript,' Smith replied coolly. 'I was only going to draw my conclusions.'

'Barker will want sight of them,' Hamilton retaliated.

Smith nodded in agreement, and for a few seconds his pen hovered uncertainly over the paper then began to move swiftly. He tore out the page and handed it to Hamilton. 'You can give him this,' he said.

Looking at it, Hamilton saw only a drawing of two small ovals inside a larger circle from the open end of which two vertical lines ascended to be closed off in a small cone.

'What does it mean?' he asked, subdued by a grudging respect.

Smith tapped the side of his nose with a blunt forefinger. 'Barker will know,' he said mysteriously.

Hamilton responded to the goad. 'I knew I would dislike you before I ever set eyes on you, and I am pleased to find that personal contact has confirmed my instincts.'

Smith leant menacingly across the table. 'Is that why you blew me out to Morpeth Anatole?' he murmured gently.

Open-mouthed, Hamilton recoiled into the back of his chair. Smith loomed nearer. 'You try anything like that again, Sunshine,' he heard him say as if from a great distance, 'and I'll give you what Castellain gave you ... But I won't let go.' Hamilton felt the blood drain from the innermost recesses of his brain and his eyes closed against a sickness in his stomach. When he had recovered the file on the Popkiss Intercept was lying in his lap. All his former fears flooded back. How badly he had underestimated his potential rival. Damn it all, the man was endowed with extra-sensory perception!

# Eleven

◆◆◆◆◆◆

Smith thought about the charm bracelet. Eric Popkiss had not been so high-minded after all. Not so concerned that the fate of Billy Appleby might befall him. He could almost hear Eric's mind working, 'If all the geezer is worried about are these poxy papers inside the box, he ain't going to miss this choice bit of tom which is real gear and down to me. That was the deal – The gear and readies are down to me – me and Terry. But this choice bit of gear is down to me.' Nuances!

Really nothing much in the way of nuances in the transcript. Bernie Lomax? The keyman. He might have caught hold of a nuance or two. Then there was Norah Thornton. She ought to be full of nuances.

By carefully snipping the tiny gold ring with a pair of pliers, he released the skull from the rest of the bracelet and let it drop into the palm of his hand. The ruby eyes stared dully into his.

'What have you got to complain about?' he asked, offended by their reproach. 'I've given you your freedom. Free will! That's what you've got. Free will!'

'Free will!' Snow White had laughed scornfully when he responded to his question; 'If we approve your release on licence, what do you look forward to most on the outside?'

He had replied, 'I suppose the ability to exercise my own free will.'

'The ability to exercise your own free will?' Snow White

repeated, glacial incredulity freezing his loose jowls. He had melted almost immediately. 'My dear man,' he protested guiltily. 'If all you have gained from your enforced sojourn with us is an illusion about the existence of free will, then I'm afraid we have failed you badly.' He paused, stretched his arms above his head, and prepared to make amends.

'I know it is fashionable these days to speak of the quality of life,' he postulated slowly. 'But even at its best, it does not contain free will. In a dream state you may find the power to leap over tall buildings, to glide effortlessly through the air, high above the heads of an astonished populace. But in wakeful reality you, like the rest of mankind, are more likely to find yourself in the social equivalent of that other common dream state; the one in which you suddenly find yourself in the middle of a busy street, naked from the waist down, desperately trying to cover a protuberant backside with an inadequate shirt tail.'

Briefly reflecting on the soundness of his proposition and finding it valid, Snow White offered an interesting aside. 'Odd thing is,' he said to the ceiling. 'In all my research into that type of dream state, not a single subject has mentioned genital exposure as a cause for concern. Their efforts were solely directed towards an avoidance of anal display. It was as if they had no genital awareness whatsoever. As if they had no genitalia in any shape or form.' He came down to earth. 'What about you,' he enquired hopefully of Smith. 'When you encounter such dreams, do you crouch in a position of genital priority?'

'I never have dreams like that,' Smith maintained stoutly.

'Remarkable!' Raised eyebrows greeted his denial sceptically. 'But you *do* feel that free will is a reality?'

'It can be found,' Smith had replied. 'Somewhere beyond the Bricks. Outside the Wire. Once I fulfil my contract to my new employer, I will be a free agent. Able to exercise free will.'

'Balderdash!' Snow White exploded. 'Naive balderdash. Your mind may be repaired ... But I'm afraid,' he added with sinister emphasis, 'some people here have softened your brain in the process.' Smith was sadly ignorant of the long and bitter debate that had raged over the ever-turbulent psychiatric seas for years, sometimes with hurricane force, as the *determinists* and *indeterminists* fought for supremacy. Finkel, the number two White, from whom he had received psychological therapy whilst behind the Bricks was a positive *determinist*: Snow White, his chief, a determined *indeterminist*.

'I can only assume,' Snow White said hoarsely, appalled by the revelation of yet another instance of his subordinate's treachery, 'from your known record, that this is a temporary aberration. A desire fixation engendered by confinement. One that will be quickly relieved by a return to the harsh realities of the outside world. You know, my dear fellow –' he went on, busily scratching minute hieroglyphics on Smith's case-history, before putting aside his pen to administer complete exorcism. 'We are conveyed through existence, each of us in our own little dodgem car. We go careering along life's broad highway, no brakes, no control over the speed, and only a rudimentary, and ineffectual steering-wheel to keep us out of trouble. We sideswipe others and they in turn bash into us. More often than not the damage is slight and we continue merrily on our way. But occasionally we die, or are crippled, or find ourselves in prison, or if we are especially fortunate, in a place like this. Oh yes, from time to time we manage to maintain a desired course, sailing along quite happily. But sooner or later the wonky steering will go haywire, and off we go again, crashing and banging into this, that, or the other.'

'Hopefully, it will be the other,' Smith interrupted, unable to resist the bargain. However, it was an interruption Snow White left unchallenged, preferring to drive home his own point.

'So you see, Mr Smith,' he went on. 'No one possesses free will – thank God for it. What a boring life we would otherwise lead. You think that a contradictory analysis? Not at all. About the only species in the animal kingdom that possesses free will is the common earthworm. That is, until the early bird happens along. So take my tip, when you get out of here, be a good chap and climb into your little dodgem car, and simply go banging and crashing about like everyone else. In other words, forget this free will nonsense. Just try to lead a normal life.'

Once more pressing the point of his pen against the tiny ruby, Smith watched fascinated as the top of the skull flew open revealing the tight roll of microfilm inside. He had still not removed it from its hiding place. That would have to wait until he found a projector. There is no hurry, he told himself. No rush. No point in working yourself out of a job within the first week. Besides other peoples' secrets are only good for anything if they remain secret; even from the one who has discovered them. Particularly from the one who has discovered them. It was rather like waiting to see what Father Christmas has brought. An early opened present could be disappointing. He pressed the top of the skull back into place, and gently rubbed the ball of his thumb over it a couple of times deriving pleasure from its admirable perfection. 'I wonder how much of a bang you will make when you crash into the other dodgem cars, me old mate,' he said to the skull, before slipping it into his pocket and reaching for the phone.

*26 Sept. 18.44 hrs. Subject dials out. (No. indexed.) Subscriber:*
*Bernard Gordon Lomax, 'Hill View', Deep Dene, near Epsom, Surrey.*

S.    I am Detective Chief Superintendent Owen Smith of New Scotland Yard. Is that you, Bernie?

*(pause)*

L.    What do you want? I heard you'd been bounced.

S.    You heard right. Sorry about the bullshit, but I wanted to be sure you made the connection.

L.    Last time we connected was ten years ago in number two court at the Old Bailey. I don't forget those things.

S.    You got away with it. Stop mumping.

L.    It cost me a packet.

S.    *(heatedly)* Not in my pocket it didn't.

L.    *(laughing)* Still burns you, does it? Me walking out of it. Why bung a copper when you can buy two in the jury box for the same price?

S.    You're getting careless in your old age, Bernie.

L.    So I'm kidding you along. No law against that, is there? What the hell do you want anyway? You trying to put on a bit of black to make up lost wages?

S.    Nothing like that. I'm doing some private work. I want a meet. A bit of a chat.

L.    What about?

S.    Billy Appleby, Eric Popkiss, Terry Scanlon, Frank Worple, people like that.

L.    They're dead, for Christ's sake.

S.    I know. You could be next in line.

L.     What the hell is this. You *are* at the black.
S.     No, Bernie. I've joined the Royal Life Saving
       Society. You're my first client.

*(lengthy pause)*

L.     How do I know this isn't a load of old moody. You
       trying to give me a clock job. You at the wind-up?
S.     For you it could be striking twelve, Bernie. And none
       to come. Better meet me. No charge. Nothing to pay.
       Only a bit of a chat.

*(further pause)*

L.     OK. But my ground. Deep Dene Conservative Club.
       Billiard Room Bar in thirty minutes.
S.     You are getting careless, Bernie. You could be laying
       on a reception committee. Listen, you remember that
       place where Ginger Finegan slipped you the cuttle-
       fish to make the twirls for the Hatton Garden tickle?
       Make it that one.
L.     I don't know what you are talking about.
S.     Now you're being sensible. I'll see you there. And
       listen, don't hang about. Get on your bike now before
       anyone can tie you on a string at your end.
L.     Smith, if you are trying to stitch me up, don't forget
       I've got nasty friends. I'll see you, Smith. *(He discon-
       nects.)*
S.     Tinker Bell to Bollocks. Over and out. *(????)*

They must have had a van-load on standby. He had deliberately waited fifteen minutes before leaving the flat to see if it
was on him. And there they were, already in position, backing
him each way in tight contact and over-lap. Leap-frog. The
lead was fifteen feet ahead, nice and nondescript in brown
overalls under a loose blue donkey-jacket, sticking close to the
inside, not moving too fast or too slow. The tail, twenty feet

behind in scruffy denim, hugged the kerb on the outside. Across the street the two flankers were more widely spread, a signalman, warily alert, about fifty yards ahead. The controller, in the rear, opening the gap by pausing in front of a news-stand. They had a woman on point, ahead of the lead, dithering at the lights with the 'Cross Now' sign in her favour. She would switch to close tail when they saw which direction he intended taking. The flankers would then cross over and leap-frog into position ahead and behind. The close contacts would drop back to become flankers. If there were enough of them in reserve, they could ring the changes half a dozen times.

He let them have their fun until he reached Kennington Road. There he swiftly cut across the traffic and broke into a steady lope, heading north. In front, he saw the signaller turn into a shop doorway and bury his face in the collar of his coat. He knew the man would be mouthing into his radio for the back-up vehicle. They could walk him to the end of the earth. But a runner! They couldn't go with a runner. Not all of them. Not if they wanted to keep the surveillance under wraps. If they had been any good, they would have broken it off there and then. Would have realized it had come a tumble. Berks. Stupid berks. He glanced quickly behind. The one in denim was now a flanker and the only one going with him, grimly maintaining a steady canter on the opposite side of the road about a hundred yards to the rear. Smith sprinted to catch favourable lights at Lambeth Road, hearing as he gained the far kerb, the screech of brakes, a sharp thudding impact, followed by the discordant clatter of falling glass. Pausing briefly, he saw a baker's van unnaturally balanced on two wheels before the bonnet of a huge articulated truck. For a wild moment, the van hovered at its centre of gravity, then plunged on its side, accompanied from within by panic-stricken howls and a solitary, high-pitched scream. No need to worry about the back-up now. He hoped they were not too badly hurt.

Still running, he went on into Westminster Bridge Road, the denim-clad tail clinging gamely behind. At Lower Marsh, he swung right, and with the tail temporarily out of view, he sprinted down the middle of the street and reached the narrow turning leading to the carriageway in front of Waterloo Station, getting there before his pursuer had rounded the corner. It was seven-fifteen when he entered the station. From now on it would be simple.

The late commuters were still coming through. The conscientious management types. The gin-and-tonic boys. The let's have a quickie before we go home brigade. Moderating his pace, he slipped past the throng, taking the stairs in the centre of the concourse down to the low-level tunnel into Waterloo Road and through the doors of the pub opposite.

With a whisky and water in his hand, he monitored the exit from the low level through the pub window. A good five minutes passed before the denim-clad tail emerged. By now he would have given up hope. Almost. First, he would have done the toilets and refreshment rooms in the main concourse, then the bookstalls and sales kiosks. Now, for him, it was straw-clutching time. He watched the solitary figure making a desultory examination of the bus queues and surrounding area before returning to the station. It would be the Underground platforms next, then out into York Road to try his luck there. Hoping against hope. Poor bastard.

Smith consumed his drink with leisurely smugness, feeling quite pleased with himself. He had run more than a mile at a fairly brisk pace and wasn't even breathing hard. Sweating a little, perhaps. He ordered a beer chaser; there was no great hurry. At this time of night, Lomax would require nearly an hour to get from Epsom to the appointed meeting-place.

He left the pub just after seven-thirty and caught a passing taxi.

Getting out at Camberwell Green, he settled in to walk the last few hundred yards. A precaution. They might have spread the covers wide enough to latch on to him, if the close fielders dropped the ball. Waterloo Station would have been a natural long stop ... Surely he was not that important?

At the first corner, he went down a side street until he had covered sufficient distance to bring any hidden shadows into view. Concealed in an unlit porch, he looked back, seeing nothing more than a cat scurrying across the road. Why?

Because cats always scurry across roads, he told himself, deriding his fears. And what the hell. It was merely a game. He had only run the bastards to take the piss out of them in the first place. To teach them not to put him on the tinkle. To give a bit of trust. But then, these people were not the trusting kind. Not if you hadn't been to Marlborough or Eton, Oxford or Cambridge.

He remained in the porch for two minutes, then stepped boldly out on to the pavement, pausing to mock any unseen pursuers by venting a derisive whistle. Along the street, the gathering night lay undisturbed. Still whistling, if in a lower key, he sauntered away.

There was a momentary hitch with the doorman at the Leather Glove Club, for he was not a member, but mention of Bernie Lomax's name and a fiver slipped into a willing palm gained him admittance to the bar, with the unctuous proviso that he must not buy drinks until Mr Lomax arrived to sign him in. They had named the club after the leather glove used by the train robbers in 1963 to black out the signal-light that brought the mail train to a halt near Bridegow Bridge and create the legend about the biggest tickle of all time. Two million in readies! Or was it three million? Some said it was all of six! However much it was, it was enough to name a club after. A club good villains with a few quid to spread about could use. A club actors, who played good villains, could frequent in adulatory search of role-playing menace. Where script-writers could catch up on authentic dialogue and immerse themselves in character.

But when Smith entered and quietly seated himself in an alcove, where he could see both the entrance and the bar itself, the place was practically deserted. It was early. Too early. The only action lay within a group of three at the far end of the bar. One he knew to be Tony Yeo, wheelman for any robbery team prepared to give him fifteen percent of the take, provided his end was a guaranteed five grand minimum, with two and a half bunged in the sky-rocket before take-off. The other two? Well, Tony was obliging them with a demonstration of his last getaway. From the bar stool, his right foot heeled and toed the rail, his left hand whipped through an imaginary gearbox, whilst his right brought an invisible wheel swerving round blind corners and past police road blocks. Talking the caper through, in a constant stream of words pouring from the side of his mouth. He must be in for the blag of the year award, Smith thought sourly. The audience, pig-eyed, and coarse-featured, looked bigger villains than clean-cut, sharp-suited Tony Yeo could ever be, or ever dare appear. Smith reckoned them as no more than a couple of electronic heavies, fugitives from some cop show. Tony had made it, he was in the clear and had fucked the filth out of sight to the approving laughter of his companions. One of the artificial villains got in another round of drinks. Smith looked at his watch. Bernie Lomax was late. Careless Bernie Lomax?

Another ten minutes passed before Smith caught his first sight of him. A brief glimpse of Bernie's face at one of the porthole windows in the swing doors. The face hung there, weirdly suspended. Wide pleading eyes, an open mouth obscenely crimson, disappearing behind a spray of fine red mist on the glass. The face purpling, livid, almost phosphorescent. The swing doors parted and Bernie Lomax staggered into the bar. Behind him the doorman, holding out a tentative helpless hand, as if to a leper he dared not touch. Reeling into the centre of the room, Bernie stood crouched, swinging unsteadily on his feet like a drunken cripple. His eyes focused on Smith, he straightened, a dreadful mouth opened, and from it came a half-heard strangled moan, accompanied by another spray of red mist, fainter, more delicate than before, settling and vanishing into the folds of his blood-stained shirt. He tried to raise his left arm as if to point at Smith, but the effort was too great and he toppled forward along the path of his rising hand to crash face-down on the carpet.

Smith was immediately at his side, knowing Bernie Lomax was drowning in his own blood. He adjusted the position of the head in accordance with half-forgotten lectures and began the pressure. The count thundering in his mind. Say to yourself, One thousand. Two thousand. Three Thousand. Release. Should it be up to five thousand? No, definitely three thousand! Press again. Yell at stricken faces hovering above to call an ambulance. Press. One thousand. Two thousand.

Three thousand. Release. Whenever possible, artificial respiration must be maintained until the victim recovers or is officially pronounced dead, that was the rule.

He was still at it fifteen minutes later, sweat dripping from his brow, falling on the still empurpled, blood-streaked face of Bernie Lomax. A solitary bead caught in the lash of a drooping eyelid sparkled in the light. A ray of hope? Forlorn hope. From above him a harsh voice spoke. A voice he knew all too well.

'Not a case for mouth to mouth resuscitation, eh, Owen?'

Glancing upwards, he caught sight of the scarred, twisted features of Detective Commander Joe Potch. Behind him, white-faced, stood Marion Elstow. He said nothing and went into another sequence. One thousand. Two thousand. Three thousand. Release. Joe Potch loomed nearer.

'Who do you think you are, Owen?' he said in a harsh whisper. 'Jesus Christ Almighty? I thought you were supposed to be cured. And here you are trying to raise the dead! Can't you see the guy has snuffed it. He has croaked, Owen.'

Smith continued pumping, driven by conscience. Careless Bernie Lomax. His fault? Drove straight to the meet, didn't you, Bernie. No fast shuffles. You wouldn't have done that five or six years ago. Thought the cops have no balls these days, did you, Bernie? Forgot there are other people to think of besides cops, didn't you, Bernie? No minders with you either, Bernie? No minders! Arrogant Bernie Lomax. That's what joining the Deep Dene Conservative Club does for you, Bernie. Makes you arrogant, stupid and careless. With a sigh, Smith sat back on his heels and surrendered Bernie Lomax to death. Seemingly from afar, he heard Joe Potch being the CID Commander.

'Where do you think you're going, Tony? You and your two mates can get yourselves back down the far end of the bar and wait. There are a few questions to be answered before anybody leaves here.'

At that moment the ambulance men came in with the trolley. Potch waved them away from the body on the carpet and spoke to the youngster in a white coat who was with them.

'You in a position to certify death, son?' he enquired. gruffly.

The medical student fiddled nervously with the stethoscope dangling from his pocket. 'I'm in my third year,' he said, uncertainly.

'That will do fine *pro tem*, Doc.' Potch replied jovially. 'Just give a quick listen-in and tell me if his bell is still ringing. You and I know his clock stopped long ago, but...' he saved his venom for Smith. 'There are those among us who think they can bring back the dead.' Still kneeling by the body, Smith shook his head wearily. 'Not any more, Joe,' he said, defeated. He raised his eyes and met those of Marion Elstow, seeing a pity in them that verged on contempt. She turned away, delving into her capacious bag to bring out notebook and pen, then walked to the end of the bar to question Tony Yeo and the actors, one of whom was now vomiting into an ice bucket with all the total emotional expressionism required by Stanislavsky.

'May I?' The young medical student touched Smith on the shoulder, wanting to occupy the space next to the body. As he stood up, the student dropped eagerly into his place, apparently aware of his professional importance for the first time. With stethoscope, torch and sensitive fingers, he listened, peered, and probed, halted only by Joe Potch's barked command not to move the body. Rising again, a slight pallor high-lighting the ruddiness in his cheeks, he pronounced in tones both puzzled and horrified, 'Someone has severed his tongue. Removed it completely.' He met a stony silence and seemed to take it as requiring from him a wider explanation. 'As to causation,' he went on shakily, as though before a Board of Examiners at the Royal College of Physicians, 'obviously a sharp instrument of some kind. I am satisfied he is clinically dead. Death being due to loss of blood, asphyxiation, and shock.' For a few moments he evaluated the merits of his opinion, marked it ten out of ten, and spoke again with renewed confidence.

'However, I cannot officially certify death, you understand. I am yet to be qualified,' he added with future certainty.

Joe Potch nodded appreciatively. 'Not to worry, Doc. We've got plenty that are. Have one here in next to no time.' Waving the ambulance men towards the door, he ushered the student in the same direction, affably official. 'Sorry to deprive you of a patient, Doc,' he said. 'But this one stays put for the time being. Police routine, you understand?' His good-bye was generously benign. 'I'll try and row you in as a witness at the trial, Doc. As and when, I'll let you know. And I'll see you get professional expenses, whether you've qualified by then or not.'

Returning, he strode briskly towards the body and stood astride the corpse, gazing pensively downwards for a time, a Colossus in his own right. Then he redirected his attention to Smith.

'This one was in my Action Book, Owen.' His finger jabbed accusingly at the lifeless remains of Bernie Lomax. 'He was marked up "Deferred." Isn't that right, Miss Elstow?' he bawled towards Marion at the far end of the bar. 'We've got Bernie Lomax marked up "Deferred" in the Action Book?'

'We have, sir,' she agreed reluctantly.

'You see,' he turned again on Smith, his voice dropping. 'No point in chasing after a know-nothing ten-percenter who wouldn't tell you the time of day,' Potch continued remorselessly. 'Isn't that right, Miss Elstow?' If she heard, she gave no answer. Potch sought one from Smith. 'I made a mistake, didn't I, Owen?'

'Not for me to say, Joe,' Smith said.

'No, by Christ it is not.' Threateningly jovial, Potch stepped away from the body and sat down. 'How do you come to be here Owen?' he asked. 'Did you enter as a registered villain or a paid-up performer? Come to think of it, you look like something out of those Japanese movies they show late at night on the telly. You see somebody drenched in sweat, breathing a bit heavy, a load of blood and snot lying about, and you know you are watching a Japanese movie. How does this one end, Owen?'

'No idea, Joe.'

'Odd thing is; I was just saying to Miss Elstow,' he gazed in her direction, then smiled lewdly at Smith. 'I was saying to her on our way back to the Yard, maybe we had better get in amongst these deferrals like Bernie Lomax, the way things are happening.'

'What things have happened?'

Potch waved Smith into silence, he had the floor.

'These very words are no sooner out of my mouth as we are coming along Peckham High Street, when over the air comes a shout to serious bother at the Leather Glove.' He allowed Smith time to ponder on the miracle before continuing.

'Hardly believable, is it?' he said.

'Depends where you were coming from, Joe.' Smith was geographically assessing what lay beyond Peckham, feeling uneasy and afraid.

'That's as maybe,' Potch had answered enigmatically. 'The thing is, knowing, as we do, the sort of people who frequent the Leather Glove, being as there were no local cars available to respond, and further, being as we were only a couple of miles away, I said let's go and take a look.'

'You always did have a nose for trouble, Joe,' Smith offered genuine praise. 'And you always followed your nose.' Potch took it as his rightful due, showing no gratitude.

'And what do we find when we get here?' he asked, purely of himself. 'We find Bernie Lomax stretched out on the wall-to-wall tartan. De-tongued. Stone dead. And right beside him, my former colleague, ex-Detective Chief Superintendent Owen Smith, who having been deprived of his halo, can no longer get his raising of the dead act to work.' Potch rose, thrust his massive hands deep into his pockets and went for a short stroll around the corpse; hovering over it like a hungry vulture. But one undecided as to whether it was safe to descend and gorge itself. Withdrawing a hand, he clawed at his fleshy face in despair. Turning balefully to Smith, he said: 'There are questions to be asked, Owen. Answers to be given.'

'What were you doing, the other side of Peckham?' Smith repeated, more directly.

'I meant questions from me. Answers from you,' Potch replied. 'But later on will do nicely.'

Uniforms were beginning to arrive. Potch directed Marion Elstow to take charge. Photographs. Scenes of Crime. Statements – 'Oh, and doctor. Better get a real doctor in. One who knows how to spell D-E-A-D!' Then to Smith. 'Come on, Rochester Row for you – and your answers.'

Scotland Yard is an administrative and operational head-quarters, not a police station. Prisoners and suspects are not held there, it has no cells or detention rooms. But a short distance away, on the other side of Victoria Street, a handy local nick in Rochester Row serves that purpose. 'You can await my convenience at Rochester Row, Owen.' Potch made an ominous promise. 'And I can assure you, it will not be my *earliest* convenience.'

'The Kanaka,' Lionel Peachtree was saying as he held after-noon court at his favourite bench inside the Wire. 'It was always the Kanaka our chaps were up against, when I was a lad reading *Boys' Own Paper*. The South Seas were full of blood-thirsty Kanaka cutting peoples' tongues out. Or was it the Dyaks? We used to get a goodly quota of Dyaks as well as Kanaka. Long-pig. A great deal of Long-pig. Yes, I am pretty sure it was the Kanaka who went in for cutting peoples' tongues out. Long-pig. Something of a delicacy at the canni-bals' feast. Dyaks had blow-pipes and poisoned arrows. I preferred Pathans and Afridi myself, North-West Frontier stuff. They didn't give us much of that in *BOP*. Perhaps because the Pathans and Afridi didn't cut peoples' tongues out. They did "unspeakable things". I wondered for many years what was meant by "unspeakable things". That may explain why they preferred Kanakas and Dyaks. They didn't do "unspeakable things", they only cut peoples' tongues out.'

'Why the hell would they want to cut his tongue out?' Joe Potch asked the world beyond the car window.

'Long-pig,' Smith said.

'What was that?'

'Nothing. Nothing at all.'

'Nothing, eh? Y'know, I thought they would have binned you for a lot longer than they did, Owen.' Potch waited, invited an explanation.

'I always was a quick healer, Joe,' Smith answered care-fully.

Potch laid a crafty finger along the side of his nose. 'That – and a generous smear of the magic ointment from on high, eh?'

Smith sat tight-lipped. A heavy elbow nudged him in the ribs. 'C'mon, Owen. You're talking to Joe Potch, Commander, Major Crime Squad.' The elbow went in again, harder this time. 'You think I don't know? I have been apprised,' he said, with pompous confidence. 'In my position, I get apprised of things the funny people get up to. At least some of the things. Of you, I was apprised.'

'I believe you, Joe,' Smith said simply. 'I also believe you were on your way back from Blackheath when you picked up that call in Peckham. Was it Norah Thornton, Joe?'

'What if it was?' Potch said grudgingly.

'Is she all right?'

'As right as she'll ever be. Somebody broke her bleeding neck.'

'What about Maisie...?'

'Ackroyd!' Potch's sour conceit fled in a yelp of alarmed realization. 'Head for Battersea,' he bellowed at his driver. 'Foot on the floor. And pass me that fucking microphone.' With brusque authority he ordered the Information Room dispatcher to hold for an emergency car-to-car transmission. 'Any unit in the vicinity of Battersea, acknowledge immediately,' he commanded. No answer came. 'Any unit in the vicinity of Battersea, *please* acknowledge,' he begged. Still no answer.

'Doubt if you'll get anyone, Guv,' his driver said lugubriously. 'While you were inside the Leather Glove, there was a succession of shouts to some schemmozzle at Brixton Prison. A riot: six prison officers held hostage. All cars on Lima, Mike, Papa and Whisky Districts assigned. I doubt if there is even a dog van on the air this side of Mitcham Common.'

Potch threw the transmitter aside in despair. 'There's no sense of fucking proportion left in the job today, Owen,' he lamented bitterly. 'No sense of priorities. No sense of responsibility. You're well out of it.'

Words were not needed from Smith and no further words came from Potch. The car was doing seventy behind full headlights and a banshee siren. It screamed past a red light at the Elephant and Castle and took the turning into St George's Road on two wheels, throwing Smith and Potch into an unloving embrace. Racing now at eighty-five towards Lambeth Palace Road and the Albert Embankment, Potch yelling at the driver to 'cut that fucking siren,' as they sliced through Nine Elms into Battersea.

Sedately, silently, they cruised down the street, the dim glow of artificial York stone identifying the house against the night. Where were the street lights? Vandalised! They gave it a few seconds; taking sights as they would say. Giving their ears a treat, as they would say. But they saw nothing and heard nothing. Only the quiet unlit house preening itself in the dark against its dingy neighbours.

'You go round the back, Owen,' Potch whispered. 'I'll give you twenty seconds to get set, then I'm going in the front. Straight in, no messing. Right through that front porch.' It was strange, thought Smith, how he was compelled to obey without question. Just Joe Potch and him, and the driver. The driver looked a handy fellow, the sort Joe Potch would pick for a driver. But here they were, two of the old school. Not even a stick between them. That was the way of the old school. They didn't go in like a commando platoon, the way they did these days. But then the villains didn't carry guns the way they did these days. They knew what would happen to them if they did. A further thought struck him, so funny he nearly laughed aloud. In all the excitement Joe Potch had forgotten he had been slung out of the job. He had forgotten himself ... until now.

He felt his way past the dusty Jaguar, pushed open the side gate and slid along the broken slats of the dividing fence. The darkness in the back yard was total. The crash of breaking glass was not unexpected, but thunderously loud all the same. Potch had obviously used a slab from the front garden as a key to open the tacked-on porch. Smith eased across to the back door, tight-fisted and prepared. Suddenly, down at the bottom of the yard, he saw something darker than the darkness moving, merging, vanishing, reappearing. Hovering.

There is only one way to tackle danger in the dark, if you have no weapon. You get straight in there, as Joe Potch would say. Feet first. He would tell you that in the dark your adversary would not see that kick coming straight up into his crotch.

But this one did!

As Smith ran at the nebulous black shape and lunged at it with a vicious right foot, his kick was brushed aside and forward momentum brought him onto a shattering blow thrusting upwards and inwards from below his breastbone. He heard a single explosive blast of released breath, as all the energy of his foe was expended in that one thrust. Smith found himself trapped on an airless planet. One where the night sky was full of distant, unseen birds. Birds that hissed, hooted and whined in terrible warning of their anger. Soft, sibilant and far off. Not owls. Not nightingales. But dread, reptilian birds of the night and nightmares. He lay on the wet earth fighting for air, his mouth agape in search of it, his eyes bulging for lack of it. Finding it only in short, shallow morsels that tortured and twisted his empty lungs as they demanded more. Enough to sustain his life before body fluids dribbled in to fill their empty sacs, destroying them . . . and him.

Rough fingers were gripping his nostrils, lips met his lips, and a hot soothing breath was forced into his throat. And again. More, give me more. If only there was enough for a laugh. Enough for him to say with simpering bravado, 'Oh Joe, you darling. I never knew you cared.'

'Lucky for you, you have a strong stomach,' the doctor said in the casualty ward.

'It's all those post mortems I used to attend,' Smith replied weakly.

'I was not referring to your morbid appetite, but to your abdominal musculature.' The doctor reproved him sharply. 'But for that, the post mortem would be on you.' Then with peculiar reluctance he added, 'And you don't scare easily, do you? A blow like that coming unexpectedly out of the dark could have terrified . . .' he hesitated, then brushed his speculations aside. 'Let us not indulge in unscientific speculation. I'll put your recovery down to timely mouth-to-mouth resuscitation.'

Smith gave Joe Potch a wan smile of gratitude. Potch shuffled his feet and almost blushed. 'I've still got my official halo,' he said lamely. 'Never used it in all my service. Now it comes twice in one night.'

'There is no internal damage as far as I can see from the X-rays,' the doctor went on. 'But soft tissue injury won't necessarily show. If you start coughing blood, or there are signs of it in your urine or faeces, come back and see me. Now get off home and stay in bed for the next two days. A little liquid, but nothing to eat for twenty-four hours and a light bland diet for the next three days.'

Joe Potch took his arm and helped him down from the examination table. 'Don't worry about him, Doc,' he said grimly. 'I'm the one who will be spitting blood.'

'It wasn't a vagal inhibition then, Norah Thornton?' Smith asked.

Potch's driver took the car towards Kennington at a sedate and considerate twenty-five.

'Not this time. It doesn't always come off. You should know,' Potch replied. 'But he didn't even try. Just took her jaw in one hand, the back of her neck in the other and jerked. Did the same with Maisie Ackroyd and Ma Scanlon by the look of them. Could be he gets a kick out of doing it that way on women. I'm in for a long hard night after I drop you off.'

'I am sorry, Joe.'

'You are going to be sorrier. Elstow won't be going to bed tonight either. Her, and quite a few others.'

Gingerly, Smith tried to ease the strapping over his abdomen and cringed at the touch.

'Hurts, does it?' Potch asked without sympathy.

'Like hell.'

'Good. Serves you right for mixing with the funny people. I'm stymied at every turn by the funny people. Obstructive bastards.'

'The Joe Potch I knew from PC to Detective Chief Super wouldn't be obstructed by an armoured division. If that Joe Potch met obstruction; he went round it, over it, or through it. Now you are a Commander you've become circumspect.'

'Like fucking hell, I have,' a derisive snort lent weight to his denial. Potch changed the subject. 'Nothing more comes to your mind about the geezer that put you down? God, I badly need something to work on.'

Smith said nothing about the weird and sinister sounds he had heard. Imagined he had heard? Instead, he simply enquired, 'Did they ever show you a picture, Joe? Those that apprised you. A picture of a running target. One that was to be housed but not hit?'

'Such as who?'

'You will have to ask them that apprise you, Joe. Them that warned you off me.'

'Bastards.'

'I agree. But I am grateful to them. I would hate to be waiting your convenience at Rochester Row. I know how constipated you can get. By the way, I met an admirer of yours in Wyldwood. Randolph Jenkins.'

'The poofter painter?'

Smith nodded. 'A shrewd judge, Joe. Reckons you're the Leonardo da Vinci of criminal investigation.'

'Yeah?' Potch smiled fondly. 'I was into pre-Raphaelites at the time. It's Expressionists now.'

'Buying or selling?'

'Don't try taking the piss, Owen. A bit of chat, that's all. These days we senior officers require a bit of chat, an aesthetic interest beyond the job, wide ranging, the broad outlook, the cultured copper. Some of these TV interviewers pull some right strokes to try and make us look like ignorant berks. Besides it can come in handy. There is a much better class of people committing murder these days.'

'And getting away with it, Joe.'

'Not on your Modigliani they're not.'

# Twelve

Hamilton stood aghast at the sight. Sir Desmond Rachette, riven by doubt and misgivings. His half-moon spectacles hung awry and unheeded on the end of his nose, teeth were clamped so fiercely into the barrel of his gold pen that Hamilton could almost see the indentations in the metal. His apology to Fairchild had approached the abject.

'I should have been told at the outset his price was Galahad. It was grossly improper of you to edit the tape.' Fairchild was unmoved.

'A surrender should be confined to the commanding general,' Rachette explained miserably. 'There was no need to blemish your impeccable record with the dishonour.'

'But I was deceived. Had I known, I'd have put men on Galahad. I would never have employed Smith, I would have made sure Potch's deferrals were protected. I wish to God I'd realized this post demanded human sacrifice before I accepted it.'

Removing the pen from his mouth and adjusting his spectacles, Rachette visibly summoned reserves of strength.

'Galahad is perfectly capable of looking after himself,' he said, though his voice was strained. 'The risk was explained. He was an unfilled contract. He knew that. His adversary wanted him out of Wyldwood. Obviously he did not regard killing him inside a mental institution as compatible with his sense of honour.'

'Honour! For Christ's sake. Is it honourable to kill three women? To cut the tongue out of a man's head?'

'Hamilton!' Rachette pointed at the door.

'No, Hamilton remains.' Fairchild thrust his unwilling aide, now doubling as liaison officer, back into his chair. 'I insist on a witness being present. My God, with four dead and Smith nearly a fifth, just because of some lousy cabinet papers!' His incredulity verged on panic, and as if in recognition of that, he lapsed into cynical despair. 'It might not be so bad, were it not that in another five or six years some money-grubbing minister will have them spread over the Sunday papers in his memoirs.'

'Not if the Act is still in being,' Rachette replied in suddenly realized horror. 'There are cabinet papers and cabinet papers. Besides,' his alarm subsided. 'If precedent is anything to go by, ex-ministers only reveal those matters which show them in the heroic mould. Struggling against the pressure, the wiles and cunning of less altruistic colleagues. All they are concerned about, by then, is posterity. In the present instance, none would be placed in the sarcophagus of history smelling of roses however much myrrh and frankincense they stuffed in their guts.'

Fairchild sank into his chair, suddenly exhausted. Rachette took full advantage. 'If we can ameliorate our respective attitudes and regain emotional control, perhaps we can review these tragic events in a clearer light.' He took Fairchild's sullen silence as indicating consent.

'Now, whilst I may have expedited Galahad's release to meet the demand, I would have done so in any case, had some other price been exacted. Who better than Galahad to deal with his old adversary? We kept nothing from him, did we, Hamilton?'

The man is becoming more political by the minute, Fairchild thought, relying on a repetition of dogma and subservient reassurance.

'Not a thing, sir,' Hamilton was mouthing obediently. 'As soon as I told him Hamme wanted him out only to kill him, he accepted the challenge more than willingly.' Hamilton ran a finger round the inside of his collar as though it restricted his enthusiasm. 'More than willingly, I would say. Eagerly. Desperately eager.'

'There, you see!' Rachette made no attempt to reflect Hamilton's childish zeal, but confirmed it nonetheless. 'The volunteer charging the machiné-gun nest. The pilot, ammunition exhausted, crashing into the enemy bomber. The –'

'The Kamikaze complex?' Fairchild interrupted.

'A man doing his best to serve his country,' Rachette countered primly. 'And as you now know, one who succeeded. We have now received the photographs Teasdale made of the cabinet papers as Hamme promised. In the accompanying tape Hamme apologizes for an inability to recover the original negatives. You both know what he said, "I will ensure you are not inconvenienced by it." Those were his words.' Rachette gathered himself together for an assault on his conscience.

'Whilst I will not deny possession of that degree of acumen and foresight consistent with my position and responsibilities, there was no way in which I could interpret these words as indicating an intention to murder the remaining persons who had a remote connection with the Aldwych affair and Teasdale's box.'

'But it is convenient, isn't it?' Fairchild complained bitterly.

'Only if the negatives are never found. Have not been seen by other eyes. In that regard we can wash our hands of the unfortunate Inspector Worple, who obligingly did away with himself.' Having laid Worple to rest, Rachette, with priestly solemnity, entered the pulpit of his faith to preach its creed as he saw it.

'We are bound to serve and protect our political masters at whichever end of the spectrum their colours fly. We are the providers and the keepers of their secrets. If they in return show us scant regard, and even at times unwarranted contumely, we must remember it is no more than political braggadocio for public consumption. The reality is, they fear us. For we can, if we wish, destroy them. We do not destroy them because we know others from the same shallow counterfeit mould would replace them. The self-deluding crypto-communists of the 'thirties who carried their juvenile delusions into manhood thought they could do it on a permanent ideological basis from within. They failed, thank God.

Not because the cant, the hypocrisy, the greasy compromise, the unending string of half-truths and half-lies that passes for late twentieth-century democracy, survived in spite of them. It survived because of them. Had they not existed, they would have been invented. Perhaps they were. Otherwise this battered hulk, this leaking sieve we call parliamentary democracy, would have foundered years ago in the clean honest seas of simple straightforward class warfare. Who would have won? It would not have mattered to us. We would continue to function. A civil servant does not do what he has to do out of devotion to his political masters. That is an aberrant and easily transferable emotion. He does it because it is his *function*. His professional *function*. To work as dispassionately, efficiently, and as *quietly* as a Rolls-Royce engine. We allow the politicians to ride up front whilst we remain hidden under the bonnet, or sit anonymously behind the wheel. We may allow them to think we are taking them in the direction they wish to go, but we could not allow them to drive. Rolls-Royces are much too expensive for that.'

Flushed slightly, as if embarrassed at being forced into an open declaration of faith, Rachette reached for his carafe and poured himself a glass of water. He sipped at length, not greedily, as if only to stifle a sudden flame, not extinguish a smouldering fire. Giving the ensuing silence time to peak, he spoke again.

'I believe I mentioned some time ago, that in Hamme we are dealing with a man of honour. No...' he held up a hand to stifle Fairchild's rising protest. 'I will withdraw that in the circumstances.'

'I am glad to hear it,' Fairchild said with some relief.

'Nevertheless, he is a man who recognizes an obligation to fulfil his side of a...' Rachette reared away from 'bargain' with distaste, 'his side of an agreement,' he continued hastily.

'Like a good civil servant?' Fairchild suggested, acidly unrepentant.

'Precisely,' Rachette accepted the comparison with pleasure. 'He failed to recover the negatives, therefore he was obliged, within the terms of his self-imposed remit, to put forward the next best case. That was to destroy those who might have knowledge of their substance. He chose to demonstrate the fact, albeit in rather grisly fashion, by cutting out the tongue of the unfortunate Mr Lomax.'

It was the language of official public penitence, as Fairchild recognized. This sad tragedy . . . This regrettable incident . . . This unfortunate error . . . Lamentation without tears. Remorse without contrition.

'Nevertheless he reneged on the deal,' Fairchild came to life. 'Your deal,' he added viciously. 'Therefore we are entitled to bring Castellain – I mean Galahad – to bring him in out of harm's way. There is no point leaving him in the line now.'

'I do not agree. In any case, Galahad does not want to be brought in. Does he, Hamilton? You saw him last, when was that again?'

'Two days ago,' Hamilton rushed into the role of honest broker. 'At our house in Swiss Cottage. Gave him a full brief . . .'

'Did you sort out the name with him as I asked? Hammel, Hamme or Hameh? Which is it?'

'I'm afraid he chose to be ambiguous, sir. In fact, he never even mentioned his name. He said, whatever the name it would still smell as sweetly as death. An oblique reference to . . .'

'The reference, however oblique, has not escaped me. Very well, we will stick to Hamme. Let us not further confuse our nominals with Islamic connotations.'

'I agree, sir. In Galahad's opinion, he'll return to the East. "That will be the killing ground," he said.'

'Croydon, Sydenham, Blackheath, Camberwell and Battersea don't count, I suppose,' Fairchild interjected. 'Our train of thought will no longer stop at these stations,' he added bitterly.

'What has Galahad in mind?' Rachette pressed on, ignoring the gibes.

'He intends to go to Vienna, to renew old contacts. Pick up the tracks. He's sure the brute will trail his coat. Deliberately. Knowing Galahad will take up the challenge. Will want to produce irrefutable evidence on home ground that he has at last fulfilled his contract.'

Fairchild moaned quietly. 'How much simpler life would be if Galahad had contented himself with gratifying his wife's lusts, instead of rendering himself impotent in the service of his country. Or had simply gone to bed with her and got himself decently shot, even if he couldn't fuck her.'

'I don't think coarseness will help us,' the reproach from Rachette was wreathed in a smile of victory. He turned it on Hamilton.

'You did nothing to encourage him in this, I trust. We cannot sanction his intentions officially.'

'Well, I did pass him the West German and Swiss passports we had laid on for his benefit. Together with the funding.'

For all Rachette's remonstrances, his 'oh dear, oh dear, oh dear,' and his consequent tuts of annoyance, Fairchild could see they lacked venom or even reproof.

'They were contingency measures, Hamilton. Issuable only on authority from Fairchild or myself. I thought I made that clear.'

Like hell you did, Fairchild said to himself.

'I must say, sir, I thought the decision lay with Galahad. I'm awfully sorry.' Hamilton even bent his head.

'No matter. We can put him off, can't we?'

'I tried the Swiss Cottage house this morning. No answer. I'll put up smoke signals, if you wish, sir.'

'Yes, you had better. Make sure there is a clear record.'

'Has Galahad any ideas on Slunchev?' enquired Fairchild, wearying of the fire-proofing.

'A front man, a tool, a spreader of the given word. He confirms Smith's conclusions on his interview of the Ackroyd woman. Hamme is running Slunchev. Not the other way round.'

'You told him about Smith?'

'Naturally,' Hamilton said, his eyes flickering to Rachette to show where his loyalty lay. 'He was quite pleased. Thinks Smith is a good man. "Good" meaning enterprising, competent and capable,' he added, emulating his master.

'I think we can safely sever all links with Galahad and Smith as of now,' Rachette made his closing summation. 'As far as Galahad is concerned, he is off on a private and personal vendetta. It would not be inappropriate to say he is in every sense a freelance. If we can, we will dissuade him from continuing his quest, but if he has already set out, we can only wish him God speed. May he find and destroy his dragon. As for Smith, I think a month's pay and a warm handshake will suffice. Possibly we might find him a secure niche in one of our defence establishments where he can hold the bridge against CND and other disturbers of the peace. Let him know, will you, Fairchild? Services appreciated – but no longer required.'

Does madness have a gestation period, Fairchild wondered. Do the causes – stress, strain – or whatever, mate in a healthy mind, and swell into a malignant foetus driving out reason? Or is it simply a question of electricity? Short circuits, blown fuses, bare wires? Had all the faults in Smith and Castellain been properly repaired ... or were they merely bandaged? Held together with insulating tape? Who was he to know. There was no wall around his madhouse.


Owen awoke struggling against the leaden weight of the painkilling drugs the doctor insisted he take. Slowly turning his head he saw that Elstow's pillow was undisturbed, and was not greatly concerned. With all that had happened, they would be at it all day and night. The bedside clock showed two-forty in the afternoon. For a time he lay thinking how it could best be done. There would have to be concessions to pride and courage. To sheer cussedness. To affection? Love?

As he sought a solution, he heard what might have been a slight sound. It might only have been an instinctive realization, an intangible static in the silence. But he was certain someone was in the flat – in the living-room.

Getting out of bed was not easy, the pain and the stiffness round his middle made it difficult to move. But once on his feet he felt happier. Whatever was coming to him was not going to come to him in bed. Then he heard her call.

'Are you awake, Owen?' The sound of her voice brought no relief. He dressed with difficulty. What he had to do could not be decently done in a dressing-gown.

The suitcase was back in the middle of the floor when he entered. Marion Elstow, in her street clothes, was sitting disconsolately at the table, the whisky bottle and a single glass in front of her. He knew she hadn't touched a drop. He had an eye for the level in a bottle of Scotch, with all the whisky ponces who used to drop in on him when he was in the Job.

'Pour me one while you're at it,' he said, his gaze carefully avoiding the suitcase.

She refused flatly. 'From now on, you do things for yourself. I'm pulling out, Owen, I could have left an hour ago, but I wanted to tell you to your face.' The whisky was only for him. Treatment for shock. He rejected it.

'Nice of you,' he said. 'Decent of you. But why?'

She shook her head wearily as if too tired to resurrect the fierce, frightening words that had raged within her. 'Morality, I suppose,' she said eventually.

'Obviously not the sort you can buy with a certificate?' He tried to be helpful. Kind.

'Not mine. Yours,' she flashed at him. 'On your recent lack of it. I always regarded you as a moral man, Owen. Not righteous, but moral. I tell you this, the day you took up with those people you are with now, you hung your morality on a hook like an old coat.'

'I've had that Crombie in the wardrobe ten years. I take it out every winter, but I'd look pretty silly wearing it in this weather,' he said, trying to make a joke of it.

'Don't be so damnably smug. Four people are dead because...' She softened it for him, and he resented it as he resented all unsought favours. 'Maybe, not because of you personally,' she went on. 'But certainly because of the people you are working for.'

'You can put the four of them down to me. Five – if you want to include Frank Worple.'

'Does *he* matter?' she said, with all the scorn a straight cop has for the bent one. 'I'm talking about our deferrals. The ones we were biding our time with. Waiting for a little leverage. You barge straight in and they wind up dead.' There was no mercy for him now. 'I can't afford to be seen talking to you, Owen. Let alone living with you.'

'I know that. I agree with you.'

It was an inescapable professional truth, he should have

realized that. Nothing was required of him. No subterfuge. No deceit. It was inevitable. Although in a feminine sort of way, she seemed hurt by his lack of endeavour. His failure to offer any rebuttal in his own defence.

'You understand then? Why I must leave you?'

'Yes, I do.'

With gentle firmness he prevented her reaching down for the case, and concealing the pain, picked it up himself and silently opened the door. Down in the street, he slid the case inside her car. For a long moment they stood close, looking at one another, then he kissed her softly on the cheek.

'You *do* understand?' She sought his assurance, his forgiveness.

'If I were still in the Job, I'd do the same. If things were the other way round.'

She nodded sadly, got in behind the wheel and drove away. The street was empty again, and he was glad to see the going of her. She had made it easy for him, or maybe he had made it easy for her. Either way, it did not matter. The main thing was, he would not come home and find her lying on the floor with her neck broken or her tongue cut out. He had been touched by him who made death a contagious disease and now he was a carrier. The pain in his guts grew more intense. The effect of the drug was wearing off. Removing the tiny gold skull from his pocket, he returned its blazing red stare with icy anger. 'You bastard,' he spat at it. Not to it. At it. At what it represented. Things he did not know. Didn't want to know?

He could hear the phone ringing in the flat and even though he mounted the stairs slowly, indifferent to its summons, the clamour still persisted as he entered the room.

Barker wanted another meet. Urgent and important. Immediate upon receipt of transmission. Place and directions given. Please acknowledge by repeating BARKER.

He drew out a long sneering reply. 'Bollocks.' His voice clearly indicated an arrogant, contemptuous refusal.

# Thirteen

• • • • • • • • •

'He's on rehab parole again, ain't he,' Quinlan had whined enviously when he commented on Castellain's absence. 'Well in with some bleedin' farmer, he is. Them's the ones that's got all the pull these days, them that's got bleedin' farms,' Quinlan had gone on, his malice certain and assured. 'All them big politicians? All of them's got farms. Labour, Tory, Liberals; it don't matter, they've all got farms. That's where all the pull is these days. Down on the bleedin' farm.'

'How do you know he goes to a farm?' Smith had enquired, stirred by a vestige of curiosity.

'Seen it on his parole licence, ain't I,' Quinlan spoke with crafty pride. 'Left it on his locker while he was having a shower. Amla Farm, Natching, Kent. Maybe they're do-gooders who takes in the likes of us. I was thinkin' of writin' them. See if they'd put in a word for me. Get me out on parole maybe.'

'If you think it's worth the risk of trespassing on Castellain's domain, go right ahead,' he had advised, losing interest. Quinlan made no immediate reply, had just sat there, shivering slightly. Finally, he said: 'It's that old bugger, Peachtree. He must know dozens of farmers. He's got all the pull. I'll get to work on him.'

'Peachtree can't even get himself out on parole.'

'Don't want it, do he? King of the bleedin' castle in here, ain't he? Happy as a pig in shit. That don't mean he don't have pull. Look at all them petitions he writes for anybody who will bung him a few bob.'

He could have told Quinlan no one took any notice of petitions, especially those composed inside a nut factory, but could not be bothered. He was on his feet and running. Intent on getting his time down to one hour thirty.

Beyond Maidstone, he turned away from the main road and headed south-west into a maze of country lanes, following signposts that read Nettleside, Yalding and Mockbeggar, then off into even narrower lanes where after the third unposted crossroad he had to admit he was lost. To his right, the road curled away steeply. At the bottom, a man on a bicycle raised himself out of the saddle to pedal strenuously against the slope. After a few yards he dismounted in defeat, reduced to pushing awkwardly uphill. Smith pulled alongside and saw it was a postman, sweating unhappily. 'Bloody vans break down an' we 'as to push bloody bikes,' the postman complained. 'An you're bloody lorst, I suppose?'

Smith nodded, 'Amla Farm. Know it?'

The postman halted, scratched the tip of his nose and eyed him speculatively through the car window. Smith knew he was being sized up. Assessed.

'Don't live there, does you.' It was a statement of known fact, not enquiry.

'Just visiting.'

'Ah. Knows them, does you? The Dugdales?'

'I'm an old friend of Mr Castellain.' There was a chance the name might mean something. A chance of background information. Bunce. Something for nothing. Fairchild had been singularly uninformative about Castellain's antecedents prior to the killing of his wife in Vienna. 'I've told you more than I should already,' he snapped angrily. 'And that only to give you an idea of the man's character and value.' Somehow he got the impression that his own character and value did not amount to much in comparison.

'Ah, her brother, back from foreign parts. Right sparky lad, he is. Ain't seen much of him in recent times?' There was a demand to enhance the quality and quantity of the postman's sources of local gossip.

'He has to visit the continent a lot these days,' Smith replied. 'Export business.'

'Export or die they used to tell us. Just arter the war,' the postman confided. 'Still at it, they is. Export or die. Bloody guv'mints. Wants to export them, they does. Maybe leave us in peace then.' The postman bent down to inspect him more closely. 'Got a letter for Mr Castellain,' he confided.

'Oh, yes.'

'Got a few other pieces for Amla Farm as well.'

'I would give you a lift,' Smith said reluctantly. 'But you'd have to leave the bike. And I'm sorry, I wouldn't be able to bring you back. I've got to go on to Tunbridge Wells afterwards, and I'm late as it is.' He presented temptation and rejection with solemn indifference.

'You could drop them in for me!' the postman whined, alarmed at the possibility of an unctuous refusal.

'Would it be all right?'

'Course it would. You is a friend of the family, ain't you!' he thrust the mail into Smith's hands. 'You go straight on over the top of the hill for a mile or so. Turn left an' four hundred yards on your right there's a green metal gate. That's Amla Farm.'

The postman swung his bike round, and remounted with a pleasurable smile on his face at the prospect of freewheeling downhill. Smith drove on until he reached a wooded clearing where he could pull off the road. There, he examined the bunce. For Jerome Dugdale, Esq. were subscription copies of *New Society* and *The Farmers Weekly*, two obvious circulars and a private letter. To Mrs Ziah Dugdale the *Middle East Review*, *The Arab News*, *Horse and Hound*, and four personal letters. Postal evidence of matrimonial dichotomy? Smith wondered. Then he turned over the letter to Castellain.

The handwriting hit him like a hammer blow. The florid loops, the continental configuration of the lettering. It all appeared so familiar. He brought out the application form supplied by a certain snot-nosed git for the hire of the Mercedes from Emperor Motors. The handwriting of the applicant was identical. The address given had been a stumer, the driving licence produced a forgery. But the handwriting here and on the letter addressed to V. Castellain was identical. What the Hell? What the flaming fucking fires of Hell was going on? The envelope carried four stamps of low denomination as though the sender had to scratch round to make up the postage. Nothing on the back to identify the sender. Post marked 'Giffnock.' Giffnock two days ago. Where the hell was Giffnock? At least it had UK stamps.

For a time he sat thinking about it, but it did not take him long to make up his mind. Sight of an empty beer can convinced him fate was on his side. There was water in the ditch and plenty of dry twigs lying about. As he waited for the water to boil, his mind returned to Wyldwood.

'That is simply not done!' Peachtree had awakened to find Quinlan in possesson of his brief. It had as usual fallen from his lap and there was Quinlan thumbing through the pages with bored disinterest.

'Return it to me this instant!' What was meant to be a thunderous command, full of judicial majesty, issued as an aged croak. Deceptively meek, Quinlan presented the papers to Peachtree, only to snatch them away as Peachtree held out an imperious hand. Again and again they were offered, only to be snatched back. Peachtree resorted to gentlemanly disdain.

'Really Quinlan, I have tried to instil in you some semblance of social grace, yet you persist in behaving like a guttersnipe. You must understand these are confidential documents between an advocate and his instructing solicitors. A person of breeding would no more read them, than he would read another's mail.'

'I ain't read them,' Quinlan sneered. 'Can't make bleedin' head nor tail of them.' Teasingly, he offered them again, but Peachtree, wiser now, sat dignified and aloof.

'Then I'll tear the bleedin' lot up,' Quinlan threatened.

'That would be wanton destruction!' Visibly alarmed, Peachtree turned imploringly to Smith for assistance. Manic now, with unsimulated rage Quinlan clutched the papers in his fists to demonstrate an ability to fulfil his threat. It would have to be a waiting game, Smith decided, and shrugged his rejection.

'It is most unfair,' Peachtree wailed piteously.

'Unfair!' Quinlan screamed his derision. 'For weeks you've been promising to get me a parole sponsor. You've had me runnin' round like a blue-arsed fly for you. "Fetch me this, Quinlan." "Bring me that, Quinlan." Where's me bleedin' sponsor, then? I'm sick of bleedin' waiting.'

'It is not easy, Quinlan,' Peachtree tried magisterial patience. 'I am still endeavouring to convince the Whites you are suitable for parole. I assure you I have made out a very strong case, but it does take time.'

'And you talk to me about being fair!' Quinlan shrieked.

'Reading other peoples' correspondence is grossly unfair,' Peachtree countered with still greater solemnity.

'Did you ever hear the story about the Nubian Prince and the ancient Romans?' Suddenly and quietly lucid, Quinlan posed a wildly tangential question. Peachtree considered it deeply.

'Is it a matter of Roman law?' he enquired with aroused interest. 'I am an authority on Roman law.'

'Then this should be right up your street.' For all his present calmness, Quinlan retained a firm grip on Peachtree's precious brief, before launching into his story.

'There was this Nubian Prince who lived in Africa,' he explained. 'Back in them days when them ancient Romans were conquering all over the place. But they couldn't conquer this Nubian Prince, see. Every time they comes up against him and his tribe, they knock skittles of shit out of 'em. But there comes a time when the Romans piles in everythin' they got against the Nubian Prince. Thousands and thousands of 'em go in on him until they wear him down and capture him. What do they do with him? They drags him off to Rome all bound up and weighed down in chains, don't they. Then they drags him through the streets to that circus of theirs. That Colosseum place. And all the Romans come from miles around to see the Nubian Prince get what's comin' to him. Know what they do? They digs a bleedin' hole in the middle of the arena, then they sticks him in and buries him up to his neck in the ground. There he is with just his head stickin' up out of the ground and his bleedin' great white choppers gleamin' in the sun as he yells his defiance at the crowd. They all got great white choppers, them blackies, you noticed? Any old how, into the arena they lets loose this hungry lion. This bleedin' lion goes poundin' and leapin' around lookin' for somethin' to eat. Well, it would, wouldn't it? Stands to reason. All of a sudden, it spots the head of the Nubian Prince stickin' out of the ground, and with no more ado it goes boundin' and leapin' across the arena. Goin' like the clappers it was. Definitely determined to have the head off that Nubian Prince in one lump. Know what he does, that Nubian Prince? He jerks his neck to one side and the lion goes skiddin' over his head. Know what he does then? He waits till the lion has slid nearly right over the top of him, then he opens his mouth and with one great bite of his great white choppers he bites that lion's bleedin' bollocks right off...

'Well, there is a right carry on, I can tell you. There's that lion writhin' in agony all over the arena. The mob up in the terraces is doin' their nuts, hootin' and booin'. Up in the Royal Box, the Roman Emperor is doin' his pieces. Shoutin' and yellin' all over the place. Know what he was shoutin' and yellin'? He was shoutin' and yellin', "Fight fair, you black bastard. Fight fair!"

'So,' Quinlan concluded, looking meaningfully at Peachtree. 'You goin' to find me a parole sponsor or not?' Then he placed Peachtree's brief between his teeth and with a hand on either side drew the papers taut and waited for an answer.

It was, Smith conceded, as he eased the envelope open, grossly unfair to read another person's correspondence. More than that, in these circumstances it was unlawful. But then killing people was unfair; and also unlawful. Unfolding the letter, he saw the contents were written in German. The odd word here and there, within the limits of his smattering, stood out. But complete, intelligible translation was beyond him. He was right up that well-known creek, as Fairchild had pointed out. Still, time, he hoped, was on his side.

Twenty minutes later he was back in Maidstone and had

found a printer who ran a side line in photocopies at ten pence a time. He invested forty pence on two copies of the envelope and letter. A pot of paste, separately purchased, cost him sixty-five pence, and he spent a while carefully resealing Castellain's letter. Well-knowing that if it is a simple matter to steam a letter open, it is difficult to reseal one without making it obvious that it has been done. When satisfied with his handiwork, he returned to Amla Farm.

An estate agent could, for once, with justifiable hyperbole, describe the property as a magnificently thatched sixteenth-century farmhouse, superbly placed in an attractive rural setting, fronting a delightfully meandering stream. Stable block with garaging discreetly located at the rear.

The woman who answered the door matched her domicile.

August, was the word that came to Smith's mind, then uncertain if that description could be applied in the feminine gender, changed it to Junoesque. Tall, stately and erect, just like Nurse Edith, he thought. Elderly, but showing the vigour and bloom of a more youthful woman, she took the mail from him, her imperious frown evidencing displeasure at the presumption of his trespass and the frailty of his explanations.

'You are a friend of ... Vernon's?' Momentary hesitation suggested such intimate use of his given name rarely passed beyond the immediate family. He was on his way to Tunbridge Wells, he told her. Happened to be passing. He and ... Mr Castellain ... had been patients together in the ... hospital?

'You mean in the looney bin,' she snapped, with the piercing frankness of the educated and dominant middle-class female.

'We were a couple of right old nutters together,' Smith agreed amiably.

'You'd better come in,' she said, more in the way of an order than invitation. She led him through to a low beamed parlour. Embroidered cushions. Sheraton and Hepplewhite gleaming in antique splendour. 'Are you after money?' she enquired in a matter of fact way. 'If you are, you're out of luck. We have none in the house.'

'I could always lend you a few quid if you are hard pressed,' he replied willingly.

'Or make me an offer for the writing-table or the walnut bureau?'

'I couldn't go that far. I'm strictly into Scandinavian modern myself. The cheaper the better.'

'Your name really is Smith, then? You are not another of those foul antique dealers from Brighton?'

'No, but I would consider your price on the gun you're holding.'

She removed it slowly from the pocket at the front of her sensible tweed skirt. Like everything else in the room it was a period piece. A Remington Derringer. The snub, superimposed barrels pointing into his belly. The hammer was drawn and fully cocked. He knew they no longer made the heavy .41 calibre bullets the weapon required, but then she seemed capable of making her own.

'I would be careful with that thing,' he tried to sound casual. 'Some of them came with hair triggers.'

'That's right, they did,' she replied cheerfully. 'When they were first introduced over here they sold for three pounds each or five pounds seventeen and sixpence the pair. What's your offer?'

'Peace in our time.'

'Unconditional surrender?'

He placed his hands on top of his head.

'Who are you really, and what are you after? You are too damned ... composed ... to be another mental case on the loose. Are you really connected with my brother's business?'

He lowered his hands. 'I'm handling the home market,' he said. Relief made him reach into his pocket and bring out the miniature gold skull. He caressed the top of it with his thumb, a habit he had unconsciously developed of late.

'Oh Lord,' she groaned disgustedly. 'What children you men are.' He held it out in the palm of his hand.

'You've seen this before?'

'While I am certain Vernon would never indulge in such melodramatic nonsense, it is, I presume a recognition signal of some kind. That ostentatious idiot, Henry Teasdale, used to wear one on his watch chain. I will never understand this masculine predeliction for insignia and talismans.'

'You knew Henry?'

'He called on us a few times, when Vernon had his illness. The obligatory visit to the next-of-kin. Presumptuous buffer. Tried to tell me my Charles the Second chest was a Victorian reproduction.' She indicated a long, low, coarsely carved, but age-darkened box that lay like a coffin along one wall. 'Been in the family since 1665,' she snorted. 'Got the inventory to prove it.' Smith studied it obediently, but offered no opinion.

'Henry didn't wear his on a bracelet?' he asked.

'Wear his what on a bracelet?'

'His ... talisman.'

'Heavens, no. I said the man was ostentatious. Not that he was effeminate.'

Yes, Smith mused to himself. A little bit of off-duty ostentation. But when on active service, camouflaged among the other baubles. If discovered by the enemy – if explanations were required? Present for the wife, you know. A little hedge in gold against inflation. You know what it is like in the West, Comrade.

'Now what exactly do you wish to see my brother about?'

'Obviously he's not at home?'

'He may well be. But he's not *here*. This is not *his* home. This is a place he uses to suit his personal convenience. A privilege unlikely to be extended, if my husband has any say in the matter.'

Smith resisted a strong temptation to openly doubt the extent of her husband's say in the matter. She still had that damned Derringer in her hand. Could it really be loaded? The problem only increased the dull ache in his abdomen.

'The office is rather anxious to contact him,' he said, launching a tentative kite.

'Then let the office find him. I haven't seen or heard from him for over a week. If you tell me where the office is, I'll be glad to forward his mail.' Smith followed her gaze to the mantelpiece. Nestling behind a carriage clock, no doubt French eighteenth century, were at least two other letters. On the top one, he could just see the exaggerated continental 'A' of what, presumably, was the Amla address. The same hand as on the envelope he had given Ziah Dugdale on arrival. He resisted a strong temptation to suggest he would ensure they got to him. But he could see she still had suspicions he was no gentleman. He was a mere *person,* one who might read a gentleman's correspondence. Leave it up to her, he decided.

'I'm afraid I am not permitted to divulge the location,' he confessed regretfully.

'Oh, don't let it concern you,' she replied airily. 'I worked for the Service myself during the war at GHQ Cairo. Know the rules. As someone or other said – rules are made for the blind obedience of fools and the guidance of wise men. Most of them were fools then. They probably still are.' With some relief he saw her lower the hammer on the Derringer and replace it in her pocket.

'Well, unless you want to leave a message...' She moved towards the door.

'Tell him to watch out for Mr Hameh,' he said quietly.

She stiffened perceptibly, and for the first time he saw the scars of time on her face. 'Please repeat that name,' she ordered. None of her authority had been lost in the process.

'Hameh, H-A-M-E-H. Some think it is Hamme, H-A-M-M-E.'

'The first is correct. How did you come to hear of the Hameh?'

*The* Hameh? He began slowly, 'From your brother. We really were together in Wyldwood. I was a police officer with a problem, similar in some way to your brother's. At least as to cause. He once asked me if I knew of a great avenger called Hameh.'

'And what has that to do with anything concerning my brother at the present time?'

'I wanted to be certain he was aware of recent happenings.'

'Recent *public* happenings?'

'Front page. All the headlines.'

'But they were criminals, or the women of criminals. You are not suggesting Vernon would be associated with criminals. Preposterous!'

'We know Hameh killed them. He may be after Vernon.'

She sank into a chair. 'Not he – it,' she said.

'It?'

'A bird. The Hameh is a bird. A mythological bird.'

'Could you tell me more?' he asked politely.

'Any definitive work on Arab history should contain a reference. It is a variation on the Phoenix, I suppose. Legend has it the Hameh bird arises from the blood and brains of a murdered corpse. It takes to the air seeking revenge on the murderers. According to legend, the Hameh utters a long-drawn-out sobbing cry – *Is-koo'nee* – *Is-koo'nee*. In rough translation that means "Give me blood to drink." The blood of the murderers. The Hameh never rests until it has fully satiated its lust for vengeance.' Smith marvelled at the change in her. She spoke with the soft clarity of a mother telling her child a bedtime story. One of the nastier fairy tales.

'Then how...' he began, before she shushed him into silence.

'Shortly before the war,' she continued, 'Father was killed by brigands in southern Arabia. Father had the spiritual strength to grant the world a presumption of innocence. That was his one weakness. You will have observed, I do not take after him. Neither does Vernon, though Vernon always had an indelibly romantic streak in him. He was with the expedition when Father was· killed, but was at base camp when it happened. Father was out in the desert alone, some distance away. When his murder was discovered, his retainers set out to track down the killers, taking Vernon with them. They were, of course, entirely motivated, not by a desire to avenge Father's death, but to recover the money he carried with him. Otherwise they would not be paid. Later, they put out a tale that Vernon had led them in pursuit of the brigands and had summarily ordered their execution. Absolute tosh. He was little more than a child at the time. After they returned Vernon to our people in Aden, the retainers were themselves killed in blood feud with the families of the brigands. They were found with their tongues cut out. Not at all uncommon in that part of the world in those days. Bullets were expensive then, they did not come as free gifts from Russia or the United States as they do today.'

Scathingly, she declared her aversion to the despoliation of

Arab culture by the great powers.

'How did the Hameh come into it?' Smith enquired gently, to disguise the turmoil in his mind.

'Some superstitious servant in the Governor General's house, where they had taken Vernon in, foolishly told him the Hameh had sought out and killed Father's retainers for what they had done to the brigands. They had beheaded them, I believe. The servant told Vernon the Hameh would be seeking him next.'

'Frightened him badly, I should imagine,' Smith suggested.

'Certainly not!' The idea appalled her. 'He was, not unnaturally, disturbed by the whole experience, but frightened? Ludicrous! Why, a few days after he came home one of the labourers found him in the copse one night, four-ten shotgun in hand. He was looking for the Hameh, he told him. Going to kill the Hameh before it killed him. Would he act in that way if he was frightened?'

'Indeed no,' Smith agreed vehemently. 'Brave little chap,' he felt obliged to add.

'Why the dickens am I telling you all this?' she was saying to him, puzzled and annoyed with herself.

'Perhaps you *are* somewhat concerned about Vernon,' he replied. 'And perhaps because you see the policeman in me. It's the sort of thing people tell policemen. Is that why you carry the Derringer? Because you're concerned about Vernon?'

'Don't be ridiculous!' He had been wondering if she would get round to the ridiculous. 'I carry the gun when alone in the house. My husband is working the lower meadow at the moment. You policemen do virtually nothing to protect people who are left alone.'

'They say it's because of social and economic conditions . . . Do you expect Vernon to return in the near future?'

'Vernon calls or does not call, as he pleases.'

Even when he was staying with you on parole, he wanted to ask but didn't; being a strong believer in never pushing his luck.

'What is he up to at the moment, in any case?' Her curiosity escaped reluctantly.

'I really have no idea,' he replied honestly.

'He's gone to work for *them* again.'

'I really wouldn't know,' he lied.

'If only he hadn't married that Austrian whore.' The malice ill became her. Smith wondered how often she had been left alone of late. She had seen him as a diversion, a challenge to enliven the otherwise mundane world of home and garden. It could well be some of the nasty and aggressive dealers from the arse end of the antique game had paid her a visit. Tried to put the frighteners on. He wondered what they thought when they got the Derringer shoved in their faces. It would have been a big day for her. She'd be waiting for the next one. All you need to know, Fairchild had said, is that Castellain comes from a warrior clan. Combat and culture go hand in hand with that lot. Even St Francis of Assisi killed a few people before he started talking to the birds. Birds? I believe you are familiar with the chirruping of birds, Mr Smith, that clown at the BBC had sneered? *Is-koo'nee*. Give me blood to drink. Bernie Lomax! He got his fill of it.

'I'll tell Vernon you called, Mr Smith.' She was on her feet again, her hand in the pocket of her skirt. It was chucking-out time, he realized. 'I don't think you need unduly concern yourself about Vernon. He is more than capable of looking after himself. We both are.' Her smile told him not to bother to come back. He returned it compliantly, but at the doorstep could not resist a further question.

'By the way,' he said. 'Is that Derringer really loaded?'

The movement was swift but controlled. Six feet away, an empty flower pot standing on a low wall flew into shards of clay.

With ears still ringing from the sound of the shot, Smith turned to his car, glad to have brought a little pleasure into what would have been an otherwise boring day for Mrs Ziah Dugdale, née Castellain.

Ploughing back and forth through a German–English dictionary, it took longer than he anticipated to arrive at a reasonable translation of the copied contents of the letter meant for Castellain. It carried no sender's address or greeting to the intended recipient, but it was signed 'KLINGE' and dated two days previously. When he had completed his work, the letter read:

Three occasions I have been to agreed RV. You do not appear there or at alternatives. At the post office I find no communications. Am I abandoned? Yet I feel eyes on me. Of yours? Of mine? Of the great enemy who I have not seen? I do not know. All seek me. From fear I ran North. First to Doncaster, then to Manchester, now to a suburb near Glasgow in Scotland. Against all rules I write you four times directly to RV in these towns. From you nothing. I read of serious phenomena in the papers. Your enemy haunts our every step. Have you fallen? Do I write to a ghost? Is the product which was to enlarge my esteem still in his hands? It matters little now. Your people have marked my door. Slandered me as thief and defector. I cannot enter without the product, for the lie is believed. Did you intend it thus to be? No, not after all we achieved during the good years. I impugn your honour and apologize profoundly. You see how I am compelled to write in desperation. Tomorrow I go to VZ to remove what I gained from the days of yesteryear. I have finally decided to cross the line but first I must bring out my wife and children before I go over. To the French? To the Amis? It is of little difference. But I will not go to your people. They betray me. I need the help of your old network to bring over my family. I call upon your help. I beseech you. If you live, RV in VZ. I will remain there five days.

Klinge

Three times Smith went over the pages, transposing here, inserting there, always uncertain as to the accuracy of his interpretation. There could be hidden meanings. *Nuances*. How was he to know? He fondled the skull between finger and thumb. The habit had gripped him over the past few days. Ever since Elstow had left. Forget Elstow. Klinge? Look up Klinge. A blade – of sword or knife. Blade! There was a name for a secret agent! No, a spy! Theirs were dirty spies. Ours were gallant secret agents.

For some considerable time, he sat fondling the skull. Then gazing into its ruby eyes, he said to it, 'I think we've got to give this to Barker. No, not you old son, only the letter. If a fellah is entitled to anything, he's entitled to keep what he's got hidden inside his skull. Isn't he?' He winked at the ruby eyes, and thought a trick of the light gave him an appreciative reply. 'Do you fancy a run round the Royal Parks?' he asked it. 'St James's, Green Park, Hyde Park and Kensington Gardens? Find out if the old abdominal musculature is mending. Then back to the Guards Memorial to meet Mr Barker. That's a good place for us gallant secret agents to meet, somewhere between the public shithouse and the Guards Memorial.'

# Fourteen

Why they had called it the Swiss Cottage house, Fairchild could only guess. It was at the bottom end of Adelaide Road, much nearer to Chalk Farm. According to the inventory it had once been reasonably furnished, but, despite the mortice locks and the steel shutters inside the windows, the burglars had been in time and time again. Even the addition of a sonic alarm direct to the Information Room at Scotland Yard had made little difference. All that was left in the living-room was a couch, three arm-chairs, and a much-worn carpet on which stood a stained and gouged coffee table. A large ormolu mirror survived above the fireplace mainly, Fairchild thought, because no self-respecting thief would bother with it. A safe house? Good God!

Hamilton came down from the upstairs bedrooms.

'Has he left anything behind?' Fairchild enquired sardonically. 'A farewell latter? A condom under the pillow?'

'Clean as a whistle,' Hamilton replied cheerfully. 'Galahad always liked things neat and tidy.' He felt the chill in Fairchild's look. 'At least according to his file,' he added, to avoid the contamination of close personal relationship.

Rachette had insisted they meet at the Swiss Cottage house. Damned if he was going all the way in to Westminster from Hampstead on the one night in the week he placed at the disposal of his wife for a small dinner party and bridge afterwards. Are you quite sure this will not keep until morning? It is a question of national interest, Fairchild had replied with considerable flourish.

Somehow he was not surprised when Rachette appeared five minutes after they had arrived wearing a quilted velvet smoking jacket, stiff collar and black tie. On the one night a week he permitted his wife a bridge party, Rachette would certainly dress for dinner. Throwing himself into the least time-worn arm-chair, ignoring the others present, Rachette snapped an imperative 'Well then?' into a corner of the room. Instant decisions were about to be made ... It took somewhat longer than that.

'What an abominable person this man of yours is,' Rachette said, almost admiringly, but still curling a distasteful lip in Fairchild's direction. 'Inveigling his way into Ziah Dugdale's home like some sleazy bum bailiff,' he continued. 'What on earth made him go there in the first place? Did you authorize this?' he queried suspiciously.

'No. I did not. But I fully approve. Smith is a detective and Ziah Dugdale was a logical line of enquiry.' At that moment Rachette had no time for logic. 'I have heard Ziah Dugdale referred to as many things, but never as a line of enquiry,' he carped. 'She is a woman of character, of known and admired principles. She has influence within certain *circles*.' By tonal cadence and stress he implied those *circles* were as ancient and apparent as Stonehenge and yet as mystical and enigmatic in purpose. Rachette hurriedly escaped to the photocopy of Klinge's letter. He held it between a finger and thumb at the extremities of its diagonals as if in fear of leaving his fingerprints on it. 'Disgusting,' he mouthed, displaying his dentures and his loathing. 'Are you telling me the fellow virtually stole this from a postman, steamed it open like some prying housemaid, had it copied, then bold as brass delivered it to Amla Farm as though nothing had happened.'

'I always thought the man was an unprincipled bounder,' Hamilton added his still cheerful weight to the condemnation.

'But we do it all the time!' Fairchild protested in amazement.

'Only when our security is seriously threatened,' Rachette

stung waspishly. 'And then only in the proper form. He read through the copy once again. 'It is not even in particularly good German,' he complained, throwing it aside.

'German has become a sort of lingua franca in Central Europe and the Balkans,' Fairchild said. 'And Klinge is Bulgarian.'

'We have identified him?' Rachette began to show interest. 'I can hazard a guess of course, but I would like confirmation.'

'According to records, Klinge was the work name for a member of Galahad's original network. Top of the remuneration league and well worth the money. He was chief liaison man between Bulgarian Intelligence, the 2nd Echelon KGB, and Abteilung "C" of Vfk in East Berlin. As you know, the British–US interest sections of the apparatus.'

'True identity, Slunchev?'

'Not listed of course, but it must be.'

Back in control, Rachette was prepared to be generous. 'There is certainly a prima facie case,' he said. Pragmatism, Fairchild observed mentally. Due regard having been paid to outraged form, pragmatism must prevail.

'It is beyond doubt,' he stated firmly. 'The connections all fit. The observed Slunchev–Popkiss meeting. The handwriting on the hiring form for the car used for the meeting in Albemarle Street. Now this letter to Castel – dammit – Galahad. The conclusions to be drawn are most unpleasant, are they not?'

'That Galahad was the man behind Slunchev?'

'Without any doubt.'

'Slunchev has perfect English. Why should he write to Galahad in bad German?' Like a bomb-aimer who had the vital target square in his sights, Hamilton sat back waiting eagerly for its disintegration.

'I don't know,' Fairchild only fizzed with irritation. 'But possibly in an endeavour to stop us making that judgement, or maybe,' with a glance at Rachette, 'to stop prying housemaids from reading his letters.'

Ignoring the issue, Rachette toyed with the braided cord that held his smoking jacket together. 'Damage report, please Hamilton,' he said at last. 'Stem to stern, port and starboard.'

Hamilton stirred uneasily. 'It all goes back to Teasdale, doesn't it,' he began slowly. 'I suppose we must firstly establish Teasdale's motivation and intention.'

'I did that weeks' ago,' snapped Rachette. 'Motivation: thwarted ambition, obsessive vanity and personal hatred arising therefrom. Intention: to embarrass the Government to a point where it could no longer survive. Ultimate aim: that's the one to go for. The bull's-eye.'

'Ideology?'

'Oh, for God's sake,' Rachette exploded. 'To think I put aside nineteen points and a certain four spades contract for this. Do tell him, Fairchild.'

'He would have to put a price on it, a high price,' Fairchild was also uncertain as to what Rachette wanted. 'They would think it was a snow job otherwise,' he went on.

'But the target,' Rachette wailed at such lack of perception. 'Can you not see it? I was Teasdale's target. He envisaged my destruction, and the Service with me. Thwarted ambition, my lad,' he addressed Hamilton with a schoolmaster's severity. 'It has greater explosive force than TNT, never forget that.' Now wearily to Fairchild, as if too exhausted to put his thoughts into words. 'Would you care to develop what our American friends would call a scenario out of this mess.'

'I have been working on it,' Fairchild replied more willingly this time. 'I accept your theory on motive, intention and ultimate aim.'

'Kind of you,' Rachette whispered. 'Please go on.'

'Teasdale offers the product to Dzerzhinsky Square. Probably direct to the 2nd Echelon. They have their doubts about it ...'

'Thinking it might be dodgy,' said Rachette with a wan smile.

'Exactly. But they cannot resist the possibility. So they put in an independent assessor to evaluate, not so much the product, but the vendor.'

'Hamme,' breathed Hamilton.

'Hameh!' Fairchild corrected him by cutting short the final syllable.

'I trust you are not committing *us* to a belief in Arabian

mythology,' Rachette intervened mildly enough, then went on with a shrug of his shoulders. 'But if Galahad chose to name him thus, whilst the balance of his mind was disturbed, and the fellow chose to adopt it, then let us avoid further confusion by finally sticking to Hameh. After all we have no true name for him,' he pursed his lips as if regretting his momentary indifference. 'Though I hate to imagine what such superstitious nonsense will look like in the files.'

Lightly pressing on his temples, Fairchild sought to retrieve his line of thought. 'Hameh,' he began slowly, 'decides, for reasons it is pointless to speculate on, that Teasdale is offering counterfeit coin. Lead-based and booby-trapped...' Hamilton, dithering on the side-lines as to whether it was now prudent to recommit his allegiance to his new chief, noted the hesitation, saw the spasm of panic flit across Fairchild's face before it settled into a determined stillness.

'There is an alternative,' Fairchild continued quietly. 'That Teasdale's product was twenty-two carat, *as indeed it was*. That *we* knew it was on offer and *we* put Hameh in on Teasdale to stop the sale.'

'No. No. No.' In an ascending scale, Rachette endeavoured to heighten his outrage, but there was a flatness in his voice, causing it to lack conviction. 'I told you before we do not indulge in Lubianka solutions.' Then he added a qualifying proviso, 'Not without stringent safeguards, which I assure you were not even contemplated. Regrettably, we knew nothing of Teasdale's transgression. Please proceed with your original theme. Most stimulating.'

Fairchild proceeded with some reluctance. He had the modern policeman's aversion to proceeding anywhere. Nowadays policemen simply *went* where they had to go. 'I cannot adduce a shred of solid evidence as to why Hameh should eliminate Teasdale. But clearly he did, and as we know in this game the reasons could be many. So let us leave Teasdale in his grave for the moment and return to Slunchev.'

'RIP, Henry,' Hamilton said gaily, trying to lighten the gloom. He had been hauled away from a cocktail party and the spirit lingered on. His words brought neither rebuke nor even notice.

'We know Slunchev arrived in London two days after Teasdale's murder. We know he left again four days later on an Aeroflot flight to Leipzig. We know the burglar alarm system at the Aldwych was designed by the Marshall G. K. Zhukov Electronics factory in Leipzig, although actually manufactured on licence over here. A week later, Slunchev returned to London aboard a Moscow–London flight that made a scheduled stop at Prague. The strong room at the Aldwych was made before the war, just outside Prague, by the then European subsidiary of a British parent company. State-owned there now, of course, but still in existence. What followed is confirmed by the Popkiss intercept.'

'One can only wonder,' said Hamilton in measured tones as if anxious to prove sobriety, 'why they did not make the actual keys. I mean, paying a local crook for the work. They could have saved themselves a cool two thou. Even carried out the burglary themselves.'

'How would you fancy trying to pull off a bank job in Sofia?' Fairchild asked him.

'Here, I say, I'm no crook,' said Hamilton indignantly.

'Precisely my point. They had the wit, if not the morality, to know they lacked the criminal cunning such an operation requires,' Fairchild said patiently. 'It also needed a high degree of local knowledge. Caution demanded it to be a home-baked piece of English cake. Suppose they supplied the keys direct? If it came unstuck and Popkiss and Scanlon were nicked, metallurgical examination would reveal the origins of the steel, and the tools that made them, as coming from Eastern Europe. If Popkiss or Scanlon chose to unburden themselves to the police, it would lend their story a consider-able amount of credence. Enquiries would certainly be made. Awkward diplomatic issues raised. That is why the entire op-eration was sub-contracted by Moscow. If the worst came to the worst and it came a tumble ... All down to Slunchev ... Everyone knows what these Bulgarians are like.'

Fairchild paused to observe the fall of shot. Rachette was slumped in his chair, his face without expression, examining his loosely curved fingers as though they held but an even knave-high hand, and he had to find a response to partner's forcing bid.

'That was the way the Moscow plan was supposed to work. Complete with outers and fall-back. But as we know, it never came off.' Fairchild heard his voice gradually reduced to a dull monotone. He was unaccustomed to lengthy solo perorations and was quite pleased to have Hamilton utter a single, sobbing incredulous cry as if witnessing the death of a hero.

'Galahad!'

'Exactly. Galahad came galloping into the arena.'

'There is only suspicion,' Rachette came to life suddenly. 'The vizor is down. We cannot see who is inside the helmet.'

'There can be little doubt as to identity,' Fairchild insisted. 'We know he was on parole the weekend Slunchev arrived. And from then on, those weekends were extended from Thursday afternoons to Tuesday mornings. He was at liberty before, during and after the robbery at the Aldwych Safety Deposit. Look at it this way,' Fairchild leaned aggressively across the table. 'Slunchev, work name Klinge, was Galahad's man, in what he calls the days of yesteryear. Now he is here in England, by proxy the executor of Teasdale's last will and testament. All he has to do is get his hands on the estate. There is nothing in it for him personally. He has been warned to lay off the rest of the loot. He is just another middle-grade civil servant on low pay.'

If Fairchild heard the hiss of displeasure from Rachette's lips, he ignored it. 'What a chance to get back on the British payroll. Salary required? New identity, sanctuary in the West for self, wife and family. Guarantee on pension rights. How to set about it? Who better to go to than his old guide and mentor for a suitable reference.'

'He wouldn't know if Galahad was alive or dead,' said Hamilton with an ill-concealed sneer, seeing the way Rachette's wind was blowing.

'Don't you think they keep history sheets on our people as detailed and precise as we do on theirs?' Fairchild countered hard and swift. Hamilton sunk his chin on his chest and hid behind his eyelids. His head was beginning to ache.

'Well?' Fairchild drilled it into him, having had about enough of Hamilton lately.

'Yes, sir. Point taken, sir,' Hamilton mumbled sulkily, seeing no relief charging over from Rachette's side of the table. With some effect Fairchild went on with his narrative in a more reasonable voice, glad to find its timbre restored.

'There we are then, Slunchev contacts Galahad. Old comrades reunion. Big night down nostalgia alley. Inevitably the question goes in, "And what are you doing in London, Klinge, old pal?" "I am very glad you asked me that," comes the answer. The plot is unfolded. A counter-plot proposed. Rendezvous points are fixed, schedules and alternatives arranged. Drops explored and agreed. Just like old times. "But where to find our London crooks?" Klinge enquires. "I will find them for you," Galahad replies."Have no fear, for I have been mixing with the entire range of the criminally insane for years. I have been told stories, and I have been given names. And just like in the old days, I will cover your rear."'

It was during this latter phase that Rachette's expression moved from being blandly replete to being acidulously nauseated. 'You are condemning the man without trial,' he spat out. 'Had not this Hameh intervened, a man of Galahad's breeding would have brought the plot to us, once he had established its ramifications.'

'I quite agree,' Fairchild conceded mildly. 'But in his own sweet time.'

'What do you mean?'

'As you mentioned earlier. Vanity!'

'I fail to see the relevance.'

'Galahad was no longer welcome at the round table. He had lost his armour, blotted his escutcheon, broken his lance. The only way he could get his feet under the table again was to return bearing the Holy Grail.'

Rachette could contain himself no longer. 'Absolute nonsense!' He voided all the constraints of cold courtesy. 'Pure tripe,' he declared. 'We would have listened most carefully to anything an agent of Galahad's reputation brought in, despite his unfortunate breakdown.'

'Oh, I don't doubt it,' Fairchild responded. 'But he wasn't going to play the snivelling informant. He was Galahad. Action Man personified. He was going to return in triumph, the precious documents clutched in his hand. Mission accomplished. Democracy saved. Enemy foiled and routed... Slunchev had no need to apologize to him in his letter... Galahad did intend to double-cross him. Only he never got the chance. Hameh did for him on both counts.' And with a strong sense of foreboding, Fairchild could not resist paraphrasing something he had previously heard. Words that had long persisted in his mind. 'We've got a couple of right nutters there together,' he predicted gloomily.

Surprisingly, no counter-attack came from Rachette. He had expected a rebuff or at least a resolute defence. Instead, Rachette merely writhed in his chair, silent, rather ill at ease ... even nervous?

'And Hameh?' Rachette eventually grunted. 'I find nothing to explain the actions of Hameh. Were it not for the fact he actually obtained possession of the papers, I would be inclined to doubt his existence.'

'Smith has a theory on that,' Fairchild said.

'Smith! You have discussed this with Smith?' Rachette bit back like a cornered rat.

'No, actually he discussed it with me. Much of what I have already offered came from Smith. He has a certain flair for inspired guesswork.'

'That is all I seem to get these days,' Rachette sighed, falling back wearily. 'Guesswork. Conjecture. The effluent of undisciplined minds.'

Fairchild felt the desperation in Rachette's limp aphorism. The man had thought he had won, that the battle was over. Tongues had been silenced forever. But the Hameh was still hovering. *Is-koo'nee*. It was after Galahad's blood. And Rachette did not give a damn. Hameh or Galahad. One of them would go. Maybe both, and if so, so much the better for governments, civil servants and the national interest.

'And what is Smith's theory on the Hameh, sir?' An obsequious enquiry from Hamilton broke his grim reverie.

'What? Oh, yes. Hameh!' His mind returned to Smith standing behind the Guards Memorial, the chill autumnal air converting his sweat into wisps of vapour, shivering spasmodically, like a steeplechaser after the Grand National. Not the winner, just one of the also-rans that managed to finish the course. He had appeared out of the mist drifting in from the lake, a distant wraith, moving, running with an uneasy gait that indicated pain rather than exhaustion. A hand pressed hard against his side confirmed that opinion. They had moved away to sit together on a park bench close to a nearby public convenience.

Why is he punishing himself like this? he had asked inwardly. And being a policeman for so long, considered the possibility of guilt for the hidden crime. But what crime?

Smith had insisted on speaking through his agony, as if determined to banish it by setting his mind on other things. It was nothing serious, he had said through his teeth. The bastard is not going to beat me.

'Who?'

'The Hameh!'

*The* Hameh?

He could smell the sweat on him, rich and pungent. He presumed it was sweat. As the pain eased and he became more relaxed, Smith dug a small gold ball from his pocket and began playing with it, rolling it between his fingers. Not a ball – a skull – with ruby eyes and diamond teeth. How odd, he had thought? Unlike Smith to be so ... Well, ostentatious?

And after telling him about the letter and his visit to Ziah Dugdale, Smith had voiced his conclusions on the way he saw things.

He had tried not to show his incredulity.

'Let me get this straight,' he had said, in an endeavour to retain his own sanity. 'That after Galahad discovered his wife and her lover had been shot in Vienna, it so turned his mind it brought to the surface repressed childhood fears of the Hameh's vengeance. That he imagined those people he killed were in some way its messengers?'

'I never knew he killed people over it,' Smith's nostrils were a-quiver.

'You know now,' he had answered savagely, angry with himself for voicing the answer to a problem that had long troubled him. Hammel! The East Germans had given the indistinct murmur of a dying man the only meaning they had a word for. Hammel! Mutton. Code name Mutton. Dead mutton.

On Rachette's tape it had been interpreted as Hamme. Now *the Hameh*. Like Poe's raven, bird of evil. Prophet still if bird or devil? What was the next line? Tell me truly I implore . . .

It meant that their Hameh – this Eastern bloc gunman – had taken Hammel to its mythological derivation. Had knowledge of the legend. An Arab himself? PLO? Had adopted the name? Blood and brains! Oh Hell.

'And how do *you* see this Hameh?' he had asked Smith, almost imploringly.

'The way I see it,' Smith had said stoically, 'is that Teasdale put the squeak in on Castellain right at the off. When he was performing back in Vienna. The opposition contract Hameh to do him, but he blows away the wrong people. Fuck-up number one. After the dust settles on that, Teasdale puts these papers of yours on offer. Hameh is sent in to figure out the SP. He takes a strong sus against the odds. Maybe he blames Teasdale for the fact he goofed in Vienna. Maybe Hameh sees Teasdale talking to the wrong people. Anyhow he offs Teasdale. Fuck-up number two. The comrades have convinced themselves Teasdale was putting in a true bill. Slunchev is nominated to do it the hard way. Hameh is declared an incompetent imperialist lackey, which burns him up considerably.'

'Wrong bird,' Fairchild had interjected to try and rid himself of the vision. *Is-koo'nee*. Oh Jesus.

'Well, whatever,' Smith had gone on uncaringly. 'He perches on the mast of Slunchev's boat. I mean, Klinge must be Slunchev, mustn't he?'

'It's possible.'

'Probable. In any case, he sticks to Slunchev like shit to a blanket and who does he see him meet in London? Mr Vernon Castellain, that's who.'

'We prefer to call him Galahad,' he had confessed sadly.

'Why?'

'It's the way we like to do things.'

'Very laudable,' Smith had said considerately, after trying to understand its significance. And failing.

'Do go on, there's a good chap,' he had pressed urgently.

'It's a game for nutters, isn't it?' Smith grumbled to his little gold skull. Then begged him, 'They are all nutters, Cyril, the lot of them. Get yourself out of it. Tell them to stick their knighthood up their backside.'

'I told you I am not in it for that,' he had insisted. 'Please go on. I have a committee meeting in an hour. I do have other irons in the fire besides this particular pot of stinking fish.'

'But this pot could boil over. Put the gas out. Later on, if someone strikes a match. Boom.' Smith was grinning, smugly pleased with himself. Fairchild had risen to leave, no longer prepared to put up with it. To throw his pay-off money in his lap and walk away.

'Don't go, Cyril, I'm sorry,' a plea and an apology from Smith. Genuine. A rare combination. He sat down again and waited, silently.

'It went right up his nose, Hameh's I mean.' With some effort, Smith heaved himself back on the rails. 'Hameh would have a shrewd idea what Slunchev was briefed to accomplish, so he decides to work one off on the comrades by showing them what a right berk they sent in to do a man's job. Fuck you and your secret papers, comrades, he says. I'm going to drop Lancelot –'

'Galahad!'

'I'm going to drop Galahad right in your laps,' he says to himself. 'Get myself a Commissar's commendation. Number one on the hit man's parade. You see Hameh is just another big-headed nutter, like your Galahad. Like you and me, and all the other nutters in the funny farms over there.' His arm swept across Whitehall.

'Be careful, Smith,' he had warned him.

'Oh, I've got undiplomatic immunity,' Smith had sat there laughing, throwing that silly skull of his in the air. Puzzling? Hardly, but intriguing, that's what kept him there.

'It doesn't hold water,' he had said coldly. 'Galahad was within days of being finally discharged from Wyldwood when Hameh made the demand for his release.'

'Was he?' Smith had said mysteriously. Then as if conceding the point, went on: 'Well, so what. Anyone can kill a bull in a slaughterhouse, but if you want to be awarded the ears you've got to do it right underneath the Royal box.' For some odd reason, that thought made Smith laugh again.

All this Fairchild had enlarged into more formal speech for Rachette's benefit. Concluding with a question. Searching to rid himself of an inherited fear. 'I *was* right. They were going to discharge Galahad, weren't they?'

Nodding comfortingly, Rachette proffered a condescending smile in Hamilton's direction. 'Be a good chap and see if you can organize some coffee. Hopefully they will have left some in the larder.'

Fairchild had a strong sensation of *déjà vu*.

'Well?' he demanded firmly, after Hamilton had left.

'Well what?' Rachette parried, openeyed.

'They *were* going to discharge Galahad?'

'Not exactly,' Rachette admitted carelessly. 'They *did* want to hold him back for a time. As a punishment. Discovered he had been breaking bounds whilst on parole. Been a naughty boy, had skipped from the confines of Amla Farm. Heavens above...' Rachette implored the mouldering plaster on the ceiling. 'He was still a strong virile chap. Cooped up all these years. Had a need to let it out. I mean, Amla Farm and pedigree cows, all very well...' His voice trailed into silence. Rachette had neither the stomach nor the gift for gross masculine vulgarity. He tried to restore his strength with a declaration of past policy. 'I was not going to have him gated for some petty misdemeanour when I needed him to avert a crisis,' he bellowed.

'And as a result we now have another,' Fairchild reminded him, with the quiet dominance of a victor. Rachette saw the struggle was hopeless.

'What do we do now?' he enquired meekly.

'We bring Galahad home before he goes on the rampage again,' Fairchild declared.

'He is out of range,' Rachette made a despondent gesture. 'Does not respond to signals.'

'I am aware of that,' Fairchild took up the surrendered sword. 'But we do know where Slunchev is. RV in VZ?

Rendezvous in Vaduz. In Liechtenstein. It cannot be anywhere else. About twelve Ks from the Austrian frontier. A short stroll from the town square and you are across the Rhine into Switzerland. I attended an Interpol conference there a few years ago,' he added, as if finding it necessary to explain such esoteric knowledge. Rachette merely nodded, glumly grateful.

'Slunchev will be holed up there,' Fairchild continued, with increased confidence. 'That's where his flyaway money is stashed. Where he's expecting to bring in his wife and kids. Where he's hoping Galahad will rendezvous to help them make the run. I'm sending Smith and Hamilton there first thing tomorrow morning.'

'But Galahad has hot-potatoed Slunchev,' a strident wail came from the doorway. Hamilton stood there gingerly holding a steaming cup. 'I'm afraid it's only chicory,' he said to Rachette as he placed the cup on the table. Rachette acknowledged the fact with another slow, helpless nod. 'I mean, he's never received Slunchev's letters. He won't know his intentions.' Hamilton ladled in some sugar.

'He was Slunchev's paymaster.' Fairchild said determinedly. 'He's in Vienna, or at least in Europe. I have blocked his credit cards so his contingency fund will only support him for another couple of days. He will have to go somewhere. There was nearly seven thousand Swiss francs unaccounted for in his imprest when he ran off the rails last time. That could still be in Vaduz.'

'There is no evidence, so far, to say he has run off the rails this time,' a faint whispering plea came from Rachette.

'So far,' echoed Hamilton mockingly, at sight of the wreckage, and offered his words to Fairchild as an indication of fealty and undying loyalty.

'Besides,' Fairchild added with ugly satisfaction, 'there is the possibility Galahad might phone his sister to see if there have been any letters for him,' he leaned over and tapped Rachette on the knee. 'I will have to ask you to do something about that,' he said. 'Smith and Hamilton should be prepared for his arrival. We don't want either of them finishing up with a boat-hook in the belly in mistake for Hameh.'

# MINUTE SHEET

—2—

Minister of State,

At 1A we have an urgent request from Head of Director-
ate to warrant special facilities. The reasons given are (as
usual) nebulous, but it is stated (as usual) life is at risk and
security of the state in peril. You may however evince
surprise as to subject of proposed action. I have spoken with
H of D and asked him, in view of subject's impeccable reputation and commitment, to enlarge his reasons. This he
refuses to do, other than say subject is not personally under
suspicion, but could be a conduit along which information
detrimental to a current operation may innocently be
passed. He does not feel, knowing subject's independent
mind, that a personal approach for cooperation and assistance would achieve desired objective.

C. H. NOLEGGE.

—3—

Secretary of State,

I do not evince surprise, but astonishment, and a certain
amount of horror, at this application. Subject is known to

both of us personally. If H of D is not prepared to be more forthcoming, I am certainly not prepared to recommend his application.

B. Duxworthy.

—4—

Minister,

I concur. Application refused. We must draw the line somewhere. Some pertinent words of advice to H of D would not be amiss. Plse spk.

Lassingfold-Cooper.

# Fifteen

•••••••

When it was raining they were allowed two hours in the day room during the afternoon. Peachtree was there droning on interminably about the precedures and intricacies of taking an appeal through the Divisional Court of the Queen's Bench to the House of Lords. It was difficult to tell if Castellain was listening or asleep. There was a penetrating alertness to his eyes even under half-closed lids. In repose his frame held the tension of a bent bow. Suddenly, the arrow was released. Castellain was on his feet striding swiftly across the room to where Randolph Jenkins was sitting with a sketch-pad held on a bent knee. Jenkins newly arrived from behind the Bricks. *Jenkins on walls and skirting boards.*

Castellain had snatched the pad from Jenkins's grasp, given a brief glance at whatever he had been drawing, and for the first time Smith observed the latent menace in the man. A restrained menace, but approaching the maniacal nevertheless. Crushing the drawing in one hand, Castellain then ripped the sketch-book to shreds, and only when he had contemptuously cast the fragments aside did the madness die. But the menace remained. He leaned over Jenkins and in a low voice that filled the room with suppressed fury, said to him, 'Do not ever again attempt to steal my face.' Slowly he had backed out of the room, his eyes never once straying from those of Jenkins, eyes now so dead they almost appeared sightless. All it needed, Smith thought at the time, was the dull beat of a drum. It was as ritualistic, as primitive as that. Jenkins, however, had accepted the incident with remarkable aplomb. Almost as if he had expected it. Even though he had made no protest, he had maintained an air of calm defiance that made Smith warm to him. He moved to an empty chair nearby. 'Was it as bad as all that?' he asked smilingly.

'He didn't like what he saw,' Jenkins explained with exaggerated hauteur. 'They never do, those who keep their faces hidden behind a mask. But I am an artist, I can penetrate masks, real or assumed. That's mainly why I'm in here.'

He caught the knowing twist of Smith's lips, and with evergreater loftiness had said, 'Yes, you are quite right, my dear fellow. I *am* as queer as a coot.'

'And why are you in here?' he had asked, avoiding Jenkins's challenge to his inbred chauvinism. But first, Jenkins wanted to know why *he* was in there. To his surprise he felt compelled to tell him, and did so. Thinking at the time perhaps it was because he had never told anyone before. Not even himself. And he wanted Jenkins to draw his portrait, to compare it with what he saw in the mirror. To see if he also wore a mask.

But it was Jenkins's story he recalled on the flight to Zurich, with Hamilton sitting next to him. Hamilton, who had greeted him at the briefing with such charming effusiveness it was as if their previous antipathy had never existed. 'Glad to have you with me, old chum,' he had burbled with obvious cunning, implying he was in charge of direction and purpose. 'Been absolutely yonkers since I worked with the jolly old forces of lor'n'order. SB then, of course. Not your scene at all.' He had let him get away with it. When and if crunch time came around, Hamilton would find out who was boss. And anyway, what lay underneath his enforced gaiety?

But his mind kept going back to Jenkins, who had laughed ironically when he told him he had been a CID officer.

'Did you know a Commander Potch?' he had asked him.

'Very well, although I did not know he has been elevated to the police peerage.'

'He had that rank when I met him almost a year ago,' Jenkins said in confirmation. 'And well worthy of it, I imagine. Now there's a man who has no need of a mask, his entire life is written in his countenance for all to read. Nothing too culturally esoteric, but stimulating enough. If Kipling had written of policemen instead of soldiers, I'm sure he would have found a few lines for a Commander Potch.'

'He'd be pleased to know that,' Smith had said.

'Oh, he does. I told him so. And he was.'

'How did you happen to run into him?'

'He ran into me. Or more precisely, he ran me in. But we became quite chums. Had he chosen to be awkward, I could have found myself being raped with monotonous regularity in one of Her Majesty's fouler prisons. It all happened ten or eleven months ago.'

'I was behind the Bricks then.'

'Ah,' an utterance of sympathy from Jenkins. 'Fine fellow Potch,' he backtracked hurriedly to return to a more pleasant topic. 'I think he shared and understood my artistic temperament.'

Artistic temperament? Joe Potch? Smith had stared in wonder. But for all this fusion of kindred spirits, the initial cultural collision between Jenkins and Joe Potch had been a fairly mundane, even sordid affair.

There had been a domestic spat, as Jenkins called it, over the distribution of his favours between an ageing companion in residence and a potential usurper of more tender years and smoother flesh. So jealously enraged was the existing incumbent that he had taken a kitchen knife and slashed to ribbons a newly completed work by Jenkins. The one he was certain would get him an RA after his name. So provoked by this act of spiteful vandalism, Jenkins had taken the same knife and thrust it into the guts of his once good friend – no less than twenty-seven times according to pathological arithmetic.

'Potch was most understanding when he arrived to investigate the matter,' Jenkins had said with evident gratitude. 'I was quite frank with him about the entire nonsensical business. I well remember his words. "It is such a pleasure to deal with a genius like you, Mr Jenkins, as opposed to stolid and stupid criminals. The reasoning mind, Mr Jenkins, never insults the intelligence of others by denying irrevocable facts."'

Smith had sniffed the air appreciatively at the odour of Joe Potch's bullshit, but said nothing.

'Dear old Potch, it was quite a relief to sign a confession for him,' Jenkins fondly recalled. 'He did talk such a lot of twaddle about the pre-Raphaelites. I sometimes think that was why I confessed. To stop him talking about the pre-Raphaelites. But for all that, he did appreciate the truth and beauty of my own work. At the trial he stoutly confirmed his belief that I had been temporarily driven from my mind by such an atrocity. Even if the brute of a judge did intervene to say Potch's opinions on my state of mind had no relevance.'

'The atrocity being the destruction of your picture?' Smith had enquired.

'There had been no other,' said Jenkins, mildly surprised by such an unnecessary question. 'As a reasonably astute and perceptive jury found, in declaring my responsibility for the whole silly contretemps absolutely diminished.'

With supreme confidence, Jenkins went on to declare: 'So I now await what I am perfectly certain will be Her Majesty's not overly long delayed pleasure.'

'And when you come out, they might even make you keeper of the Royal pictures,' Smith had suggested, with all due deference.

# Sixteen

◆◆◆◆◆◆◆

The sketch Randolph Jenkins eventually made of him was committed to paper reluctantly, for clearly Smith's was not a face that greatly appealed to him. Not for nothing: not without a fee. He even refused to sign it. But he did make it. After all, as he grudgingly put it, I suppose you are an elder of the tribe to which dear old Potch belongs.

The result was a face he knew, but had not lived with recently. Had conscience ploughed and darkened the flesh around his eyes that much? Nipped and bitten at the hollows of his cheeks so deeply? Well, so much for him. But what of Castellain's portrait, he wondered. What had that shown? If only he knew. The searing whisper came back to him. 'Do not attempt to steal my face.' And what of the one who had stolen the secret fear of his childhood, had stolen the name of his mad delusion . . . Hameh!

At the car-hire desk in Zurich airport, Hamilton dealt with the necessary formalities, Smith marvelling at the change that came over the man as he made known his demands in the staccato precisions of fluent German. His *Bitte* snapped punctiliously. His *Danke* was a double crack of empty gratitude. His *Warum?* a questioning thunderclap. Smith was slightly disappointed at the failure to end the proceedings in an exchange of stiff bows and clicking heels. He felt sorry for Hamilton. So clearly a Prussian born in the wrong country. 'I'll drive,' Hamilton barked, retaining his Teutonic arrogance in the transition back to English. Smith grinned complacently and slid into the passenger seat of the Audi. Poring over the map with the intensity of Rommel before the attack on Alamein, Hamilton decided on a flanking movement along the southern shores of the Zurich See, then once beyond the smaller Walensee, to swing north for Liechtenstein at Sargans.

After forcing his way through the centre of Zurich without casualties, he announced his battle plans once they were clear of the city.

'Appreciation,' he said crisply. 'The only certainty we possess is uncertainty, and we must therefore prepare to act in the face of uncertainty.'

'How do we do that?' Smith asked tolerantly.

'We consolidate uncertainty in an effort to discover where the certainties lie.'

Smith vented a low whistle of admiration at such profundity.

'It is the research that matters,' Hamilton explained modestly. 'I have been engaged on research most of the night. For instance, our selection of Vaduz as Slunchev's bolt-hole might appear to be uncertain. But if we examine those places beyond hamlet status beginning with a V and ending with Z, you will find only three. Valdez in Alaska, Veracruz in Mexico and Vinaroz in Spain. The sheer improbability of any of these places being a likely rendezvous with access to the confidentiality of the Swiss banks makes Vaduz a certainty.'

'Provided VZ is a straight abbreviation and not a backward-forward code. Half the Klinge letter could be coded from a one-time pad.'

'*We* do not think, that on balance, it is likely.' Hamilton defined the superiority of his resources. 'Our cryptographers have fed it through our ... apparatus ... without result. Our consultant psychologist considers the emotional overtones in the Klinge letter to be genuine indications of induced panic.'

'I always understood a message coded from a one-time pad couldn't be broken.' Smith had the eerie experience of seeing an eye-ball located in the far corner of Hamilton's left eye glaring at him suspiciously, whilst the head that held it pointed straight forward.

'How do you come to know about backward-forward codes and one-time pads?' Hamilton enquired, the unnatural positioning of his eye-ball making his voice sound disembodied.

'I used to read a lot,' Smith replied. 'It was all in the *Boys' Book of Spies*.'

It had begun to rain heavily, giving Hamilton an excuse to concentrate on the road, his eye-ball retracting to normality like an undercarriage. Smith relished the silence. It was still pouring when they reached Pfäffikon. Beyond the level crossing, Hamilton pulled into the side of the road and began noting the licence numbers of passing cars. He dwelt steadfastly at this task until the barriers came down, then sped swiftly away. Passing his notebook to Smith, he said, 'If you spot any of them on our tail, let me know.'

'Why?'

'Anything tailing us from behind has been held up at the level crossing. If they have us under surveillance they must be in front.'

'Who?'

'How the dickens do I know. It is standard avoidance technique.'

'They never mentioned it in the *Boys' Book of Spies*,' Smith complained. Hamilton reverted to being General Rommel.

'We hold one other certainty. Galahad. At least we are certain what he looks like. Slunchev is a reasonable certainty. We have his photograph and full description. Hameh, we must consider an uncertainty. Nevertheless, our certainties accord with the objectives of our mission. Firstly, to find Galahad and order him to return. Secondly, to find Slunchev and persuade, bribe, or blackmail him into coming over to us. Thirdly, to avoid if possible confrontation between either of them, and ourselves, with this Hameh creature.'

'And if it should prove impossible? Avoiding confrontation, I mean.'

'We withdraw in good order, having attained at least our first objective.'

'And what about killing people,' Smith ·persisted. 'If Galahad refuses to obey orders. If Slunchev doesn't submit to persuasion, bribery or blackmail, and Hameh keeps coming.

Have you got orders to kill people?'

'My dear man,' Hamilton laughed without humour. 'I suppose that's from chapter ten of your *Boys' Book of Spies?* Now look here, Smith,' he added seriously. 'I may not be a religious chap, but I am a Christian. C of E in fact.' It was as if that explained everything.

'Method.' Hamilton pressed on with his operation orders. 'We establish ourselves in separate, but reasonably adjacent hotels in Vaduz. You may wish to find one within the price range of our subsistence allowance. I will stay at the Sonnenhof and pay the excess out of my own pocket.'

'Which leaves me a wide range of third-class doss-houses, I suppose?' Heavy sarcasm came from Smith. 'Our passports say we are company executives. Who do I tell them I represent? The ancient and honourable company of ragpickers and bottlewashers? Or maybe British Rail?'

'Method,' Hamilton repeated, undeterred. 'Having established our respective bases, I will make a quick recce of the town to select RVs, fall-backs and suitable dead letter drops. Are you familiar with these terms? No, don't answer that. It would be in your idiotic book. I don't know why we bother to have an Official Secrets Act and 'D' notices these days.'

'There is a green Lancia with Zurich plates right behind us,' Smith grunted.

'What about it?' Hamilton asked.

'It's on your list.'

'How the devil did it get there?'

'You overtook him two minutes ago.'

'Well, it must be all right then, mustn't it?' Hamilton monitored the rear-view mirror. 'A man, a woman, and three children in the back. All perfectly normal.'

'You said to . . .'

'I know what I said, but you must learn to differentiate.'

'Sorry. Next time I'll wait until I see their black capes and slouch hats.'

'Please be serious and try to pay attention. Now, once I've got the picture over the ground, I'll allocate RV schedules. Do try to arrive precisely on time. I will only allow for a two-minute delay. If you cannot make the RV then you must show at the fall-back not more than forty minutes later.'

'And if I can't?'

'Why on earth could you not?'

'I've no idea. Look, why don't we stick together on this? It would be much simpler.'

'And dreadfully unskilled workmanship. The thing is; if one of us goes down, the other is left to carry on.'

'Goes down where?'

'Are you being deliberately obtuse? Vaduz is a small town, less than five thousand inhabitants. At this time of year there will be practically no tourists about. The winter sports set will not arrive until January.' Hamilton was struck by a sudden thought. 'Chas learned to ski in Liechtenstein, you know.'

'Chas?'

'HRH.'

'Oh...'

'So with only the local populace about, our targets should stick out like boils on bums. We will not make the same mistake.'

'The majority of people place primary importance on bum cover.' Smith told him gravely. 'That is a psychological fact.'

At Sargans on the Swiss side of the Liechtenstein frontier, Hamilton insisted they separate, with Smith completing the fifteen-kilometre journey to Vaduz by taxi. There is in fact no formal frontier check for people entering from the Swiss side, as the Swiss border police and Customs attend to that, and quite a few other policing responsibilities on behalf of the Principality. Thus, having cleared a Swiss port of entry, one is free to enter Liechtenstein unhindered. Hamilton had explained all this to him before consulting his watch. 'I have sixteen ten and forty seconds. Prepare to synchronize on sixteen eleven... Now! Right? At nineteen hundred we will meet in the café on the north side of the square. Leave it to me to make the recognition signal. Good luck.'

Smith was coming to the conclusion that it was an increasingly good idea on Hamilton's part that they go their separate ways. He could not have stood much more of him. It was still raining when he arrived in Vaduz. High above the town, the castle of the Prince von und zu Liechtenstein, Duke von Troppau und Jaegerndorf, sailed through the swirling mist like a ghostly galleon. After surveying the discreet luxury of the Sonnenhof beneath the castle walls, Smith left it to the taxi driver to find him a modest Gasthof nearby. 'Not so many English come now in the year,' the gratified proprietor told him. 'To yourself you have the place.' It was a business trip, Smith explained. A matter of business, then a few days rest. The proprietor treated him to a massive wink, full of conspiratorial jollity. 'Ach yes, the taxes,' he laughed. 'They all come not to pay the taxes. The Italians, when they change the government come four, five times a year, as many as fleas from a dead dog. The French with their relatives come, like to a picnic. The Americans come in threes. One to carry, two to watch the one who carries. Always the English come alone, but very regular they come. Every year since the war they come.'

He seemed surprised by the weight of Smith's suitcase. 'You have not yet been to the bank?' he enquired anxiously. To allay his fears, Smith patted his breast pocket as if it held the deposit book. The proprietor's bonhomie returned. 'Good. Good,' he said. 'Now you can die rich.' He laughed again. Uproariously.

Through the rain-drenched windows of the café, Smith watched Hamilton's approach. Even though he could not see him, he knew it was Hamilton. The vivid blue and yellow hemisphere of the golfing umbrella, held low against the driving rain, seemed to be moving through the night of its own accord, like some weird segmented moon. If it was not the only golfing umbrella in Liechtenstein, Smith surmised, it certainly must be the biggest. He had noticed it strapped to the side of Hamilton's suitcase at the airport. Cover? He had pondered at the time. Outside the door of the café, the umbrella was lowered and shaken vigorously before Hamilton entered. A few paces beyond the door, he halted, his face and smile going directly to the counter whilst his eyes gyrated round the interior. Only when this had been accomplished did he turn his head in Smith's direction. The smile on his face became wider and sillier.

'Hello there,' he said loudly. 'You must be English? Seem to recognize that tie. Old Harrovian, isn't it?' It was only an ordinary striped tie from a multiple store, but Smith, knowing he was participating in a farce, nodded his agreement. 'Thought so,' Hamilton burbled on. 'Mind if I join you?' Smith indicated the chair opposite. Hamilton removed his raincoat and sat down. 'What do you think of the weather, eh?' he said.

'Jolly for boating,' Smith replied.

'Wrong school,' Hamilton hissed back.

The waitress came over. 'What's that you're drinking?' Hamilton peered into Smith's glass. 'Cognac? Yes, that will do nicely. You'll have another?' He held up two fingers to the waitress. 'Two cognacs, miss,' he said loudly in the English the English use on foreigners, wagging his fingers in confirmation. 'Two! Compris?'

'What happened to the Deutsch spreche?' Smith asked when the waitress had left.

'Unless operational conditions make it necessary, always give the impression you do not understand the language of the country in which you are working. Useful information can often be gleaned from indiscreet remarks that would not otherwise be made.' It sounded like a quotation from an instruction manual.

'That's reasonable and logical,' Smith acknowledged, having taken a liking to the phrase, maybe because Elstow had used it, maybe because it formed a useful closure on boring conversations. It did not succeed in this case.

'Not mentioned in your *Boys' Book of Spies?*' Hamilton replied, smugly amiable. Fortunately the waitress returned with the drinks. After she had gone, Hamilton raised his glass and leaning across the table whispered, 'Anything to report?' as if by way of a toast.

'My room is clean, though sparsely furnished, the bed is lumpy, the shower at the end of the corridor doesn't work. The cognac is good, the weather is lousy.'

'I meant any sighting reports,' Hamilton moved nearer.

'For Christ's sake I've only just got here,' irritation made Smith snap the words. Hamilton withdrew, making a placatory pout of his lips. Over by the *Kasse*, the waitress and the cashier were watching them, indulging in a giggling interchange. Smith saw Hamilton's face reddening.

'What's up?' he asked.

'They think we are having a homosexual assignation,' Hamilton answered, hurt and offended. Smith laid a comforting hand on his wrist, 'Just ignore them, darling,' he crooned soothingly. The giggling verged on the uncontrollable. Hamilton snatched his hand away and stood up abruptly, donning his raincoat with a dignified flourish. Pulling a newspaper from his pocket, he threw it on the table. 'Today's *Times*,' he said, his voice unsteady in an effort to be both masculine and convincingly friendly. 'Interesting leader on the steel industry. I've finished with it. Yours if you want it.' He picked up his golf umbrella and stalked towards the door. Smith watched the blue and yellow mushroom receding into the darkness, suddenly realizing the bastard hadn't paid for the drinks.

The middle pages of *The Times* contained Hamilton's battle plan, written on the Sonnenhof's notepaper. It ended in large capitals with the words, MEMORIZE–THEN DESTROY BY FIRE, underlined in red. Attached was a Tourist Bureau map of Vaduz, in which the town had been divided into two parts called Blue Zone and Red Zone. Smith had been allocated the Red Zone. He wondered if there were political implications. Keeping the map, he flushed the battle plan down the lavatory before going to bed.

Next morning, he did the hotels first, not in accordance with Hamilton's order, by going round personally and enquiring without arousing interest or suspicion if anyone resembling Galahad or Slunchev was in residence. How that was to be accomplished without arousing interest or suspicion was unexplained. Fairchild had said Galahad had been supplied with two passports, one Swiss in the name of Peter Josten, the other, West German in the name of Erich Leimer. He phoned round the hotels, barking at the telephonist, 'Herr Peter Josten, bitte,' in a manner Hamilton would have envied. When the answer came bearing a distinguishable *nein* or *nichts*, he would ask, plaintively this time, for Herr Erich Leimer, and on receiving an obvious negative, would say, '*Ach du lieber...*' and hang up. He became quite good at saying '*Ach du lieber...*' for all he ever got by way of reply were incomprehensible sentences containing the key words *nein* and *nichts*. Then he left his *Gasthof* to keep the scheduled morning RV with Hamilton.

Should you have a report to make, the orders stated you will walk with your hands clasped behind your back as in the 'stand at ease' posture. If I have information or further instructions to pass, I will carry my umbrella (open or closed according to weather conditions) in the 'slope arms' position. Nothing so old hat about blowing one's nose or carrying a copy of *The Times* about Hamilton, he was pleased to note. Although he wondered what Hamilton would do with his umbrella if it happened to be raining and he had no information or further instructions to pass. He would probably invent some, he concluded.

In the event of a positive signal by either party, the orders continued, both will gather in front of the nearest shop selling stamps. Information will be exchanged under cover of discussing the merits of the stamps displayed. Appropriate gestures should be made to lend credence to this cover. Afterwards both parties will leave the scene in opposite directions, exchanging such formal courtesies as are appropriate to a casual encounter between persons with a mutual interest. It would, Smith thought, be less conspicuous to lay on the Trooping of the Colour. Particularly as Vaduz was virtually a one-street town, and almost every shop sold stamps. Luckily, when he saw Hamilton, the rain had stopped and he was marching along head held high, eye-balls working overtime, his umbrella furled and carried at the short trail. Smith passed him on the opposite side of the street, with his hands thrust firmly into his pockets.

Returning to the *Gasthof*, he got busy on the phone once more, in English this time. There was the name Slunchev had given to Eric Popkiss, the same one he had used to hire the Mercedes. And Galahad? There was always the chance he might go in straight. 'Do you happen to have a Mr Trench or a

Mr Castellain with you?' 'No. We are most sorry.' The identical answer each time, as if they had all been on the same course in hoteliers' English.

'You look sad,' the proprietor mourned in sympathy as he emerged from the cubicle. 'You have sold, when you should have buying been? Buying, when the selling was correct to do?'

He stood listening to himself muttering something incomprehensible about rates of exchange, coughing heavily to conceal his ignorance. 'Up to the mountains why don't you go,' said the proprietor, suggesting a remedy for financial asthma. 'Here is a clear day with no rain. Wrap yourself warm. Many pretty villages there are in the mountains. From the Platz the mail buses go to Triesenberg, Steg and Malbun. Pretty villages. To them have you been?' And to his great astonishment, he saw his guest strike his forehead with an open palm and heard him say: 'To stupidsville, I have been.' Then he had watched him go through to the bar and sit morosely sipping a glass of cognac. The proprietor turned away to other things, offering a '*Gott sei dank*' for the steadfast solidity of the Swiss franc and the equitable demands of Liechtenstein's tax laws.

It had all happened too fast for considered thought. Fairchild personally dragging him out of bed at five in the morning. The car ride through deserted streets to Camden Town and Chalk Farm. The dingy detached house, passing on its steps a distraught figure he recognized as Sir Desmond Rachette, a senior civil servant they had brought in years ago as a caretaker Commissioner of Police who, a year later, quietly returned to the obscurity from which he had sprung. Nodding distantly to Fairchild as he left, then turning at the foot of the steps, looking up at them, incongruous in his black tie and dark velvet smoking jacket, saying, 'I'm sorry about the deception. But it really was in the national interest.'

'Sorry about what deception?' he had asked Fairchild once they were inside the house. There was a stench of decay about the place. Not strong. The sort of smell you get used to after a time.

'Galahad. Your friend Castellain. They wanted to hold him

in Wyldwood for further observation. They thought he displayed signs of regression. Nothing conclusive, but enough for them to want to be sure. Only pressure was brought to bear to get him out.' He didn't bother to ask who put on the pressure.

'You've got to get him back,' Fairchild speaking, alone and lonely. As brittle as glass in his endeavour to remain calm, but so taut he had the impression that if he flicked his earlobe with a playful finger it would ring like glass. 'Not easy, I know,' he was saying stiffly. 'Vaduz? Ever been to Vaduz in Liechtenstein? We think he might show up there. Yes, VZ. We're sure it means Vaduz. Hamilton will go with you. Do stop flaring your nostrils. He speaks excellent German, knows something of Switzerland. Not around that area I'll admit. St Moritz and Klosters are more his scene, but he can get things done through consulates, the embassy even.'

'It won't be easy. Not with people like Castellain and Slunchev,' he had said.

'I know that. Remember what they told us in the job when we first joined. "By the use of tact and discretion, the public can ordinarily be induced to comply with directions." Something like that. We had to learn it by heart. Remember?'

'I remember. I also remember the next bit. "But should a resort to force become necessary, it should be applied with sufficient strength to achieve the object in view." Something like that, as you say. It was all a long time ago.'

And there had been a long silence. A fond silence.

'You see what I am getting at?' he finally had to ask.

'Yes, I think so.'

'I won't do it. Not that way.'

'No. I don't expect you to. But I want you to come back. You will protect yourself. You're entitled to protect yourself.'

'I'll do that all right. I can run a long way as you know. If necessary in the opposite direction.'

'Yes, if it comes to that. We can't give you anything in any case. Not in Switzerland. Upset Switzerland and you upset the world. Strict neutrality, Red Cross, all that sort of thing. That's what makes it so difficult. Do anything like that in Switzerland – it's like raping a nun – bayoneting babies. For all that a great deal of espionage goes on in Switzerland. More spies to the square inch than edelweiss. But all they do is listen, it's the ear of the intelligence community. No one acts. Not forcibly. To act is a professional foul, you get sent off the field. Suspended for life. *We* don't want that.'

'We?' he had sneered, disappointed to find Fairchild seeking refuge in plurality.

'It would recoil on us diplomatically. I have to act in the national interest.'

He had looked round at the front door. 'Him out. You in?' he had asked.

'I'll put it this way,' Fairchild had answered. 'I'm partly responsible for this mess in the first place. Guilt by association, as it were. If it is not cleaned up, I am out also.'

He had felt sorry for Fairchild. He had been a good Guv'nor. Even if they hadn't always seen eye to eye. For a moment he was tempted to make him a present of the skull. What it contained might serve to alleviate Fairchild's troubles. He had even taken it from his pocket, rolling it between finger and thumb. Caressing it ... until a withering glare from Fairchild made him put it away again. No, he decided, what was inside the gold skull was no longer a panacea for Fairchild's ills. Nothing inside a tight roll of microfilm could bring about a cure now. As always, the trouble was with people. Bad mad people. Mad bad people. Bad because they were mad? Mad because they were bad? The dead are too numerous to be listed in the indictment, my lord. Their wounds too terrible to contemplate. Can there be any doubt the defendant's reason was impaired, his responsibility diminished far beyond the realm of guilt?

Lost his buttons?

Buttons! It was a question of who had all their buttons ... And the fingers to press them with.

He drained the remainder of his cognac in one quick gulp. Back on the rails you have to get, his mind emulated the proprietor's English. He had wandered way off-track. Allowed himself the indolent luxury of tagging on to Hamilton's naive idiocies just for the cheap self-indulgence of taking the piss out of him and what he represented. Another world, an unseen world. That was the trouble with other unseen worlds, they exerted a gravitational pull on the real world out of all proportion to their size. How big were they in any case?

Quickly leaving the bar, he walked briskly down to a stationer's in the main street, bought a map, returned to the bar, and ordered another cognac. Fifteen minutes later, with his shoulders sagging somewhat, he was fully aware of the enormity of the problem facing him. Vaduz may only be a small town in a comic-opera principality tucked in between Switzerland and Austria, but it seemed to lie at the centre of the earth. It was Getaway Land. A springboard to anywhere. One long leap to Zurich international airport. A short sprint across the Rhine to Buchs, and the railway to Vienna and all points east – change at Salzburg for Rome, and the south. A hop, step and jump to the north and the ferries across Lake Constance from Romanshorn and Rorschach into Germany. Rorschach? Main export – Ink blots? To test the minds of nutters like himself?

He sipped his drink and gazed out of the window. The clouds had lifted and broken into pink and white marshmallows, and for the first time he had sight of the mountains! Many pretty villages are in the mountains! And the map showed the roads and tracks leading to them. Dozens of them within a fifty-kilometre radius of Vaduz. Roads! He hadn't even given a thought to the roads. The trouble with being a little Englander is that, despite the continental holidays, you still imagine all roads end at the seaside. He returned to the lobby and the telephone cubicle. The proprietor saw him and heaved a sigh of despair. Those Englanders and their money! About their money was all they thought. Not that much of it they had.

'You really are being most insecure,' Hamilton admonished after he had openly identified himself on the phone. 'You may well have blown my cover.'

'I'll blow your balls off, if you don't listen and do as I say,' he threatened vehemently. 'Get on to every car rental firm at Zurich Airport. You are the Chief of Police at St Gallen, and they are to get busy on their computers to see if they, or any of their subsidiary offices in the area, have rented a car on a

British driving licence to a Mr Trench. You will hold the line while they *schnellmachen mit den Aufträgen, verstehen Sie?*' He felt, rather than heard Hamilton wincing at the other end of the line. He rubbed it in by adding, 'And it might *machen* them *schnell mit grösse Energie* if you tell them, if Mr Trench is not found within forty-eight hours, he will put into operation a financial coup that will make Bernie Cornfeld seem like an embezzler of the proceeds from stolen piggy banks, bringing about a fifty per cent devaluation of the Swiss franc.'

It was some time before Hamilton surrendered to his brusque tirade. Finally, he said, 'I will report at the second RV in precisely one hour. I hope you realize what you are asking me to do.' He made it sound akin to cheating at cards.

The second RV was outside the open-air swimming pool on the edge of town. Hamilton was there when he arrived, sitting in the Audi, fingers strumming nervously on the steering wheel. The pool was closed and the Audi the only car in sight. Boils on bums! Smith got in quickly and said: 'Move it out.'

'Where?'

'Anywhere. Just drive.'

Once on the road, he waited until Hamilton's left eye-ball had orbited in his direction. 'Well?' he demanded.

'He rented a green Opel the day before yesterday. I've got the number.'

'Good lad. For how long?'

'Five days.'

'Returnable at Zurich? Any local address?'

'I never got that far. They became suspicious. The Swiss always suspect officials. Especially one whose German is not quite Swiss German. There are distinct differences, you know. I mean, neither you nor I could fool a Yorkshireman into believing we came from Bradford, could we?' It was a plea for mercy.

Smith granted it reluctantly. 'Nay lad,' he said slowly. There would be no point now, in trying for a repeat performance in either of the names Galahad was using.

Still, it was a gain. A major gain. It proved Slunchev was here – somewhere. A known car can always be found. Yes, but only if you have enough people looking for it. With only the two of them, it would be difficult, but not impossible, given enough time. At best they had forty-eight hours. Action? They could go back to Zurich and sit outside the car rental office until Slunchev brought it back. But would he bring it back? Returnable where? In any case, Slunchev was on the trot. He would dump it and run. A road watch? He looked at the map. On the Liechtenstein side of the Rhine, the road ran from Balzers in the south past Vaduz to Schaan where it forked. One road went to Feldkirch and Austria, the other arm followed the river to the north. On the Swiss side, the autobahn went parallel with the river to Lake Constance before swinging south again in a wide loop to Zurich. They could sit on the bridge at Vaduz. But what about the other bridges? Six or seven to the north, more to the south. The roads coming down from the mountain villages? Hell, a static watch was useless, it would have to be a good old-fashioned punt around the manor giving the eyes a treat.

As there was still three hours of daylight left, and as they were heading north in any case, he told a quiescent and surprisingly amenable Hamilton to keep on going. They drove to the Austrian frontier at Feldkirch, turning south again short of the customs post, taking a different route for luck. Several times their hopes rose at the sight of a green car ahead. Rising further when it became clear it was an Opel, falling again when the number plate failed to correspond. But always overtaking to get a good look at the driver. 'Hardly likely he would change plates,' Smith said. 'But you never know.' They would stop for a time at the bridges over the Rhine watching optimistically. 'You never know,' Smith would repeat the incantation, and Hamilton would nod grimly and try to look both ways at once. 'My first job in the field,' Hamilton admitted, obsequious now, almost fawning on Smith, whose age and experience had led to such a positive lead. 'I do hope we succeed. I could get a good overseas posting out of this.'

'Moscow?' Smith had enquired.

'Good Lord, no. Washington.'

Smith had smiled, recalling his own first job in the field. Plainclothes aid to CID at West End Central. 'Get out and find your meat in the gutters,' the old Detective Sergeant in charge of

'Aids' had said. 'That's where the villains live. Catch them at it. Get 'em with the gear on 'em. Give them a pull, turn the buggers over. Keep 'em on the hop. Bring the work in or you're back in uniform. Susses don't count. Anyone can nick a sus. And shoplifters, they don't count. Neither do any other perchers. Anyone can nick perchers given into custody.'

Three days later, with not even a 'percher' in the back of his book, he had begun to wonder if he was cut out for CID work. The other 'Aids' had been bringing in whiz mobs, as they called teams of pickpockets, van draggers, as they called villains who nicked gear from unattended delivery vans, kite flyers, who were those who uttered forged and stolen cheques, and even the occasional shopbreaker and burglar, which then were cases that had to go for jury trial at the Inner London Sessions. At three in the morning he was on his way back to his room in the single men's section house, after a fruitless fourteen hours on the streets, when he spotted a dark figure coming out of Great Windmill Street into Brewer Street and unbelievably, he was carrying a sack on his back. Though it did not bear the word 'Swag' it was enough for him. Bang to rights, that one was. What's in the sack? It writhed and moved in his hand. Something living! What had he tumbled into? A white slaver? A kidnapper? Christ, it's a dream. He'll wake up in a minute.

'What's in the sack?' Repeated in a fearful, ferocious shout.

'Chickens.'

'Chickens! Live chickens?'

'Released them five minutes ago, back of the Chinese restaurant in Old Compton Street. They keeps them in cages. Cruel it is. I'm reporting them to the RSPCA.'

'You are nicked – Official.'

'That's what you gets for being kind to dumb animals. Bleedin' well nicked. Ain'cha got no finer feelings?'

So he had marched him back to West End Central. The charge room full of drunks, prostitutes, and a team of spielers from a gambling raid on a basement in Wardour Street.

'What have you got there, lad?' the Duty Inspector enquired.

'A chicken thief, sir.' It drew a keen hard look from the

Inspector. 'Don't try and be funny, lad. Not with me. I eat "Aids" for breakfast, and I don't even like them. I detest "Aids". You have been posted to West End Central, the hub of the universe. This is not Much Muck Spreading in the Wold. We don't have chicken thieves in West End Central and we don't have lippy young "Aids" either.'

So he had tipped up the sack and nine chickens flew about the charge room in a frenzy of new-found freedom. Three of them crowing and screeching atop the charge table, others fluttering among the light fixtures, two fighting and scratching in the middle of the floor. 'I've got chicken shit all over me leopardskin coat,' a tom, which is what they call a prostitute, complains. Towering aloof, and menacing above the chaos, stood six foot four of Duty Inspector, dignified and silent, only the glacial stillness of his face foretelling an ominous future.

The next morning, for it was in the days when the Department looked after its own, even the 'Aids', he was transferred from the Washington of West End Central to the Moscow of 'C' Division at Tottenham Court Road to keep him out of trouble. Eighteen months later, with sixty-three arrests following the chicken thief into the back of his book, he was appointed as a fully fledged Dectective Constable. And it was all down to these bloody birds, he remembered. Birds!

The dream vanished. Hamilton was gripping his arm with excitement, peering intently at a green Opel crossing the bridge from Buchs, saying with increasing intensity, 'Five, two, seven . . .' Then bewailing in chagrin, 'Oh, dash it, the last digit doesn't match.' Smith watched the man behind the wheel of the green Opel. A portly burgher on his way home from the office, lost in that look of almost uncomprehending complacency they all seemed to wear around here. The final figure on his number plate, a three. If only it had been another five. If only the man's features had a square, yet sly solidity, instead of a round, open vacuity. If only . . . He must be slipping. He had never been one to wish *if only* before. With a resigned gesture, he dismissed the good burgher to his waiting *Blutwurst mit Kartoffeln*.

'Let's get back to Vaduz,' he said. 'After dinner, an early

dinner, we'll punt around the other hotels and restaurants. The man's got to eat somewhere.'

They dined at the Sonnenhof. 'My treat,' Hamilton insisted as he perused the oversized menu. Smith pulled it to one side. 'Wienerschnitzel and chips for two,' he said. 'We haven't time to wait for the four-course cordon bleu.'

RV in VZ! the enigma kept flickering round inside his head, on and off, like a neon sign. But where? When? An RV in police parlance was simply a meet. Nothing frenchified. Escalope de veau Viennoise, et pommes de terre frites, Hamilton had ordered. Wienerschnitzel and chips, indeed! Laughing. Nothing malicious now. A good-humoured laugh. A meet. It was only a frenchified meet and he knew all about meets. He had covered plenty of meets during his time in the job. Knew all about them. The villains cautiously circling to make certain the filth hadn't got it ready-eyed. Then in – contact – and it was off and away. He had no reason to think spies did it any differently. To cover a meet, to take it on un-detected from its source to its unknown destination and purpose, you had to know the where and when. Merely to be on the wrong side of the street at the wrong time meant you were down two nil before the game had started.

Not that it always meant you had lost the entire match. There was that time when John, that shrewd young detective sergeant on his team, the great 'V' Section... Years ago it was, when he was DI on the Flying Squad, back in the days when there was a Flying Squad. Strike fast, strike hard, and hang on to your bottle. There was himself in charge of 'V', with Tam the Slam, Reg, John, Steve, Ken and two young DCs, what were their names again? Faces? – he could recall their faces. But their names? *You have stolen my name*! John had a snout, a good 'un. Reliable. The blag was set for a Thursday at eleven in the morning. Where? The snout doesn't know, John said. But after they've done the blag, they are going to dump the bent motor, split up and make their way on foot to meet at the spot where they have a straight car parked, then share out the readies. The straight motor will be parked in a street to the north of St Pancras. And Tam the Slam said John ought to nick his informant for false pretences because north of St

Pancras was all the kingdom between there and John o' Groats. Even if it was dumped within one square mile of St Pancras, there were at least ten thousand cars left in the streets there any time of the day or night.

Ah but, John had said. My snout's got the make and number of the straight car! A blue and white two-tone Zephyr. All we've got to do is punt round the manor until we find it. Then we sit on it and wait for the meet.

It had not been all that difficult. Not with 'V' Section in its three cars and nondescript van quartering the ground. They found it with half an hour to spare before the blag was due to go down. And sweet as a nut, there happened to be a space right opposite the straight car to park the nondescript. It could not have been better. Channel six was open and the car-to-car transmissions were going across loud and clear. At three minutes past eleven a shout came over the air from Information Room. A wages robbery in Euston Road, about a mile away. Four men involved. A grey Transit used for the getaway. Fifteen grand in readies nicked. Attention all cars.

The plan was simple. They would let the villains get in the Zephyr. It was lodged fairly tightly between other cars parked front and rear and would have to manoeuvre to get out. As soon as the villains were spotted approaching the Zephyr, the shout would go in to crews in the Section's big Rover, Mk 2 Jag and the Triumph 2500, who were cruising out of sight ahead and behind the meet. The Rover would steam in and block the offside doors, the Jag would drive along the pavement and deal with the nearside, the nondescript would swing over and block the front. The Triumph would float and observe. Simple. Sweet as a nut. No need to worry about tailing anyone to anywhere. The caper had been pulled, all they had to do was sit on the meet and wait. It didn't quite work out that way.

Controlling from inside the nondescript, he saw two of the villains coming in at the top end of the street, carrying a hold-all between them. Inside it would be the coshes and ammonia squirters. Villains were not fully into sawn-offs, ·Smith and Wessons and Walther P-38s in those days. He saw them give the hi-sign in recognition of the other two homing in over the railway bridge. One was clutching a plastic travel bag which would contain the readies. The other was doing a little skipping jig of delight. All four met at the straight car, exchanging playful shoulder punches and joyful whoop-de-do's.

It was at that juncture it went wrong for the Section, who were all poised and ready to go. The big Rover, the Mk 2 Jag and the Triumph were already in motion. But the villains, instead of getting into their car, suddenly and quite unconcernedly went up the stairs into a large Victorian apartment house. Gawd Almighty, one of them must live there, John said. Bang; the huge oak door slammed shut as the big Rover came tearing down the street, and the Mk 2 Jag delicately threaded its way along the pavement. Hold everything, he had yelled over the radio, they have gone into number seventy-three. Tam, get round the back with two others. The rest of you to the front door.

As they huddled out of sight under the portico, he realized it would need at least two ounces of jelly to open that damned door. Start knocking and the gear would come flying out of a window. All they would get would be the wide-eyed and innocent: Who me? A narrow ledge above the basement led to a half-open window on the ground floor. John said it was his snout, his job, so it was up to him to get in through the window, and along the ledge he went. In next to no time he was opening the front door from the inside. But frowning, either aggrieved or puzzled. Boy and girl in bed in the front room, he whispered. Shagging their heads off. Never took a blind bit of notice of me!

Four floors ahead of them. Two apartments on each floor. Which one were the villains in? How to do it quietly? CRASH! The back door flew apart. Tam the Slam was never a patient man when villains were behind closed doors. So it was all on top now. Storm up the stairs, hammering on doors, kicking them in when necessary. Nothing on the second floor. The same treatment on the third. Nothing. Nix. Nowt. Up to the fourth. A door flies open under a well-placed boot, and there they are, the villains sitting round the table, one with tattooed arms dealing out the readies, three for you and three for you and one two three for me. Slack mouths hanging open in horror and amazement. You are all nicked – official.

Afterwards they had asked the villains how they had never heard them. They had made enough noise to waken the dead. Tattooed arms pondered the question for a long time before replying sadly, 'Guv'nor, there is nothing so deafening as the crisp rustle of nice new readies.'

So it had all worked out as sweet as a nut after all. Fifteen thousand, two hundred and ninety-five quid nicked. Fifteen thousand, two hundred and ninety-five quid recovered. Four villains in the bin. Bang to rights. Let's get across the Red Lion and get pissed.

Unlawful? All this kicking in doors and creeping in through windows while people are quietly shagging in bed? No, not exactly. The archaic law of hue and cry says police may break down doors and enter premises in hot pursuit of fleeing felons, provided they have demanded and been refused admission. Provided? Well, they would have been refused in any case, wouldn't they. Besides, nobody complained. They didn't in those days. The villains toed a line drawn for them by police. The public knew it and the Courts knew it. All the checks and balances worked until the politicians got into the act, realizing that crime was controversial. Good for TV exposure. That the criminal vote was worth having. Or that the get tough with criminals vote was worth having. So between them they rubbed out the line and now they have something like four million criminal votes and nobody spends a lot of time out in the streets. But in those times *when he had been young and active in the job*... Why did they keep coming back... Those times when .. ? He was out of it now. A nutter. A part-time spy.

'A memento mori?' Hamilton enquired as they waited near the Schlössle Hotel to see if a green Opel came by.

'A what?'

'A memento mori. That little gold skull you keep playing with?'

He thought of Frank Worple. 'Yes, you could call it that,' he replied. Then wanting to forget it, said, 'We've given this one long enough. Let's go and have a look at the Falknis and the Landhaus. If there is still no joy, we'll have a general punt round the cafés and bars. If still no joy, we'll call it a night.

With so little traffic about, we're beginning to stick out like . . .'

'Boils on bums?' Hamilton suggested.

# Seventeen

◆◆◆◆◆◆◆◆◆◆

They were on the road early next morning. It was a day of autumnal beauty. One of those particular days, found only in mountainous country, when in the clear air, vision and senses are enhanced, horizons clearly etched and defined, and all the crags and peaks seem within reach of an outstretched hand. Across the valley, the river was partially hidden under a blanket of mist, but now and again there was a gleam of silver where the sun, higher now, had burned the mist into tattered rags. To stand in the sun meant discarding coats and jackets in order to be comfortable, yet it was also unwise, for in the many shadows the chill of the night lingered and persisted. For all that, it was, as Hamilton remarked, 'A simply glorious day.'

They began at Triesenberg on the lower slopes, Smith leaving Hamilton in the car to watch the mountain road, while he explored the village in search of the green Opel. If he saw it, he would come and tell. If it passed Hamilton, he was to give three quick blasts on the horn and Smith would come running. Not to worry about the delay, he said, on these narrow twisting roads a driver of Hamilton's ability would soon get on its tail. Hamilton had preened modestly and nodded in confirmation of an obvious fact. But there was nothing for them in Triesenberg. Not even an Opel, let alone a green one with the right number plate. Not to worry, Smith said again. There are many pretty villages in the mountains, in one of them our man must be.

After Triesenberg, a problem. Do they fork left to check the hamlets of Masescha and Gaflei, or do they keep on going over the ridge and across the steep Samina valley and climb the next range to Steg and Malbun? Smith lowered his gaze along the plain of the Rhine to the mountains on the Swiss side of the river. Many pretty villages there are in those mountains also, he mused. This was not like St Pancras. Down below, Slunchev could, at this very moment, be driving across the bridge to RV in VZ whilst he was poncing about up and down the wrong mountain. It was too hit or miss. The worst kind of police work. Ah, what the hell, he was 'aiding' again. Finding his meat in the gutter. Remember the sack of chickens, he consoled himself. 'Straight on up to Malbun,' he directed Hamilton, 'Steg is no more than a few houses along the road. We can check as we pass through. No need to stop.'

Malbun was slightly larger than Smith had anticipated, though still no more than a village. A forlorn village, ominous even, in its low-season solitude. The hotels, charming yet desolate, spread in and around the outskirts. Empty ski-lifts stalked the bare slopes, like gallows expectantly waiting execution day ... And then it was third time lucky.

At the third hotel there were three cars parked outside. A blue Fiat, a white Toyota and a green Opel bearing the right number plate. Smith told Hamilton to roll the Audi tight in behind it so it could not be driven away. Then they remained in their own car to consider the next step. One they had not prepared for, for it seemed unlikely they would ever take it. 'Now what?' Hamilton asked, bewildered by their success, his athletic eyes flickering nervously.

Smith remained silent, thinking. Yes, Sunshine. Now what? It's over-the-top time. Zero hour. Poke your head out and the parapet will be swept by diplomatic shell-fire. Your career will be severed at the neck. He waited for Hamilton to make the first move. It was, after all, his party.

'Perhaps, we should pull back? Wait for him to come out. Let him drive away and follow him to somewhere quiet where we can stop him. Have a chat. Negotiate from a position of strength,' Hamilton suggested tentatively.

'What strength? Suppose he doesn't want to stop. Or chat.

And what is there to negotiate about? We need him more than he needs us.' And yet, Smith conceded there was a great deal of sense in Hamilton's proposals. If they tailed Slunchev away, he might lead them straight to Galahad. But would Galahad show? He had ignored RVs in Doncaster, Manchester and Glasgow, why should he show up in Vaduz? He didn't even know his mole from the golden age of conspiracy was above ground and in Liechtenstein ... *Or did he?*

'We tried to put the line at Amla Farm on the tinkle,' Fairchild had said. 'But the pols wouldn't wear it. Ziah is a cog somewhere in that wheel within a wheel.'

'The one where they stand round in a circle scratching the back of the one in front?' he had asked sourly.

'That sort of crudity will get us exactly nowhere,' Fairchild had put him down firmly. 'The fact remains, if Galahad phones his sister to ascertain if enquiries are being made about him, if she tells him of your visit, if she lets him know his mail is accumulating and he asks her to open it and let him know what is inside, we will be none the wiser.'

'So why don't you hammer the sods again to put her on the bell?'

'That is exactly where Sir Desmond came unstuck. He finally had to explain matters he had kept from them. That he had even kept from me. Like putting *you* on the bell. As a consequence, Sir Desmond has been kicked out. Appointed to the Arts Council. I am in control.'

'Arise, Sir Cyril,' he had grunted.

The realization came to him slowly and he cursed himself for a fool. They had not been expected to find Galahad or Slunchev. He and Hamilton were paper people to be plastered over the cracks. To cover the *if and when* eventuality. If and when it came on top. If and when the questions were asked, the explanations demanded ... Someone ... Fairchild? *Someone,* would solemnly aver, 'Skilled, resolute and experienced agents were sent out in an effort to resolve the situation brought about by the irresponsible actions of the previous incumbent. Regrettably, despite their dedicated and strenuous efforts carried out under the most difficult circumstances, they failed to achieve their objectives. No blame can be attached to ...' and it would go on and on until the whitewash was thick enough to present a seemingly solid surface. It could even be they did not want Galahad and Slunchev found. Finding them would pose more problems than it solved. Like now? Finding them meant confrontation in a neutral and highly sensitive country. By the use of tact and discretion ... Bullshit! Finding them meant only one thing, capital T for Trouble. To the people that played this game there were easier, more efficient ways of dealing with that kind of Trouble. Away to the east, behind *those* Bricks, beyond *that* Wire, the automatic rifles and machine pistols could take care of this kind of Trouble. It only needed someone to point them in the right direction. The wheel within the wheel. A back-scratching exercise.

Well, whether Fairchild liked it or not, they had them on the perch now. One of them at any rate. All they had to do was knock the bastard off. Hamilton? Was he really the blithe berk he seemed to be? No, he couldn't be anything else; a performer who acted like him would be going in for Academy Awards, not for a life in the secret service. What had they told Hamilton that they hadn't told him?

'What have you been authorized to offer in the way of persuasion?' he suddenly wanted to know from his pensive companion.

Hamilton considered the Act before answering, then apparently deciding two persuaders would be better than one, he came out with it. 'An offer, financially reasonable, without being extravagant,' he explained, as if announcing government policy. 'Fifteen thousand on verification of a historical debriefing. Gossip and conjecture to be thrown in for nothing. A further ten thou a year for two years, and an entry permit and good papers for any country of his choice in the West. A guarantee to bring his wife and kids out of Bulgaria as soon as circumstances permit.'

'How soon will circumstances permit?'

'As soon as they can get themselves from Sofia to any Black Sea port where we can buy a Turkish skipper to bring them across to Istanbul. The price, of course, will be deductible from his emolument. Luxury goods, you see?'

'Won't the secret police have his family under surveillance?'

'Probably. But we must expect them to use their initiative. I mean, that's what life is all about these days. Initiative.'

'Death also, it seems. What's the blackmail alternative?'

'His brother in the Ministry of Culture and a cousin in the Post Office. We will blow them if he refuses to cooperate. Slunchev used them both as couriers when he worked for Galahad.'

'How do we know that?'

'We don't. But we will threaten to say they did. Slunchev knows it will be believed.'

Smith got out of the car feeling a desperate need for clean air. Hamilton wound down the window and spoke to him. 'Aren't we going to wait?' he asked, then said pleadingly, 'I really do feel we should wait.'

Smith turned on him bitterly. 'What the hell for,' he rasped. 'If it's a choice between you, Galahad and Hameh, I'd give him to Hameh every time. He'll die quicker.'

Swinging away, he marched through the front door of the hotel. Drawn blinds had turned the reception area into a gloomy cavern. White shrouds made ghosts out of the furnishings. He stood for a few moments to get accustomed to the dim light. From somewhere near the reception desk a voice spoke quietly. Two factors brightened his dull spirits and almost brought a smile to his face. One was that he caught the meaning of the words first time, the other, that they were uttered by a plump little cherub of a girl, who was wielding a polishing block exactly like the one he had used in Wyldwood. Behind him he heard the hollow thump of Hamilton's shoes resounding on the bare boards. Stout shoes they were. Veldtschoen, Hamilton called them, forty years old they were. Belonged to his father when he was with the colonial service in British East ... East what? He had left that unsaid as though everyone knew where British East was, or had been. Everyone who was anyone, that is. Into his father's shoes, Hamilton had assuredly stepped.

'The girl says the hotel closes today until December,' Smith explained to him. 'Tell her we have called to see our good friend Mr Trench, who must still be here, for his car is outside. But be nice to her. *Machen mit der* courtesy.' He heard the girl laughing as she turned to the reception desk and switched on the lights. Smith took hold of the abandoned polisher and sent it skidding expertly across the floor. '*Gut, ja?*' he said to the girl in praise of his own efforts. '*Wunderbar,*' she agreed admiringly as he spun the heavy stone through a full circle.

'Well, get chatting to her then,' he admonished an open-mouthed Hamilton. 'Tell her we are very good friends of Mr Trench and we want to surprise him in his room, for we are mad Englanders who play silly jokes on their friends.'

He continued to work the polisher as Hamilton spoke to the girl, relaxing in the rhythm of the strokes, gratified by the sheen that came through in response to his efforts.

'He's in room two twenty-four.' Hamilton was at his elbow. 'She's surprised he has not checked out yet, but we may go up. And she asks if you would like a job as chief floor polisher when they reopen.'

Almost regretfully he surrendered the polisher to the plump chambermaid. 'On that offer, I may take you up,' he told her, gently pinching her cheek. She got his meaning wrong, blushed and fell into a fit of the giggles which she made no effort to suppress. She was still laughing merrily as they ascended the stairs.

He could, as Smith later explained to Fairchild, smell it in that dark corridor on the second floor. No, not smell it, he corrected himself, so much as *feel* it. The fever heat of death. That heat you get from a corpse newly dead from asphyxia, a fractured skull, or a vagal inhibition. The heat you get when death comes suddenly, unexpectantly and violently. When the body temperature shoots up to a hundred and ten and more; and you almost expect the flesh to melt. He could feel that heat in the corridor. Oh, it might only have been the build-up from the radiators with everything shut tight, but he felt in his guts, it was *that* kind of heat.

And then there was an overwhelming moment of incomprehensible sadness. Joe Potch should be here, Tam the Slam, John and the others from the old days, *from those times when . . .* Instead he only had Hamilton. And then he realized Hamilton was carrying his golfing umbrella, holding it furled across his chest like a victory flag to be duly raised on a conquered height. Why was he carrying that damned brolly? The tiny gold skull screamed from his pocket. *They actually do things like this!* Raging once more, he roughly snatched the umbrella from Hamilton's hands. He had seen walking-stick guns and umbrella guns before. Knew how they worked. You twisted the handle and pulled it to the rear exposing the breech. There would be a tiny retractable trigger slotted into the brass ferrule at the top. He twisted and tugged at the large bulbous handle but it refused to budge. He probed the ferrule with his fingers but felt only smooth unbroken metal. Reluctantly, he returned the umbrella to a silent but clearly offended Hamilton.

'Two twenty-four should be further along on the left,' Hamilton said stiffly. 'Do we announce ourselves formally or just barge in? I expect you are more accustomed to the protocol of these matters than I.'

'It depends on whether the door is locked or not,' Smith answered.

'That need not be a problem,' countered Hamilton. 'I borrowed the girl's keys while you were giving her lessons in domestic science.'

'Not just a pretty face, are you?' Smith said, taking the keys from him. 'Keep on like this and they'll give you a gold-plated pen full of invisible ink.'

Slowly Smith tried to turn the handle. It remained fast, as tight as the one on Hamilton's umbrella. The lock was of the usual continental type set in the door knob. He spat on the key, rubbed saliva into the grooves to provide lubrication, then slid the key into the lock, holding the door steady with his free hand until he heard the click. Twisting the handle to its full extent, he eased the door open. A short, narrow passage with another internal door at the end separated them from the room. Stepping boldly forward, Smith flung it open, heard a sharp intake of breath from Hamilton, and threw a hand over his mouth before it could emerge in a shriek of revulsion.

'Schtum, you stupid prick,' he hissed in his face. 'Not a peep out of you. Do you understand.' Hamilton nodded weakly, his face pallid. He removed his hand slowly and went over to the bed.

He had seen more than a few head-splitters in his time.

From hammer and hatchet jobs, to the simple brutality of lead pipes and iron bars, but this one was a classic. The weapon lay on the floor under the lifeless dangling legs. An ice-axe! Its curved steel blade was covered in an obscene compote of blood and brains. But it was the post-mortem nature of the wound that absorbed his professional interest. The top of the head had been prised apart after the initial shattering blow. Fragments of bone had been torn away and carelessly thrown aside. He walked round to the far end of the bed to make a closer examination, hearing Hamilton panting in the background like a spaniel left out too long in the hot sun.

'Breathe slowly, more deeply,' he advised softly without looking at him, his eyes inside the riven skull. The exposed brain had been curiously ravaged, gouged out; reminding him of a half-eaten pomegranate he had once seen discarded by a caged ape. Claw marks?

As he pondered on the cause, he at first considered the sound to be the involuntary prelude to Hamilton disgorging the contents of his stomach on the floor, but as he listened, spellbound, it filled the room with a growing insistent sibilance; slavering and unearthly. He was on the airless planet and the reptilian night birds were in flight.

'*Is-koo'nee.*' The call came plaintively, yet pitiless.

'*Is-koo'nee.*' It came again, whining, mewling and murderous in its intensity. He looked at Hamilton standing rigidly against the far wall, his furled umbrella clutched tightly across his chest, his eyes, fixed for once, staring intently at the half-open door of the bathroom.

'*Is-koo'nee.*' The call slithered round the door and into the room as though it had form and substance. Smith drew himself upright, went quickly over to the bathroom door and kicked it wide open. Then, as if propelled by an unseen force, he recoiled several paces, his fists raised in a gesture more fearful than aggressive.

It was crouched on its haunches between the shower curtain and the bidet, red-rimmed eyes blazing, lips drawn in a vicious defiant snarl exposing heavily stained teeth; and in the dribbling saliva that hung from its jaws, Smith found a horrifying answer to the lacerations inside the ruined brain of Vaclav

Slunchev – code name Klinge.

Rising imperceptibly, the thing in the bathroom got to its feet and assumed human form. And was no less menacing or murderous in the metamorphosis.

'Galahad! Oh, Galahad!' An anguished sob broke from Hamilton's lips. It evoked no change in the manic form that advanced to fill the doorway. Blood-stained hands clawed at the lintel. Smith thought of going in with the boot, but the residual pain in his belly made him retreat as the figure advanced, an arm swooping down effortlessly to scoop up the ice-axe from the floor. Holding it poised, the madman, who was Galahad the hero, held them locked in the fury of his unblinking eyes. It is a matter of selection, he is sorting out which of us is going to get it first. The thought was clear in Smith's mind, as driven by desperation he prepared to launch himself forward, only to be restrained when magically, two tiny darts appeared imbedded in the stained shirt in front of him. Thin wires trailed from them to the base of Hamilton's umbrella. He saw Castellain stiffening, his spine arching as the current heaved him to the tips of his toes and threw him down at Slunchev's feet. *They actually do things like this!* Smith nearly howled it in relief. A stun gun. A power pack that forced the charge from a dry battery through a miniaturized impulse generator to give a paralysing high-voltage, low-amperage shock. He had seen one before in its original form, no larger than a heavy-calibre pistol. They had tried to sell them to the police. Got the strong rebuff. Quite affronted they were. The effect is only temporary, they said, very humane. Lasts just long enough for you to put your would-be assailant under restraint. Always make sure you can get the probes home, you may not have the opportunity to insert fresh batteries. Fresh batteries! There would be no fresh batteries for Hamilton's electronic umbrella. Now it would only keep the rain out. There was a slight whirr as the wires snaked back into the root of Hamilton's umbrella. Its owner knew its power had expired, and with it his own. Why don't we run for it, he asked him with his eyes. Why don't we?

Castellain was stirring on the floor. There was still time to put the boot in. Put him out of action completely. He went forward and kicked the ice-axe under the bed. It was the best, or the worst he could do. Galahad sat up.

'Good God, how on earth did you two manage to get here?' he enquired calmly.

Tense, yet fascinated, they watched him climb unsteadily to his feet, unable to go near him, apprehensive, for now he stood between them and the door, staring down at his blood-stained hands, his expression falling into a fragile mixture of doubt and disgust. He clawed at the awful mess around his mouth and chin. For a long moment the snarl returned, then settled into a grimace of angry loathing.

'Oh, you foul brute,' he whispered to a place beyond the ceiling. 'Now you degrade me!' Hiding his face under folded arms, he stumbled into the bathroom.

'Shall we make a run for it?' Smith heard Hamilton say above the sound of splashing water.

'To where?' he replied. 'We came to do a job, remember?'

'But, don't you see...'

'Don't worry. You've just accomplished a miracle cure by the use of electro-convulsive therapy. You've stopped the clock on the bomb. For a while at least. You don't have a tranquillizing hypodermic in your shoes, by any chance?'

'No, only the umbrella and that's useless now.'

'I know. All we are left with is my mouth, so keep yours shut and leave the talking to me. It's the best chance we've got.'

Galahad came back into the room rubbing his face vigorously in a towel. He stopped and stood over Slunchev's body. 'Dear old Klinge,' he said without emotion. 'Sorry I couldn't make it in time. The brute must have struck me down as I came into the room.' He fingered his chest where the electrodes had been. 'Don't quite know how...' he hesitated and the fragile expression flitted across his face once more, only for its weakness to be recognized and instantly banished. 'I want an explanation as to how you came to be here?' he demanded.

'Klinge left a forwarding address in Glasgow,' Smith said quietly. It drew an imperious frown.

'I doubt it, but never mind. Let me put it more positively. *What* are you doing here?'

'We came to bring you home, Galahad,' Hamilton intervened despite Smith's warning glare. But the reply suited Galahad's temperament exactly.

'And how do you propose to do that?' he sneered. 'Trundle me across the Alps in a perambulator? Do you think I need a nursemaid?' He swung away and, holding his hands towards the bed, offered them Slunchev's corpse.

'See what has been done to him. Do you imagine for one moment I will let this abomination go unpunished?'

'If we don't get out of here pretty quickly, we are going to finish up in the local jail.' The air of calm authority in Smith's voice did not go unrecognized. Nor did Galahad fail to read its challenge.

'My dear uninsultable Smith! Is it really true you cannot insult a policeman? Don't worry, I do not intend to try. You are quite right. We must get out of here. The fire escape should be the most convenient way.' He looked at his stained clothing, then went to the wardrobe and removed a loose-fitting tweed coat.

'You won't deny me a parting gift, will you old friend?' he said to the ghastly ruin that had been Slunchev's head. 'No more for you the ecstasy of terror,' he went on, as he slipped into the coat. 'No more the delicious stench of your own fear. But, rest assured, I will find the one who robbed you of your honour. I will deliver him straight to you in your own little corner of hell and there you may pick at *his* blood and brains for all eternity.'

Something not unlike a suppressed cackle fell from Hamilton's lips, but his tormented features declared he had no intent to abuse the rites with indecorous impiety.

'You have transport?' Galahad wanted to know.

'An Audi outside,' Smith replied.

'Good. My valise is deposited at the railway station in Buchs. We will stop there.'

'You take the fire escape with Hamilton,' Smith told him. 'The chambermaid knows we're up here. I'll tell her Hamilton is helping our friend to pack. That should keep her out of the room for a while.' He looked at his watch. 'Nearly an hour until mid-day. She won't start wondering before then.'

'Had *I* not better speak to her,' Hamilton implored. 'At best, you have little more than pidgin German.'

'Don't be silly, man,' Galahad snapped. 'Sight of Klinge has scared you shitless. One look at your face and a ten-year-old child would know something is wrong. You are coming with me.' Smith silenced a desire to add, 'And may God have mercy on your soul,' as he watched Galahad propel a reluctant Hamilton along the corridor to the fire escape.

Downstairs the chambermaid was working away at the floor. Smith paused on the landing to envy the beatific rapture on her face, coming as it did from the monotonous tranquillity of her task. He spoke to her gravely, not involving himself with the intricacies of explaining how his friend was helping their other friend to pack his luggage. Confining himself to simple words and phrases which she had no difficulty in understanding, but to his regret, totally destroying her smile and peace of mind.

Outside, Hamilton sat grimly behind the wheel, revving the engine as if waiting for the start of a grand prix. Like a prince of the blood, Galahad was relaxed in the rear seat staring fixedly ahead. Smith did not like that. He had it in his mind Galahad would prefer to sit next to Hamilton.

It would have been much better to have had him in front with *his* neck and head vulnerable instead of the other way round. As it was, he had no sooner settled in the passenger seat than Hamilton let in the clutch and took off, jerking the side of his head painfully against the upright pillar. 'Take it easy, Sunshine,' he growled in the other's ear. 'You've saved our skins once today. Don't bugger it up by throwing us off the side of the mountain.' Lowering the sun visor, he cast a glance behind at Galahad. A face graven, almost peaceful. His eyelids hooded but not quite closed.

It was not until they were within a mile of the bridge across the river leading to Buchs that Galahad opened his eyes and spoke. 'I have no intention of returning home with you,' he said. 'You had better understand that. I will not return until I have squared the account. Even in this day and age there is such a thing as a debt of honour.'

'Your code name,' Smith digressed deliberately. 'Did you

assign it to yourself or did it just happen to be on the list? I mean, did you invent Galahad?'

'Are you *that* ignorant, my insult-impervious friend,' the voice chuckled tauntingly in his ear. 'Galahad was not invented. He existed in a golden age when honour was hard won. When it could not be bought, or given as cheap recompense for favour. He lived in a time when pride never came before a fall.'

'I quite agree Galahad existed,' Smith answered with conciliatory mildness. 'At least in mythology. A legend... Like the Hameh!'

He watched Galahad sink into his seat, dull leaden eyes stared into his own. *You have stolen my face!*

The eyes clung to him as they crossed the bridge into Buchs. They were still there when they stopped outside the railway station. Smith broke the bond reluctantly to get out of the car. As he closed the door he saw a hand reach out and fasten on Hamilton's neck. 'You will take this key and recover my valise from the locker,' Galahad was saying in a voice Hamilton had heard once before on a recording. 'Before going, you will pass me the car keys.' Smith stood watching Hamilton make his way into the station, turning now and again to look at him, as if at odds with his conscience and his courage.

'Does that one have the guts to return, I wonder?' The voice in his ear had darker tones now, as though dragged from the innermost depths of the throat. Galahad was behind him, embers starting to glow in the ashes of his eyes.

'He'll be back,' Smith said cheerfully. 'Why shouldn't he?'

Galahad raised a hand across his brows as if to shut out the light. When it dropped the fires were even brighter, the knuckles were folded inside the palm and locked in position by a powerful thumb.

'You will please stand absolutely still!' A new voice, accented and precise spoke to them.

They must have been lying on the floors of the cars parked nearby, their disturbed dignity being restored as they approached. Uniform caps being replaced on heads, tunics being adjusted and pulled into shape... Guns being drawn. It was the one with the stars on his shoulders who had spoken.

They came closer, but not too close. Smith was impressed and relieved.

'You will please come!' a gesture indicated the interior of the railway station. Galahad seemed to swell, to grow in stature and majesty as he confronted the policemen surrounding them. And such was the effect that those holding the guns found it necessary to adjust their stance, apply a two-handed grip and tighten their fingers on the triggers.

'Please come!' the policeman with the stars said again. Two sharp, distinct words that only the Germanic tongue can utter in English as both request and command. Galahad nodded, perhaps in approval, and stalked into the station with Smith following behind. They were led into a waiting-room which contained two more policemen and Hamilton. A profoundly affected Hamilton, one proclaiming his British citizenship and status as executive on the board of a multi-national corporation, together with vehement denials of any knowledge or connection with, 'Whatever other people you have outside, whoever they may be . . .'

'Save your breath,' Smith told him. 'I arranged for them to be here.'

'*Ach so*,' the one wearing the stars exclaimed. Smith decided he must be a captain. He had all the qualifications. A lean intelligent face, a sharp voice and three stars on each shoulder. 'Are you of the name Smith?' his captain enquired.

'I am of the name Smith,' he agreed.

'My name is Diehl. I command the police in this region. You understand?' Understanding clearly meant he was not therefore to be trifled with.

'I understand,' Smith replied.

'We earlier had a telephone call from the housemaid at the Hotel Grunenberg in Malbun. She said an Englishman of the name Smith told her certain facts. Certain serious facts. Repeat them, please.'

Yes, I like it, Smith thought. No leading questions. No re-iteration of what he had been told. No hints. Let me hear it from your own lips, Englishman. A professional.

'I told her,' Smith went on evenly, 'that in room two twenty-four was the body of a man who had been murdered. That she was not to enter the room but to call the police and tell them we were on our way to the railway station at Buchs in a blue Audi with the Zurich number 658312. That with us would be a very dangerous madman who had committed the murder.'

'Sooo.' Diehl made a sentence out of a syllable, and clasping his hands to the rear in what Hamilton would call the stand at ease position, he rocked thoughtfully back and forth on the balls of his feet.

'And please, which one of you is the dangerous madman? The murderer?' he finally asked.

'HAMEH!' It came as a grinding metallic scream from beyong the grave. Transfixed against the wall, Galahad slid slowly to his haunches in a posture both bestial and contrite.

'Hameh,' he said again, and this time it came as a defeated whimper. But the fire was still in his eyes, his teeth were still bared. Something snapped inside Smith. He towered accusingly over Galahad.

'Fucking grow up,' he yelled at him. 'You are not a schoolboy in the desert any more ordering the beheading of brigands. You are a compulsive psychopathic killer who began it all years ago when you did in your wife and her lover. A sordid commonplace domestic murder. She had rejected you, you useless impotent clown. But you wouldn't accept that, would you? Damsels don't ditch Galahads. Galahads are in the damsel-saving business. Provided they are virtuous. Was that it? Did you never give her one? Was she to remain virtuous all her days? Then when you found she was only human after all, you slaughtered both of them. But because Galahads don't go round slaughtering damsels in distress, you summoned up the Hameh out of your childish nightmares and put it down to the great avenger. Then you slaughtered your way across half Europe to justify your own inadequacy.'

Galahad cowered under the shield of his protecting arms.

'Please,' Diehl said, making a request of it. 'This is not to be permitted.'

'Like hell, it isn't,' Smith was beyond recall. He turned his fury on Diehl. 'They get this ... *thing* back to England. They stick him in a madhouse for a few years then they let him out ... this will make you laugh, *mein Kapitän*. Do you ever laugh, *mein Kapitän?* Never mind, it's not that funny. They let him out to clear up a job he planned himself. He wanted to play at being Galahad again. Feats of derring-do, done to order. Enemies to be struck down. Dragon Hamehs to be pursued and slain. But he carried this dragon around inside his head. He could produce it whenever he wanted an excuse to kill people. Not a reason, you must appreciate the difference. Only an excuse. This fucking *thing* never needed a reason for killing people.'

'You must be quiet, please,' Diehl roared. 'It is most confusing. *They?* Who are these they? Hameh? Who is Hameh?' He shook his head, '*Mein Gott,* which one of them is mad?' he asked himself in German.

In the background, Hamilton laughed wildly. 'They both are!' he screeched in triumph, cleaving into a mordant silence.

Galahad was on his feet again, gliding slowly forward, his steps exaggerated, prancing, almost balletic, now dropping down and slithering toward an outstretched knee, now rising into a swift pirouette, making multiple changes of direction to the accompaniment of hands and arms moving in counterpoint. His wrists guiding fingers into graceful, yet threatening flourishes, the arms swirling in convoluted arcs, then suddenly thrusting at the air, as powerful and controlled as steam pistons.

In his subsequent report to his superiors, Diehl dealt with this particular part as follows:

'As you are aware, I represent our Service and my country in the martial arts of Aikido and Karate and have studied the various other forms of this science. In the actions of this madman, I recognized a most advanced and arcane skill. That of 'H'sing I,' believed to have originated in the ancient cultures of the Middle East over two thousand years ago and later introduced into the temples of China by practitioners among the Arab traders. There it was developed and refined by Buddhist monks into a defensive and aggressive ritual of the most deadly nature. Today, only a few dedicated masters and teachers of its secrets still exist.

'From the subject's manner and movements it was apparent

to me he was adept in this art to the highest degree of expertise and proficiency. His preliminary steps were of "Ti Chei", a preparatory form of complex exercises in which the practitioner reaches a transcendental state, preparatory to a descent into the swift and merciless aggressions of "Pa qua", where by striking at precisely determined vulnerable points in the nervous system and organic structure of the human body, death will invariably supervene in most cases.

'At this juncture, I must admit to a tactical error in placing my men and the three English suspects within the relatively confined space of the waiting room. In such closely assembled company, I could not order my men to open fire in the event of violent attack without placing them in danger from misplaced shots. Indeed, I was, with the possible exception of the Englishman, Smith, the only one who recognized the potential danger posed by the madman. My men only saw in his gyrations the harmless antics of an insane person.

'To avoid breaking the spell, as it were, I issued no verbal orders, and not without some difficulty in making my intentions understood, I eventually succeeded in clearing the room by pointed signals and gesticulations and placed my force on guard outside. This was accomplished without hostile reaction from the madman, who nevertheless was now displaying external indications of frenzy by the increase in speed and ferocity of his movements and by the terrifying aspect of his facial expression. Thus having extricated all, with the exception of the madman, from the room it was necessary to plan and decide my next move.

'The madman could of course have been shot without difficulty. A technical point I merely mention, there being no present cause for extreme action. The man was, at least to the uninitiated, harmless and was offering no direct violence at the time. My alternative was to endeavour to subdue and restrain him by sheer force of numbers. This I dismissed despite my own prowess as it was clear to me that the madman was capable of inflicting death or serious injury on one or more of my men before he could be overpowered. I therefore decided to await the arrival of tear-gas canisters from the central armoury in Zurich, and in the meantime set about securing the windows and doors of the waiting-room with such materials as were to hand.

'I had sight of the madman before a weighty packing-case was positioned over the last window. By now he was standing quite still in the meditative position. A posture indicative of the gathering of spiritual and mental resources to enhance the prodigious spasms of physical energy and strength such masters of the art of "H'sing I" are capable of producing. Therefore I was, at the time, extremely concerned as to whether my improvised barriers would be sufficiently robust to contain this person.

'Within a few minutes my worst fears were realized when a door seemingly exploded outwards, and a number of heavy cartons of tinned food, used to reinforce it, were scattered like chaff. The madman emerged, his demeanour terrifying and implacable, akin to one in the grip of demonic possession. In panic, several shots were fired by certain of my men without my order. The shots were hurried and inaccurate. The madman then ran along the platform and on to the railway track pursued by the Englishman, Smith, with myself and my men behind . . .'

Smith ran steadily behind Galahad with no intention of closing the gap. He would run this bastard to the end of the earth. Sooner or later he would tire, his wind would give out, and then . . . And then?

To the rear, he could hear Diehl shouting at him to move to one side. Then calling ahead to Galahad to halt or he would order his men to open fire. Smith looked round briefly, the police were falling away, some stumbling on the uneven ballast, one tripping over a low cable, only Diehl and two others were still in the chase, some fifty yards behind. Well beyond the range of accurate pistol shooting. Ahead, Galahad was moving with tireless ease, light-footed as a gazelle. No contour or ridge on the track seemed to impede his stride. No backward glance was cast at his pursuers. It began to look to Smith that the bastard *could* run to the end of the earth. He had abandoned the tweed coat he had taken from Slunchev's room and his blood-stained shirt billowed in the wind. The stain on the upper left shoulder caught Smith's eye; it looked like the head of a vulture. Rorschach! They were running towards Rorschach! Had he passed the test? Given a normal interpretation?

The rails seemed to stretch away to a point where eternity was defined by a speck on the horizon. A growing speck, that became a monstrous engine approaching at high speed. He saw Galahad move to the side of the track and halt. He stopped himself when still twenty yards away, edging clear of the rails. Galahad turned and faced him, for a moment, dead leaden eyes gazed into his. The lips moved. He could hear nothing but the roaring whine of the approaching train, yet was certain of what the lips were saying.

'*Is-koo'nee.*'

Dropping to his knees, Galahad kissed the surface of the rail as tenderly as one kisses the cheek of a dying love.

The head simply vanished beneath the train, the body whipped and spun violently until the spinal cord reluctantly severed, and Galahad's remains were discarded in a heap at the side of the track.

Diehl reached Smith, breathing heavily. 'Yes, it is good,' he panted. 'Much easier this way for me. I hope also for you.' It was merely a wish, not a promise.

'For me personally, it is easier,' Smith said. 'But for me as me, I am not sure.'

Diehl looked mystified; as he was entitled to be.

Afterwards, when the body had been stuffed into a black plastic bag, together with the more obvious fragments scattered about the track and the pieces carried away, Diehl and Smith walked back to the station at Buchs. Some way down the line, Smith turned to look once more at the spot where Galahad had died. A large black bird hovered over the place before settling in the middle of the track and starting to peck among the ballast. Diehl saw that Smith was shivering.

'It is a bird,' he felt it necessary to explain. 'A *Rabe*. I don't know how you say in English.'

'A raven,' Smith said. 'It could be a raven.'

'A raven. Yes, they are carnivores, you know. It is not surprising. Unpleasant, but not surprising.'

Well muffled in coat and scarf against the chill wind sweeping in from the Zurich See, Fairchild sat at the far end of the bench and opened his newspaper with a flourish.

'Are you quite certain they are not keeping an eye on you?' he asked anxiously from behind its pages.

'Pretty certain,' Smith replied from the other end of the bench.

'Where's Hamilton?' Fairchild was still anxious.

'In the hotel room. He doesn't go out much these days.'

'How long do they require you to stay?'

'A few more days. There are still some formalities.'

'What have you told them?'

'A tale of industrial espionage. Slunchev and Galahad nicked some plans from the company. We came out to make a deal for their return. When we got to the hotel in Malbun, Galahad had gone crazy and killed his partner. A lousy plot. A right load of old bollocks.'

'They believed it?'

'Let's say they accepted it. They prefer to stay neutral. Other killings in other countries are not their concern. The Swiss are very civilized people.'

For appearances sake, Fairchild turned the pages of his newspaper before saying, 'I suppose he killed dirty when he was Hameh and killed clean when he was Galahad?'

'Yeah. The age of chivalry is dead. Thank Christ.'

'I thought for the moment you were going to say something awfully trite; about him being just a crazy mixed-up kid.'

'It never entered my mind.'

'No? Well, I suppose it could have been worse. A lot worse.'

'You mean as far as the national interest is concerned? Do I get a bonus?'

'All those conclusions you offered in the park. By the Guards Memorial. Remember? Not very accurate, were they? Do you really feel you are entitled to a bonus? You didn't even recover the microfilm.'

Fairchild watched as Smith delved in his pocket to produce the tiny gold skull. Watched him play with it for a time, caress it fondly with his thumb. Saw him rise, walk to the edge of the quay and throw it far into the lake. It glinted in the weak sunlight before entering the water with an audible plop.

Overcome with astonishment, Fairchild lowered his newspaper. 'What on earth did you do that for?' he asked when Smith returned. 'That thing must have been quite valuable.'

'But ostentatious,' Smith replied. 'A bit too ostentatious for my taste.'

# THE GLITTER DOME

## Joseph Wambaugh

'BRILLIANT AND TERRIBLE.
Wambaugh is a historian of the American underworld
like no other that ever dipped pen in blood. A stunning
read.'
*The Spectator*

A compelling blend of wild humour and powerful
drama, this is the story of the cops who work the
Hollywood Division, a grim world of vice, drugs, child
abuse and bizarre murder. For these men, a visit to the
Glitter Dome — a bar of kaleidoscope lights and
plentiful groupies — is the only way to recover from
the fear and violence of their day. And when two
veteran detectives are assigned to the murder of a
studio president, they too discover how much they
have been seduced by Hollywood.

'An addictive blend of human and flinty realism.
Wambaugh is a master artist.'
*Publishers Weekly*

'Superb. Mr Wambaugh is a writer of genuine power,
style, wit and originality.'
*Evan Hunter, New York Times*

Futura Publications
Fiction
0 7088 2161 8

# SOLDIER ON THE OTHER SIDE

**Patrick Alexander**

Mitchell is dead. After a bizarre escape from Italy's top security jail, the terrorist's headless corpse has been washed up on the Calabrian coast.

All of which makes for problems. Latimer is making a film of Mitchell's life and wanted to interview him. Now that won't be possible. Opting for second best he sets of with his beautiful but troublesome actress wife to look for locations in the South of France.

Latimer shouldn't have jumped to conclusions.

SOLDIER ON THE OTHER SIDE — A subtle and spell-binding novel of suspense by the award-winning author of DEATH OF A THIN-SKINNED ANIMAL and SHOW ME A HERO.

Futura Publications
Fiction
0 7088 2571 0

**TRIPLE**

**Ken Follett**

The No. 1 Bestseller by the author of EYE OF THE NEEDLE.

'Sizzling narrative . . . One of the liveliest thrillers of the year.'
*Time Magazine*

A Jew, a Russian and an Egyptian meet briefly in Oxford in 1947. Twenty years later a shipment of uranium disappears between Antwerp and Genoa. And the man who returned from death takes on a mission that will lead him back into its gaping jaws.

'Ingenious, sentimental, violent . . . '
*New York Times*

'Highly imaginative . . . fascinating.'
*Washington Post*

'A compulsive page turner.'
*Associated Press*

Futura Publications
Fiction/Thriller
0 7088 1804 8

**DANCE FOR DIPLOMATS**

**Palma Harcourt**

'Palma Harcourt's novels are splendid' *Desmond Bagley*

Catherine Rayle, history don at Oxford, becomes Britain's first-ever woman permanent representative to NATO in Brussels. But her initial instinct to refuse the position was a good one, for Catherine gets drawn into a cloak-and-dagger world involving a defecting Russian ballet dancer; suddenly all are dancing, to a tune they have not called.

'The story unfolds with pace and excitement' *Evening News*

Futura Publications
Fiction/Thriller
0 7088 2573 7

# A FAIR EXCHANGE

**Palma Harcourt**

'Palma Harcourt's novels are splendid' *Desmond Bagley*

Derek Almourn, first scretary of the British Embassy in Washington, is deeply involved in NATO affairs when he marries the beautiful daughter of a Democratic senator; when a terrible 'accident' gets the couple posted to Oslo he begins to suspect his wife of working against him.

'bubbling readable little thriller' *Observer*

'a good story' *Daily Telegraph*

Futura Publications
Fiction/Thriller
0 7088 2498 6

# THE MIDAS MEN

## Jonathan Evans

£150,000,000 in South African gold. It took three days to count it. The Russian aircraft that contained it had crashed on take-off. But where was it bound? And why?

In MOSCOW, panic: famine is inevitable, and the Praesidium faces destruction.

In WASHINGTON, crisis: the oil supply is threatened, the dollar is slumping, the Presidency is under siege.

In RIYADH, scandal: a Saudi prince has lost a fortune, and jeopardised his claim to the throne.

In JOHANNESBURG, James Collington. Only his expertise and fast footwork can ward off an international catastrophe. But his business partners want him eliminated. And someone wants him dead.

Futura Publications
Fiction/Thriller
0 7088 2297 5

**FRIENDS**

**Thomas Hauser**

By the time the police find the young man's mutilated corpse in the apartment across the hall, it has been decomposing for weeks. Aggy can't tell the police anything. She can't remember.

But she is beginning to have the most terrifying dreams. Nightmares that tear at her memory.

Her boyfriend tries to reassure her. His brother is suddenly very concerned. But the police keep coming back . . . hounding her for answers . . . refusing to leave her alone.

Suddenly Aggy's world seems very unsafe. Somewhere buried in her subconscious she knows who the murderer is – and the murderer knows she knows . . .

Futura Publications
Fiction
0 7088 2554 0

# MURDER IN THE TITLE

## Simon Brett

'Mercilessly witty send-up of threadbare stage whodunnits'
*Guardian*

Playing the corpse in a wooden murder mystery at the Regent Theatre, Rugland Spa, is not exactly a triumph for Charles Paris, actor: in fact his career could hardly sink any lower.

But suddenly the mystery spilled over into real life when a bizarre sequence of events culminated in the Artistic Director's apparent suicide. And the talents of Charles Paris, amateur sleuth, were called into action.

'every page is gentle fun'
*Daily Telegraph*

'the sounds and smells, the ambitions and frustrations, of a provincial repertory company . . . a neat homicide, and an economic, uncontrived, satisfactory solution'
*Financial Times*

Futura Publications
Fiction/Crime
0 7088 2520 6

All Futura Books are available at your bookshop or newsagent, or can be ordered from the following address:
Futura Books, Cash Sales Department,
P.O. Box 11, Falmouth, Cornwall

Please send cheque or postal order (no currency), and allow 55p for postage and packing for the first book plus 22p for the second book and 14p for each additional book ordered up to a maximum charge of £1.75 in U.K.

Customers in Eire and B.F.P.O. please allow 55p for the first book, 22p for the second book plus 14p per copy for the next 7 books, thereafter 8p per book.

Overseas customers please allow £1.00 for postage and packing for the first book and 25p per copy for each additional book.